CAPTURED

Also by Marissa Farrar

The 'Serenity' Series

ALONE
BURIED
CAPTURED
DOMINION
ENDLESS

The 'Spirit Shifters' Series
AUTUMN'S BLOOD
SAVING AUTUMN
AUTUMN RISING

Stand Alone Novels

THE DARK ROAD
UNDERLIFE
THE SOUND OF CRICKETS

CAPTURED

Book Three in the 'Serenity' Series

Marissa Farrar

CAPTURED
By Marissa Farrar

Paperback Edition
ISBN: 978-0-9928504-3-2

Warwick House Press

License Notes

Publisher's Note

I'd like to dedicate this book to all the readers of the 'Serenity' series. Each and every time one of you has contacted me, whether it be by email, facebook or twitter, to tell me how much you're loving the series, it has inspired me to continue. When I first wrote 'Alone', I never imagined there would be a second book, never mind a third.

I may have created Serenity and Sebastian, but it has been you, the reader, who has brought them to life.

CAPTURED

Acknowledgments

Many thanks to my editor, Shontrell Wade of Wade-Staten Services. I always appreciate your hard work, keen eye and kind words. Thank you for picking up on all those British-isms that always seem to slip through, no matter how immersed I am in American culture. Going through your edits always reminds me that no writer should ever be without an editor.

I would also like to thank John N. Dillon, Lecturer of Classics and Ancient History at Exeter University, for his translations from English to Latin. I'm going to take a guess that the context the words are spoken in is probably a first for you! Thank you for humoring my strange imagination.

A special thanks to Glynis Elliott and Rebecca Treadway for providing proofreading/ beta reading services in return for a sneak-peak at the next chapter in Serenity and Sebastian's life. I hope the experience proved more pleasure than work.

CAPTURED

CONTENTS PAGE

CAPTURED

Chapter One

Her hands dug into soft, damp earth. Dirt wedged beneath her nails, almost painfully hard, pressing against the delicate skin. The tips of her fingers were calloused and split from digging, but she didn't notice the pain. As she knelt on the ground, the damp soaked through the knees of her jeans, cooling her already frigid skin.

Her master stood above her, his looming presence a devil on her shoulder. They spent only a few nights in one spot before relocating to the next. They moved from place to place with her clinging to his back as he ran, fast as the wind. Wherever they went, her master always needed to go back underground.

At each location, Serenity dug their resting place.

"Faster," he growled, and she forced her arms to move, clawing farther into the ground. It didn't need to be deep, just enough to cover them with clods of soil; encasing them in Mother Nature's womb.

Serenity only knew her name because her master used the title. There were other words he addressed her by—bitch, whore, slut—but she recognized 'Serenity' as being the one he used the most.

"The sun is coming up, Serenity," he said from above. "You wouldn't want me to get caught in it, would you? Just because I can walk in the light, doesn't mean I want to."

She recognized the threat in his tone, the one that told her to do as he wanted or she'd earn her repercussions—a slap to the face, a kick in the ribs, a bite to her breast. Not that it mattered anymore. She was nothing now. Even pain meant little, as though her senses had been dulled to the point of non-existence.

Serenity was sure things hadn't always been this way. Her memories were filled with her master's beatings and presence—his rotten stench, his cruel words. Yet she felt certain there had once been something else.

When she tried to search her memory, she found only darkness; a world that had imploded only to leave a gaping void.

He nudged her with his foot. "That's enough now. I need my rest."

She sat up and surveyed her work. A little over six feet in length and wide enough to fit them both, the hole looked like a shallow grave. Above her head, the branches of trees creaked and groaned in the fall breeze, the now dry russet and copper leaves rustling together. A couple of star-shaped leaves spun through the air and landed on the freshly turned soil.

Serenity was unable to appreciate their beauty.

Her master sank down beside her and gathered her in his arms, pressing her torso to his chest. She turned her face away from his neck, avoiding as much intimate contact as possible. His strength matched none and he lifted her with no exertion.

She made no effort to hold on to him as he crawled to their resting place. Though the stench of death filled the air, she'd grown immune to it; in the same way a pig farmer no longer smells his livestock.

He laid her in the shallow grave with something close to tenderness and then squirmed down beside her.

Serenity's back pressed against the earth, moisture seeping through her thin shirt. She should feel the cold, have some sort of physical reaction, but she didn't. Whatever her master had done to her had left her immune to many of the things that would normally kill—starvation, the cold, a lack of oxygen. Though she recognized her discomfort, she couldn't generate any emotion about it. It was as if her heart had been frozen inside her chest.

She lay with her hands folded across her breasts. Small stones and uneven ground dug into her bones. He lay beside her, but she drew no warmth from the proximity of his body. He was as cold as death.

Her whole body stiffened as he pressed his hideous body against her and nuzzled her neck. She heard the wet licking as he ran his fat, blackened tongue over his cracked lips. She knew what was coming. While he didn't feed from her every night, he did so on a regular basis. That was the reason for him allowing her to live. He kept her close to supply him—in part anyway—with the blood he needed.

Serenity had seen the times he'd killed; the women he'd murdered. They always seemed to be the same—young, dark-haired, pretty. Each time, she'd stood by as they screamed and begged for help. But what could she do? She wanted to scream and beg for help herself. At least the torture of these girls was swift. Serenity's seemed to be never-ending.

She took one comfort from the times her master fed—when he took blood from her, the number of killings decreased.

Cold lips pressed against the delicate skin of her throat, probing for an area not encrusted with scabs. Like a kitten searching for its mother's teat, he pressed and sought until he found a smooth patch of skin. He darted at her, teeth nipping the skin at first. With a low growl, he bit deeper. Warm blood flooded down her neck—the first heat she'd experienced for a few nights—and the sucking started. Pressure on her throat, the sucking almost painful, drew the blood from her artery.

The repetitive feeding had changed her. Her heart was slow now, at times almost stopping, yet she maintained consciousness. Her need to breathe had lessened; she found herself often going for minutes at a time without needing to draw in air.

Her master brought back food for her from the cities— old packaged sandwiches that had passed their sell-by date or half-eaten slices of pizza someone had dumped in the trash. Though she had patches of a memory of being starving, the hunger seemed to have dissipated. Now, she struggled to eat the food he brought her. Even placing the food in her mouth turned her stomach.

The thought of leaving didn't even occur to Serenity. She only knew her existence with him. She knew nothing of the world outside that which he chose to show her. Occasionally, he would take her with him into a city or town, but those occurrences were rare.

Her master slurped and sucked at her throat, taking just enough blood to abate his appetite yet keep her alive. Serenity lay powerless, her mind blanking the horror of what was occurring, just as she'd blocked it so many nights before.

When he was done, he lay back, allowing his body to adjust to the fresh hit of blood. Then he sat up and clawed the earth over their bodies.

From nowhere, a small, warm hand touched her cheek. Serenity lifted her own hand to cover the one she felt, but her fingers touched only her own cool skin. Sadness overwhelmed her, an anguish clutching at her soul, though she kept the emotions hidden deep.

A tear ran from the corner of her eye and trickled down the side of her face, running a clear line through her dirty skin. She missed something terribly, like a gaping hole in the center of her chest, yet she didn't know what.

Often, she felt as though she wasn't alone. Another presence seemed to exist near her, hovering close but remaining unseen. Sometimes a warm gust of breath would brush against her ear or she'd hear a faint voice, like someone calling her name from a great distance. On occasions, the sensation of having someone standing beside her was so strong she believed she could have reached out and touched them.

But now wasn't one of those times. As quickly as she'd sensed the warm touch on her face, it vanished and she was left alone with her nightmare.

Serenity lay still as a corpse. Earth and clods of dirt scattered over her and weighed down her legs and torso. Sprinkles hit her cheeks, forehead and nose and she instinctively held her breath. She covered her face with her arm, creating a small pocket of air. It wasn't much but it was enough to last her through the day. Because of their shallow depth and non-compressed covering, air still permeated the earth.

With her eyes closed, she allowed herself to drift to sleep.

Confused and anguished nightmares plagued her. She dreamed of being chased and of chasing something she desperately wanted. Yet, always that something remained out of reach, hidden in the shadows. The same longing that filled her when she felt the presence near, haunted her in her dreams. That time spent away from her master—if only mentally—opened up a part of her she kept shut off when she was awake, but all it did was increase her emptiness. During her dreams, the certainty that something was missing filled her like a physical thing.

On some level she couldn't explain, not being able to remember hurt even more than remembering.

When the sun set once again, her master rose from the ground, shaking the dirt from his body. His lank, dark hair hung down by the sides of his face like drapes. His pale skin rippled with the darkness that lived beneath—the darkness that made him what he was—not vampire, not human, but something in-between. A milky film covered his brown irises so he looked as though he were blind; an irony considering his remarkable senses. His vision adjusted to the dark—not perfectly, but enough to make out the features on a person's face. His hearing was more sensitive than that of any animal and he could distinguish the sound of a coin being dropped on the sidewalk several miles away. Razor-sharp, pointed teeth filled his mouth, designed to slash and tear flesh as much as puncture it.

Her master was the ultimate being: a creature who existed only to kill. He had no weaknesses, at least none Serenity had discovered.

Serenity sat up, feeling no different than when she'd gone to sleep. She existed in a numb haze, unable to focus on either the past or the future. She struggled to link her thoughts coherently together, only experiencing the emotion of intense loneliness.

"You're coming to the city with me today, Serenity," he said. "I've got plans on how to upset humanity more than simply murdering individuals. There are people everyone else look up to. Do you know what I mean?" She shook her head and he continued. "There are powerful people in this world, important people, and if something were to happen to one of those people—one man in particular—the rest of the world would be in chaos."

"I don't know anything about these people," she said quietly.

"No, you wouldn't, you stupid bitch. But then you're not here to think, are you?"

Serenity remained silent, knowing no answer would be the right one.

"Anyway, for your treat, I'm taking you to a city today. I have plans, Serenity, plans that will change the world. If you behave yourself, you could be a part of them."

She nodded, her waist-length, dark hair hanging in her face.

He held out his arms to her. The embrace was not one of tenderness, but practicality. Obediently, she stepped into the circle of his arms. His cold fingers wrapped around the backs of her thighs and lifted her onto his hip. Serenity draped her arms around his neck, holding on for safety, knowing the breakneck speed they would be achieving.

Her master ran with a sudden burst of speed, snapping her head back and ripping the air from her lungs. There was no bounce to his gait. Instead, he ran with fluid motion, almost as though he were flying, his feet barely touching the ground.

Serenity was used to traveling at such speed now and where the sensation had previously left her confused and disoriented, it now barely affected her at all. She squeezed her eyes shut and curled against the horror holding her, trying to protect her face from the force of the wind his motion created.

The forests they'd slept in bordered the outskirts of the city. Within a matter of minutes, he slowed. Serenity allowed herself to open her eyes and he dropped her to her feet.

Together, they passed through the city's wide streets. Tall, leafy trees lined the walkway. The night's sky remained unlit by stars, the city's lights masking their natural luminescence, but the moon hung fat and low. Streetlamps lit either side of the street sending spotlights onto the ground.

In the distance, a huge rectangular spire reached into the sky. Arranged in a circle at the base, numerous flags

17

surrounded the monument. Huge spot lamps shone upward, lighting the area.

People of different creeds and colors milled around, large cameras hung around their necks or maps in their hands. They gave a wide berth to avoid the strange, rank-smelling couple. Serenity and her master received curious and distasteful glances, but they ignored the stares. Human repulsion meant nothing to them. Serenity had no capacity to care and her master viewed them to be little more than cattle.

As they walked at human pace, her master taking in everything with a keen eye, Serenity suddenly became aware they were no longer alone. The presence she sensed so often accompanied them, hovering beside her shoulder.

She spun around, almost certain she would see someone, but no one was there. Yet, she felt a small patch of warmth left on the night air and the emotions of love and affection washed through her as surely as if someone had placed their hand on her heart and injected her with their adoration. The moment caught her breath and she let out a little gasp of shock, her heart stuttering in her chest. She experienced a rush of emotions and, for the briefest of moments, her head cleared.

Panic caught her heart as she dove into her memories, searching for the thing she had lost. But as soon as tried to remember, the sensation was gone again.

She stood in the street. Her master continued to walk until he realized she'd stopped, allowing him to proceed without her. He turned back, a frown marking his already hideous face.

"Serenity," he hissed. "Come."

She didn't want to move, terrified she'd dispel the magic, but her master's voice controlled her and her legs moved of their own accord.

Before long, their feet crunched on gravel. Maintained gardens stretched as far as the eye could see, round spotlights and streetlamps lighting the area. After walking farther, they stepped onto a wide sidewalk. A road was on one side, the headlights of traffic sweeping past. On the other side, a tall fence, the black railings tipping with curved points, separated them from a beautiful, white house. It was two stories high, with elegant pillars. In front of the building, a fountain spurted water into the air.

Something about the place inspired awe in Serenity, though she couldn't understand the reason for her reaction.

Her master stood before the immense building, taking in its grandeur.

"This is where I'll make mankind take notice," he said. "This is where I'll expose the world of the supernatural for being what it really is—the ruler of humanity."

"What city are we in?" she asked. The answer would mean nothing to her, but somehow she thought it was the right one to ask.

He smiled, revealing his horrific teeth. "Washington D.C."

Chapter Two

Elizabeth Bandores lived in fear of forgetting her mother. Some days she struggled to picture her mother's face in her mind or remember the sound of her voice. If she closed her eyes, she tried hard to recall the feel of her mom's soft palm against her cheek, or the way she'd stroked Elizabeth's hair as she drifted into the arms of sleep.

Elizabeth was lucky. Her part-vampire genetics meant her memory was better than that of a full-human. She'd only been four years old when her mother disappeared into the void of the mine and she was lucky she remembered much of her at all. But two years had passed since she'd last seen her mom and even those fractured recollections were starting to fade.

Still, her memories of events after her mother's disappearance remained clear in her mind. It had been a frightening time for her, filled with serious conversations between the remaining adults in her life, when long words such as 'custody' and 'residence orders' seemed to spike through their muttered tones. However, after her daddy, Sebastian, and Uncle James went through her mother's things, they discovered Sebastian's name on Elizabeth's birth certificate. After that, the problems over who would take care of her and the scary, intense conversations subsided. Uncle James still acted strange at first, but once he saw how she lived—with her nanny, Bridget, taking care of her during the day—things had gotten easier.

On the big double bed before her, her backpack lay open, partially covering her rose-embroidered quilt. Now an expert in packing light, Elizabeth began the monotonous task of filling the bag with enough items of clothing to see her through the next couple of days. She added her favorite teddy and then snuck in the muslin cloth she still had as a comfort blanket. She felt like she was too old to still have a security blanket, but she couldn't bring herself to give it up. Should she have a friend around to play, she hid the blankie under her pillow.

Her daddy told her the room that was now hers had also been the one her mother slept in. It gave Elizabeth comfort to know that when she put her head on the pillow at night, her cheek rested on the same spot her mother's once had.

Elizabeth's gaze traveled to her white nightstand, where a photograph of her and her mom stood front and center. Her mom had caught her up from behind, her dark eyes looking directly into the camera. From the way her arm reached out, Elizabeth guessed her mom had turned the camera around to take the photograph herself.

Elizabeth knew her mother had dreamed of a normal life for her, but that was never going to happen. Elizabeth's ability to predict the future made living in the present difficult. She'd learned from a young age that people didn't like to hear her thoughts and dreams. Hearing predictions about their future—ones that always came true—made them fear and hate her.

The sound of her bedroom door swishing open made Elizabeth turn around. Her nanny, Bridget, stood in the doorway, one hand on her chunky hip. Her wrist jangled with numerous turquoise bracelets and a long braid of almost-white hair hung down one side of her body.

"Almost done?" Bridget asked, her British accent softened from the number of years spent living in America.

Elizabeth's shoulders sagged. "Nearly."

Bridget crossed the room and sat on the edge of Elizabeth's bed, the soft mattress sinking beneath her weight.

"Getting a bit sick of racing around the country, huh?"

Elizabeth put down the long-sleeved tee she was holding and climbed up onto the bed, huddling beside Bridget's solid form.

"I just keeping hoping we're going to find her, but then we don't and I feel even sadder than before."

Years had passed, yet her father hadn't given up. They both knew Serenity was still out there alive somewhere and he swore he'd continue the search until he brought her home.

Because Elizabeth dreamed of Serenity.

Sometimes it felt as though she were watching her mother from afar, as though hovering above her or lurking in the distance like a spy in the shadows. Other times, she saw the world from Serenity's eyes, experiencing what she did, feeling her emotions. Yet she was never able to see her mother's face. Naturally, when she watched the world from her mother's perspective she wouldn't expect to, but even when she watched from afar, her mommy's face was always cast in shadows.

At first, the dreams came to her sporadically and fragmented. Elizabeth struggled to make sense of them, to pin down Serenity's exact location. As she got older, she learned how to control them more; how to look for clues as to the whereabouts of her mother—names on buildings, street signs or landmarks Sebastian might recognize.

Sebastian was tireless in his search. Each time Elizabeth saw something in a dream or envisaged something about Serenity, he immediately sat her down in order for her to break down any leads she might have picked up on. Time and time again, they'd left in search of Serenity—New York, Phoenix, San Francisco—anywhere Elizabeth gave a clue to where she might have seen. Each time they missed Serenity, though on several occasions Sebastian had found clues to suggest they'd been there: a stinking hole in the ground, or worse, an unexplained and horrific murder of a young girl. They'd been on innumerable trips now, Sebastian racing across the county with Elizabeth clutched to him, but still they'd not so much as caught a glimpse of Serenity. Somehow Jackson knew to stay on the move, that if he stayed in one place for any length of time, they'd track him down.

Elizabeth's dream the previous night had placed Serenity in Virginia, so now they would head to that city for a couple of days to search for her. Elizabeth slid easily into her father's sleeping pattern while they were away—as though the sleep she didn't need normally was saved up for the times they were away. They always made sure the hotel they stayed at had blackout blinds or shutters and Sebastian would sleep under the bed to reduce his chance of exposure. The amount of money they had meant almost anything could be bought—including privacy—and the staff would be warned to stay out of the room until nightfall.

At night, they scoured the city and surrounding area, trying to pick up on a trail or hoping that Elizabeth's proximity to her mother would increase the strength of her dreams and visions so they could pin her down to a more specific location.

Bridget offered a smile of sympathy and rubbed Elizabeth's leg. "You know, I'm sure your daddy wouldn't want you to be upset. If you want to stop all this, you should tell him."

Elizabeth glanced up at her bedroom wall to where her clock hung, the face covered in colored diamante butterflies. The huge house in the Hollywood Hills seemed imposing to many, but her daddy had done everything he could to make the place her home, including decorating her bedroom just how she wanted. Of course, he'd gotten in some designers to take care of things—shopping for pink wall paper and princess furnishings was just a step too far for his vampire personality.

Six thirty-two p.m.

Only another minute before sunset.

Elizabeth knew the exact moment of sunset, whatever the time of year. It wasn't that her body was attuned in the same way Sebastian's was. She simply liked to know when her father would get up.

Having a vampire father didn't exactly help integrate her into society.

In order for them to live as much like a human family as possible, Sebastian had been diagnosed with a rare skin condition—one that made him allergic to the sun. Bridget took care of her for most of the day—doing the school run and feeding her dinner—but as soon as the sun fell, Sebastian was all hers again.

As Elizabeth got older, her need for sleep had diminished. Where most six-year-old girls would need ten to twelve hours a night, Elizabeth only needed eight. Her lack of need for sleep meant she still got time to spend with Sebastian. He would take her on excursions, moving in that way she knew no one else understood and she needed to keep a secret. She loved nothing more than clinging to her father as he flew across the city, holding her in his arms as though she were the most important person on earth.

The other kids at school still teased her about her family life, despite her obvious wealth. Picking up on mainstream culture, they didn't hesitate to call her daddy a vampire because of his inability to be exposed to the light. Of course, they had no idea how close to the truth their mean, childish jibes were. At night, as she snuggled down in bed, Elizabeth fantasized about showing each and every one of the mean kids just what a vampire really looked like.

A gentle knock on the door made both Elizabeth and Bridget look up. Her father's handsome, pale face poked around her bedroom door.

"Ready?" he asked, his green eyes flicking over the half-packed bag.

"In a minute, Sebastian" she said.

"It's Daddy to you."

"Yes, Daddy," she grinned.

Sebastian's attention turned to her nanny. "Has everything been okay?"

"Yes, fine. She's been good as gold."

Sebastian smiled and Elizabeth beamed back. "I wouldn't expect anything less. You can go now, Bridget, if you're ready. Thanks for everything."

"Same time tomorrow?" Bridget asked.

"I'm not sure when we'll be back, but if you could be here just in case."

"Of course." Bridget planted a kiss on top of Elizabeth's head. "See you, sweetie."

"Bye, Bridget," said Elizabeth.

Sebastian opened the door further and stood aside to allow Bridget past. The nanny's footsteps echoed down the hall. He stepped fully into the room and closed the door behind him.

"What are you doing?" he asked.

"I want to take my things with me."

"You don't need to pack, Elizabeth," he said. "If you need anything, we can buy it when we get there."

"Yeah, but I want *my* stuff," she protested, her lower lip pooching out. "I can't sleep without my things."

"It's easier for me to carry you without a bag."

She folded her arms across her narrow chest. "You're strong. You can manage."

"Hmm," he said, only partly disapproving.

Elizabeth knew she'd get her way. While he limited things like junk food and too much television, when it came to things she sought comfort in, he rarely said no. His compliance stemmed from guilt; guilt for what happened in the mines two years earlier. Elizabeth lived with her own guilt. She remembered breaking free from her mother's grasp and running in the total darkness, only to suddenly plunge into icy cold water. If she'd have stayed with her mother as she'd been supposed to, her daddy would never have been forced to come after her, leaving her mommy alone and unprotected.

In the weeks and months following Serenity's disappearance, Elizabeth cried many times about what happened. Her father tried to reassure her, telling her it wasn't her fault, she was just a child, but nothing soothed the sickening, aching hole in her heart.

The psychic connection she had with her mother meant she could not escape the pain, neither her own or her mother's. Serenity had become a shell with no memory of her family. Jackson kept her as his companion and she followed him around, making no attempt to escape. His regular bites kept her half drained, making her physically weak. The repetitive bites also had another effect—they'd made her forget who she was. She only knew of her existence in that moment.

"How much longer are you going to be?" Sebastian asked.

"I'll be ready in a minute," she said, her voice sharp with irritation.

Sebastian put up his hands in surrender. "Okay, okay. I'll wait for you downstairs. Just make sure you don't pack everything you own."

She gave an over-exaggerated sigh. "I won't."

He left the room at human speed and Elizabeth jumped back off the big bed to finish packing.

She picked up her shirt, preparing to add the item to her bag. The room around her blurred as though she were suddenly looking through a frosted window. Everything tilted, the floor sloping out from under her like the deck of a big ship in an ocean storm. She stumbled and steadied herself on the bed, but her world continued to change.

"Daddy?" she tried to call out, but her voice came out as only a whisper.

She glanced down to find the pink carpet of her bedroom had been replaced with gravel. As she raised her head, her bed disappeared. The walls of her room continued to ripple and blur, growing thinner and more transparent by the second.

Elizabeth squeezed her eyes shut, trying to bring her world back to normal. However much she knew they relied on her visions to find her mother, they always frightened her while they were happening. But when she opened her eyes again, her bedroom had completely vanished.

She stood on a long, wide street. Leafy trees flanked her on either side. In the distance, a tall spire reached into the sky, bigger than anything she'd ever seen before, lights shining up from its base. The structure was unusual because it wasn't circular but square.

Voices from behind made Elizabeth spin around.

In front of her was the back of a man she recognized as Jackson. Beside him stood her mother, her hair longer than she recalled, brushing right down her back. It was dirty and bedraggled—nothing like the soft, fragrant curls she remembered.

The stench that always surrounded Jackson filled her nostrils and she clamped a hand over her nose, trying to breathe through her mouth. It did no good and she tasted his rottenness on her tongue, cloying at the back of her throat.

Elizabeth's senses were more acute than most and the hideous reek made her want to gag.

"Mommy," Elizabeth said. "Mommy, I'm here. Can you hear me?"

Serenity had never been able to hear her before, but still Elizabeth needed to try. Normally, when she appeared near her mother, Elizabeth was little more than a ghost; an apparition no one could see. Yet, she was sure her mother sensed her somehow and this time was no different.

As she spoke, Serenity stopped walking.

Elizabeth paused, her heart thumping. She'd not seen her mom's face in all these visions and she longed for her mother to turn to her, recognize her and run with arms open wide, to squeeze her so hard it hurt.

Serenity turned.

Elizabeth screamed and stumbled back.

Her mother's face no longer looked like her own; it didn't look like anyone's face. A black, moving mask of shadows hid her features, like clouds racing across the moon. *What had she become?*

Elizabeth covered her face with both hands, no longer trying to avoid Jackson's stench, but to hide from the terrifying sight of her mother. Was she no longer the person Elizabeth had known? Had Jackson turned her into the same monster as him?

Tears flooded her eyes, blurring her vision and she stumbled away. Muted by her emotion, she distantly heard Jackson calling to Serenity. Elizabeth just wanted to be away from there, to be back in the warm safety of her home and her father's arms.

Her feet caught around each other and she fell, her face about to smack the rough gravel. Instead, she hit the soft mattress of her bed, the springs bouncing beneath her. Her own familiar scent welcoming her home.

Relieved to be back, but still horrified by what she'd seen, Elizabeth curled up on her bed. Her whole body trembled and her bowels felt loose and watery. She crushed her face into the soft feathers of her pillow and allowed the tears to come. Sobs wracked her body and her hand unconsciously sought her comfort blanket, forgetting she'd already packed it.

"I hope you're done already," her father's voice called from outside the door. Elizabeth didn't answer. She felt a slight breeze across her forehead as her father pushed open the door, and, finding her in tears, used his vampire's speed to be instantly at her bedside.

"Elizabeth?" he said from above. "What's wrong?"

She couldn't answer him and only continued to cry into her pillow.

"Elizabeth!" he repeated, his tone slightly brusque. "Tell me what's happened."

She lifted her face to him and he wrapped his arms around her narrow waist, pulling her onto his lap. Grateful to be held in his solid, very real embrace, she choked back the tears enough to speak.

"I saw Mommy, but she didn't look like herself. Her face was all dark and scary."

"Shhh," he said, rocking her. "What you saw wasn't really your mom. It was a projection, something your mind picked up on."

Elizabeth shook her head against him. "No, it was her. She's different now."

His finger touched the bottom of her chin, tilting her face up to his.

"Elizabeth, if all this is too much, if you can't face the thought of still looking for her, if everything is too upsetting, then we won't. You know how much I love your mother. I love her as much as I love you, but I won't see you upset by all of this." He squeezed his eyes shut, and then opened them again. "You're only a child and you need to be allowed to act like one. Your mother would never have wanted you to be growing up scared of her."

29

"I don't have a choice," she said. "I can't control it. It's like she's calling to me and I can't help but find her."

His cool lips pressed against the top of her head. "I wish I could take it away from you," he said. "I wish there was some way I could make you a normal girl."

"I don't. If I was normal, we'd never be able to find her and bring her home."

He nodded against her head. "I know. I just hate this."

"Me too."

"Any time you're ready to talk about what else you saw, you tell me, okay? And don't worry; we're not going anywhere tonight. I'm not about to start dragging you around the country when you're so upset."

Elizabeth sat up. "I'm okay. I can tell you what I saw. I want Mommy home too."

"Are you sure?"

Elizabeth nodded and took a breath. "I was standing in front of a huge spike sticking up into the sky. Loads of people were hanging out, Sebastian—"

"Daddy," he automatically corrected.

"Daddy," she repeated, and then carried on. "People with cameras, maps and books. And I saw a really big house—even bigger than our house! It was white and had pillars like the ones in the books at school when we were learning about Greece. There was loads of grass, all cut short and perfect."

"Hang on. Tell me more about the house."

"I don't know anything else. The front was round. It was more like a castle than just a big, white house."

Sebastian's face widened with recognition. "The White House? Are you telling me you saw the White House?"

Elizabeth wrinkled her small nose and rolled her eyes to the sky. She smacked her forehead with the palm of her hand. "Duh, yeah, of course it was the White House. Why didn't I recognize it right away?"

"You were upset and disoriented. It's not surprising you didn't recognize it. But what the hell is Jackson doing there?"

Elizabeth pursed her lips and shrugged.

"Maybe he's visiting the President."

Chapter Three

Sebastian decided they couldn't wait another night before searching for Serenity. Elizabeth's vision had been too powerful to ignore. Such a precise location as the National Mall meant pinning her down might prove easier than before.

Another thing worried Sebastian—the reason for Jackson being in Washington. He was pretty sure Jackson wasn't just sightseeing. What possible reason could Jackson have for being right in the center of things like that—for taking Serenity right into the middle of everything? Serenity was officially a missing person and anyone might spot her. Perhaps Jackson didn't care, but even so, something set Sebastian's nerves on edge.

"Are you sure you're okay to travel?" he asked Elizabeth as they stood in their vast hall, preparing to leave. "If you feel ill or dizzy in any way, you'd tell me, wouldn't you?"

"I'm okay," she said. "I'm just a bit sad about Mommy."

Sebastian's heart broke. He wished he could make things all right again, but he was doing what he could. He hated that their little girl had been forced to grow up without a mother and he felt her pain as clearly as his own.

Bridget went some way to being a stand-in mother for Elizabeth, but they all knew no one would ever replace Serenity. Bridget had come recommended to him by another vampire who lived in San Francisco. Though she was one hundred percent human, her son had been turned when he was in his late twenties. Her son told her everything and, as a spiritualist, she'd accepted the nature of his existence. Sebastian offered her an inordinate amount of money to come and take care of Elizabeth, and of course as soon as Bridget met the beautiful child she would be looking after, it was impossible for her to say 'no'.

But Sebastian lived with his own pain. How he'd let Serenity down made him feel sick every time he thought of it. He'd promised to keep her safe, but he'd failed her by being part of the circumstances that had allowed Jackson to kidnap her.

Though part of him argued with himself that he'd made the right decisions at the time—that Serenity would have always chosen for him to save Elizabeth from the water in the mine before thinking of her own safety—he couldn't help questioning the choices he'd made. If he'd never taken them into the mine, Serenity might still be with them now. He'd been a fool to take them to such a dangerous place and assume the only danger would be from Jackson.

Sebastian lifted Elizabeth in his arms. She wrapped her arms tight around his neck. Sebastian moved fast enough to not be seen, but he needed to slow slightly to accommodate both Elizabeth's presence and her fragility. Her part-vampire genetics meant she withstood the speed in a way most humans could not, but she was still only a six-year-old girl and he wanted to protect her.

Even at his supernatural speed, it would still take hours to reach Washington. If they wanted to catch Jackson and Serenity in the same place Elizabeth had envisioned him, they needed to move fast.

With his daughter clutched against him, Sebastian left the house at human pace. The huge front gates to the property opened before them and he passed through. Once on the sidewalk, Sebastian broke into full gait. Within moments, he'd left the city far behind. He had no need to stick to the roads or highways, and instead cut across wilderness areas, traversing across roads when he needed to.

Sebastian didn't tire; his body wasn't capable of such a thing. Elizabeth, however, did. As they cut through New Mexico, the city of Albuquerque in the distance, he felt her arm around his neck loosen and he slowed to human pace.

"Are you okay?" he asked, setting her down for a moment.

"Yeah, my arm was just getting a bit sore."

"Okay, let's rest for a while."

"But what about Mommy?" she said, a hint of panic heightening her pitch. "We might miss her."

"We'll be able to pick up her trail easily," he said, though he wasn't sure how much he believed that. They'd missed her on numerous occasions before and always lost whatever trail they found. Jackson's ability to move in the light when Sebastian needed to shut himself away gave Jackson an advantage.

They sat side by side on a boulder on a hillside, the shadows of rock formations all around. In the distance, the twinkling white and gold lights of the city spread out before them, looking like something out of a science fiction movie.

Before Elizabeth had come into his life, Sebastian had forgotten how it felt to love a daughter. He'd forgotten the total forgiveness and acceptance that came from the love of a parent for a child. There was nothing Elizabeth could ever do to stop him loving her. The protectiveness he felt toward

Elizabeth was fierce and powerful, and as he'd gotten to know her more and more over the past couple of years, his emotions had only grown in intensity.

He still hated that he would never be a part of her daytime life. When Serenity first disappeared and Elizabeth came to live with him, he had considered home schooling her and keeping her to his schedule. However, the possibility only flashed briefly in his mind. He didn't want Elizabeth to miss out on the normal experiences of childhood—to play in the sun, to go to the beach, to attend birthday parties with her friends. Because of this, he'd had no choice but to employ Bridget to take care of Elizabeth during the day.

He found the summer months to be the hardest, when the days were long and the nights short. He hardly got to see her and found he almost looked forward to the times they went away in search of Serenity. During those times, Elizabeth lived to his schedule and he got her all to himself.

Beside him, Elizabeth stretched out her arms, rubbing at her aching shoulder muscles and wiggling her fingers. Sebastian sat, trying to remain patient and ignore the bubbling pit of nerves that roiled in the pit of his stomach.

I should have left Elizabeth at home, he thought. *I'd be in D.C. by now.*

But he needed Elizabeth. If they got to the city only to find Serenity and Jackson had vanished again, Elizabeth may well pick up on something else.

Sebastian was keenly aware of the passing of time. Well over an hour had passed since Elizabeth's vision and with Jackson's speed Serenity could be miles away by now. Yet, something about the precise location made Sebastian think Jackson had more of a reason to be there than simply taking in the sights; a reason that might keep him there for longer than a fleeting pass-through. When he'd been human, Jackson had been a bully who'd enjoyed nothing more than watching others—in particular, Serenity—suffer. Now, in his supernatural state, what would stop him from wanting to continue his bullying ways on a whole new level? The idea of creating fear amongst the whole of humanity would surely be something that would give Jackson an entirely new sense of purpose.

Washington D.C. was one place he could do exactly that.

"We can go now," said Elizabeth. "My arms feel better."

Not wanting to wait any longer, Sebastian jumped to his feet and pulled Elizabeth up with him. He picked her up again and took off at a burst of speed with his daughter huddled against him.

A couple of hours later, they hit the outskirts of Washington. It was still late evening and traffic flowed at a steady stream through the city's wide streets.

Not until they reached the National Mall and he saw the monuments Elizabeth had described did he slow to human pace. A couple of people walking nearby started in surprise at the sudden appearance of the man and little girl, but, as most people do when they see something they didn't quite believe, they shrugged it off as 'imagining things' and kept walking.

Sebastian crouched to Elizabeth's level. "Are you all right?"

"I can sense her close by," Elizabeth shivered despite the unseasonably warm night.

Sebastian nodded. Jackson's rancid scent tainted the air, like rotting trash cans left open in the sun. The odor gave him hope, but he didn't want to give in to it. They'd missed Serenity so many times before; to allow himself to hope would only mean heartbreak once again when they couldn't find her.

Tourists meandered around them, unaware of the horror in their midst. They stood and posed in front of the monuments, flashing billion-watt smiles or double handed 'victory' signs. None of them looked at Sebastian and Elizabeth with anything amounting to suspicion. The good-looking father and daughter appeared no different than any other tourist. Sebastian knew Jackson and Serenity wouldn't be blending in so easily. They were close by, and wherever they were, they'd be catching people's attention.

"We need to catch him by surprise," Sebastian said, keeping his voice low. Although they were nowhere near Jackson yet, the monster had the hearing of a vampire. If he were listening out for them, he might pick the voice of another immortal out from the crowd.

"What do we do when we find them?" Elizabeth asked, her tone matching her father's.

"I'll take out, Jackson," he said. "As soon as Serenity sees you, I'm sure she'll remember who you are. Just take her hand and run away as fast as you can. Don't worry about what direction you're heading in. Just put distance between your mommy and Jackson."

Elizabeth nodded, the head on her shoulders far too mature for a six-year-old.

"And, Elizabeth," he continued.

"Yes, Sebastian?"

"Whatever you do—whatever you hear—don't look back and don't try to come back for me. I'll find you."

"What if you get hurt?" Worry turned her voice into a whine.

"I'll heal. Don't come back for me, Elizabeth," he warned again. "You're only six years old." He held himself back from saying; *you know what happened last time.* The guilt she'd lived with for the past two years was already far too great for any child to bear. He suspected any normal child may have forgotten some of the event—after all, she'd barely turned four when everything happened—but Elizabeth was no normal child and she remembered the events with a clarity that was unnerving.

"I won't," she said. "I promise. I'll do what you say."

He pulled her close, squeezing her in a hug he needed to restrain for fear of crushing her with his inhuman strength. He dropped a kiss on top of her head, relishing the feel of her soft hair against his face and the innocence of her smell.

Sebastian stood up straight and took Elizabeth by the hand. Together they walked, their feet crunching on gravel. Tourists wandered past them, relaxed and happy, but Sebastian and Elizabeth were caught in a bubble of tension.

"There!" exclaimed Elizabeth, pointing into the distance.

Serenity stood in front of some iron railings, her arms wrapped around her skinny frame. Her voluptuous figure was nowhere to be seen. She'd wasted away and was emaciated. If Sebastian hadn't known better, he would have immediately thought her to be someone suffering from anorexia or a severe drug addiction. Her hair hung in dirty ropes around her face and down her back, almost brushing the tops of her non-existent buttocks. Her cheeks were hollowed, her cheekbones sharp beneath her dirty skin. Her eyes were sunken, dark and haunted with abject misery.

Jackson stood beside her, his hand wrapped around Serenity's upper arm. Even from this distance, Sebastian could see Jackson's fingers digging into Serenity's flesh. The hold was clearly not one of affection.

Jackson looked no different than the last time Sebastian had seen him; his face white and cracked, his eyes milky. The monster's hair resembled Serenity's in texture, though was much shorter.

Something about the similarities of their appearances snapped the band of rage he'd kept tightly strung within him for the last two years. Fury boiled through him like nothing he'd felt before and he dropped Elizabeth's hand.

"Jackson," he growled, his voice a low rumble deep in his chest.

Serenity's captor turned at the sound, his eyes narrowed. Before Jackson even had a chance to consider who'd uttered his name, Sebastian leapt. Where two years ago the idea of sinking his teeth into the monster's throat had repulsed him, he no longer cared. He would rip the evil brute who'd done this to Serenity to shreds.

Jackson had become complacent. He'd not given Sebastian another thought, whereas Sebastian had spent two years nurturing his hatred for Jackson. Now, seeing what he'd done to Serenity took his anger to a whole other level.

Sebastian ran between the tourists in a blur and collided with Jackson, knocking him away from Serenity. The creature let out a yelp of surprise and the two fell backward, Sebastian landing on top of Jackson.

Around them, tourists cried out in shock.

Sebastian's fangs elongated, his jaw jutting forward, morphing the shape of his face. He felt his eyes burn and knew they would be glowing yellow; a terrifying vision for anyone who might catch sight of them in his pale face.

Sebastian's sheer anger made him stronger than Jackson, but that didn't stop Jackson from fighting back. The monster bucked under Sebastian's weight, his head twisting from side to side, trying to snap at Sebastian with his pointed, yellowed teeth. Sebastian's strength, fury and dominant position kept Jackson beneath him.

With one hand, he pinned Jackson's head down, pressing his cheek to the ground. Jackson's eye—the only eye visible— widened in shock when he realized who his attacker was, but before he had the chance to react further, Sebastian lunged down and bit.

The bite wasn't that of a vampire about to feed, but the bite of an animal intending to kill. He sank his teeth deep, forcing his body not to react to the repellent blood flowing over his teeth and tongue. He fought against the desire to expel the substance from his mouth and forced himself to rip across. A huge chunk of flesh came away in his mouth. Jackson tried to shriek, but the sound came out as a wet gurgle.

Sebastian sat up and wiped his face with the back of his hand. He looked down at the wounded monster below him and his nose wrinkled in disgust. A dark pool of blood crept out from beneath Jackson's head, edging toward the people who'd gathered by.

The tourist's yells of surprise had morphed into screams and curses of "What the fuck?" The group of bystanders began to back away, some turning to run. Others seemed unable to tear their eyes away from the scene, some sense of morbid curiosity keeping them close.

Elizabeth, Sebastian thought. *Where's Elizabeth?*

But he couldn't allow himself to be distracted by her or Serenity. Not this time. He needed Jackson dead.

As though he knew not to touch the gaping hole, Jackson's hands fluttered by his throat. He didn't make any attempt to turn his head to look up at Sebastian or fight back. The vicious attack had left him stunned and seriously wounded.

Somehow, the speed of the attack didn't feel satisfying enough for Sebastian. Even though their previous encounter had ended badly and he'd known he needed to take Jackson out quickly, part of him wanted Jackson to fight back. He wanted to take out all the grief and rage he'd experienced over the past two years. He wanted to bite and hit and claw until he'd purged himself of all the pain Jackson had caused his family.

Though there was a gaping hole in Jackson's neck, Sebastian knew it wouldn't be enough. Given time, his throat would heal.

He took Jackson's chin roughly in one hand and twisted his face so Jackson had no choice but to make direct eye contact with him. A thrill went through Sebastian as he saw the panic, pain and fear in Jackson's eyes.

When he spoke, his voice was level, all of his anger channel into his actions. "This is for what you've done to Serenity. This is for all the years of torture you put her through. For every time you hit her, or called her names, or even looked at her in the wrong way."

Jackson's eyes began to flutter shut and Sebastian gave his head a brief but vicious shake. His eyes opened and despite the extreme blood loss, he managed to focus on Sebastian.

"For the last two years, you've taken a mother away from her child. You've forced a little girl to grow up knowing and experiencing her mother's pain. This is your punishment."

With that, Sebastian drew back his arm and punched forward, his fist plunging into Jackson's chest. His knuckles smashed through Jackson's ribcage, shattering bone. Thick, viscous, cold blood surrounded Sebastian's fist. His fingers closed around the monster's motionless heart and, with one swift movement, he yanked it out, tearing arteries, muscles and connective tissue.

Jackson bucked, convulsing.

All around them, total panic had taken hold. People screamed and pushed to get past each other. Sebastian glanced up, trying to spot Serenity and Elizabeth but they were nowhere to be seen. *Good, that was good.* He didn't want Elizabeth to see what had just happened, though it wouldn't surprise him if she'd seen it in some other way or would dream about it later.

Still holding the cold heart in one hand, his fist and arm drenched with black blood, he got to his feet. This place was full of security and they'd be here any minute.

He flung the heart away and wiped his hand on his pants in disgust.

As he stepped away, what looked like a gray mold started to creep over Jackson's body. Like rapidly growing tree roots, the mold sent out tendrils of itself, spreading over Jackson's cheeks and forehead. It rippled across his skin, filling in his eye sockets, creeping up his nose, masking his already hideous features. The gray substance met in the middle, completely covering his face and, only a second later, Jackson's thrashings ceased.

Sebastian stepped forward and drew back his booted foot. With one move, he kicked the monster's corpse. Dust exploded around him—a cloud of death.

The few tourists still hanging around ran from the dust, afraid they'd inhale whatever the freakish material was.

Sebastian's shoulders sagged in relief. Finally, it was done. Jackson was dead and they would be free to get on with their lives as a family.

The wail of a police siren cut through the night air, quickly joined by a second, and then a third. In this high security area, with the threat of terrorism never far from people's minds, something like a murder out in the open was always going to bring the cops running.

Of course, the witnesses would struggle to describe what they had seen, and now, with Jackson as little more than dust in the air, they didn't even have a body as proof. Sebastian knew people would start to question what they'd seen before long. In order to save their sanity and hang onto the fragile facade of what they thought they knew, they'd block out the truth in favor of a more realistic explanation—two men fighting, only for both to take off before the cops got there.

With Jackson dealt with, Sebastian's attention turned to locating the whereabouts of Serenity and their daughter.

Chapter Four

The moment Sebastian attacked Jackson, Elizabeth ran to Serenity's side.

"Mommy?" she said, taking Serenity's hand. Her fingers felt like bone, as though she'd taken hold of the hand of a skeleton.

Serenity glanced down, but no recognition or pleasure lit her dark eyes. She stared at Elizabeth as though she not only didn't know who she was, but that she barely believed a little girl was holding her hand at all.

"It's me, Mommy," Elizabeth said, tugging on her hand. "Come on, we've got to go!"

Serenity didn't even look back to where Sebastian now crouched on top of Jackson, to where the vampire was about to tear out the throat of the monster who'd held her captive for such a long time. Instead, she walked forward, shuffling along like an old woman, allowing herself to be led.

"We've got to go faster," Elizabeth said, dragging her along. Obediently, Serenity picked up her pace.

Elizabeth didn't know where she was headed, only that she wanted to disappear into the crowds and get as far away from Jackson as possible. Sebastian had told her to get away and she planned to do exactly that. Tourists stood, gathered around the fight, watching with a mixture of distaste and captivation. When Sebastian's teeth flashed white and he raised his head briefly before striking, his yellow eyes glowed in the dark and a rippled murmur went around the crowd, a nervousness that had not been present before. A second later, Sebastian struck and screams echoed around them.

Elizabeth pushed through the crowds, people pressed in on every side. She couldn't see above them so simply pressed forward. Then the people started to move, scrambling to get away from the scene unfolding before them. Elizabeth and Serenity were carried along in the crowd.

The thought that Sebastian wouldn't find them again never crossed Elizabeth's mind. The past two years spent in her father's company had shown her how powerful he was. Sebastian was like a superhero she saw on television—with his ability to move so fast she sometimes couldn't see him, and he had amazing hearing and sight. He was stronger than anyone else's daddy, though Elizabeth knew she wasn't allowed to talk about it, however much she wanted to boast about him to her friends. Both he and Uncle James had warned her if anyone ever thought there was something different about him, people might come and take her to live with another family. Elizabeth didn't need to be told twice.

Bodies buffeted her on every side and Elizabeth stumbled, losing her grip on her mother's hand. She thought she was about to fall and panic fired through her. Hands caught her from behind, holding her upright and propelling her on. Elizabeth glanced back to discover Serenity had caught her. She flashed her mother a quick smile, but she still saw no recognition in her fathomless eyes. Serenity had reacted but perhaps only through instinct. Even so, this small amount of awareness, amount of *care*, made Elizabeth want to cry.

Her mother's hands remained on Elizabeth's upper arms and Elizabeth reached up and covered one with her own.

More screams came from behind and they hurried on. Despite the mass of people, Jackson would still find them if he somehow managed to get away from Sebastian.

As they increased the distance between them and the fight, people dispersed over the huge landscaped area, leaving them with breathing space. Still, Elizabeth didn't stop. Her mind was programmed with one thing—*get away, get away, get away*. Losing her mother two years earlier had been her fault and, while that might be a hard thing for a six-year-old to carry on her shoulders, she had no intention of bearing the same guilt twice.

Someone suddenly appeared in front of them. Elizabeth almost collided with the set of legs, but a hand reached out and caught her before she did. She shrieked, then realized who it was and the scream turned into a relieved laugh.

"Sebastian!" She took in the sight of the black blood covering his face and one of his hands. A rank stench came off him. She wrinkled her nose. "Ugh, gross. You really stink."

Sebastian tore a piece of material from the bottom of his shirt, his eyes briefly flicking to Serenity as he did so. He used the cloth to wipe his face and hand and then dumped it in a waiting trashcan.

"Better?" he asked and Elizabeth nodded.

"Is he dead?"

Again, Sebastian's eyes focused on Serenity. "Dead and gone. For good this time. But we still need to get out of here. The police will be here soon, asking questions. None of us should be anywhere close when they get here."

"Can we go home?" she asked, her heart giving a happy little skip.

Sebastian's gaze once again flicked to Serenity but she made no attempt to protest or ask any questions.

"Sure."

Sebastian pulled Elizabeth to his side and faced Serenity. He reached out and touched her cheek, her skin cool and waxy beneath his touch. She didn't react to his touch—neither flinched, nor leaned into his hand—her eyes remaining impassive.

"I've missed you so much," he said, but Serenity didn't respond. "Do you know who we are?"

Her eyes darted between him and Elizabeth. Finally she spoke, her voice a mere whisper. "I don't know who *I* am."

"We know who you are," Elizabeth piped up, full of enthusiasm. "We'll help you remember."

Sebastian nodded. "She's right. This must all be terrifying for you, but we'll make you better. We'll make everything better again, I promise."

Inwardly he recoiled, his words reminding him of the promise he'd made to protect them two years earlier and how badly he'd failed.

He wouldn't break another promise.

"I have to carry you to get us home," he said, studying her face. She was so different from the woman he remembered. When they'd first met and Jackson had been beating on her, he'd still seen a fire behind her bruised and beaten exterior. Even worse was comparing her to the strong and balanced woman he'd been reunited with two years ago. Serenity had been through so much—alone—and yet she'd survived and not only built her own life, but had raised a beautiful daughter by herself.

This woman was a shell. He could see none of Serenity in her.

"I understand," she said. "I had to travel that way with my master."

Sebastian physically flinched at the term. "Never call him that! He wasn't your master. He was your kidnapper and he doesn't even deserve to be given a name. He's nothing but dust now and he'll stay that way."

Doubt flickered across her still beautiful, yet ravaged face. "I don't know how to believe anything anymore."

He reached out and took her hand. "You can believe me—me *and* Elizabeth. We won't lie to you."

"You feel like him," she said. "You're cold like my master."

Sebastian's heart almost tore itself in two and he gritted his teeth, trying to suppress the emotion raging within him. To be compared to Jackson from Serenity's own lips hurt in a way he couldn't fathom. He kept his eyes lowered, knowing they would be burning in the night and his fangs threatened to elongate.

"He's not your master," he growled. "He never was."

Elizabeth warm palm slipped into his and he looked down at their daughter. Her wide, dark eyes stared up at him and she gave him a small smile.

"She doesn't remember. Let's just go home now, okay?"

He nodded. "Okay."

Sebastian tentatively drew Serenity toward him, worried about her reaction. But she allowed herself to be pulled to his side. With one arm wrapped around the top of her thighs, he lifted her onto his hip. Automatically, she folded her arms around his neck and he had to stop himself turning his head and burying his face against the crook of her elbow. Jackson's scent still surrounded her, though he imagined it also clung to him.

Elizabeth reached for him and he bent and scooped her up.

Across his chest, she reached out and touched her mother's hair. "I missed you, Mommy."

Serenity didn't answer.

His heart broke for the tenth time that night.

With his family back in his arms for the first time in two years, Sebastian took off through the night. He still had several hours till dawn but he didn't want to leave Elizabeth and Serenity together without him being able to spend some time with them first. Plus, he needed to let Bridget know what was happening. She'd freak at a strange, vacant woman suddenly wandering around the house.

Sebastian expected Serenity to sleep during the day, keeping to the routine of a vampire—or whatever half-breed monster Jackson had been. Just because Jackson could walk in the light, didn't mean that he did as a habit. His kind was always drawn to darkness and the fact that the sun didn't harm him didn't mean he would have wanted to bathe in it.

He'd keep Elizabeth off school for the next couple of days. She deserved to get to spend time with her mother after everything they'd been through. With her nocturnal adventure, she'd probably end up sleeping all day as well, but Sebastian still wanted Bridget around in case Elizabeth woke before nightfall.

He ran; his two loves clutched to his body, close to his heart. Wind caused by his velocity tore around his body, whipping his clothes back, pulling the skin back from his face. The miles flew beneath his feet, leaving the city and forests behind them. He was focused on his house in the hills, in getting Serenity and Elizabeth within the four walls. For the first time, he realized, he'd thought of the place as a home, as a place of sanctuary. Before, the house was only a building, yet now he craved to be back there.

Serenity didn't recognize the identity of the people who'd taken her into their lives. By the way they smiled and spoke in calm voices, she assumed they didn't plan on causing her any harm. They told her they knew her and she took some comfort in their words, but the confused void she existed in hadn't dispersed.

Being held in this man's arms felt strange, but not in a bad way. His masculine and heady scent caused her slow beating heart to trip faster. The hard muscle of his bicep curved into her waist, holding her close with firm tenderness. She rested her face in the crook of his neck and closed her eyes. Her lips pressed against his cool skin, the tiny hairs at the base of his neck tickling her nose. Only inches from her head, on the other side of the man's broad throat, the little girl's head was buried into his shoulder. Her dark hair flew back in streamers and she clung to him as though her life depended upon it. The presence of the child stirred something deep inside of her—not recognition—but *something*. The aura the child gave off made her think of all the times she'd sensed someone close. When she'd felt as though she wasn't alone.

Though thankful for her master's death, it also made her nervous. She was incapable of thinking either forward or back, and now, even the small amount of her life she'd come accustomed to had vanished. Even though she'd despised him, she'd only known life with her master. The idea that he was gone left her feeling as though she were suspended above a void with someone about to cut the rope.

The pale-skinned man with the piercing green eyes flew through the night, perhaps no faster than her master had moved, but certainly with more grace. With her master no longer around, Serenity became aware of the stench her own body gave off; a result of being kept so close to her master for so long. The smell also clung to the man, but not at the strength she emitted, as though it were entrenched in the depths of her pores.

Her body odor embarrassed her. Something inside her gut writhed in a tight knot. Everything made her self-conscious now. What sort of person was she to not know anything—that she was so forgettable she'd even forgotten herself?

They stopped on the outskirts of a city she could not name, allowing them a respite, though the man did not seem affected by the long journey. Serenity sat on the cold, hard ground; her arms wrapped around her legs.

She watched the man and child exchange glances. The man removed his jacket and wrapped it around Serenity's shoulders. She flinched when his hands made contact with her shoulders, unused to any touch that didn't inflict pain.

"I don't know your names," she admitted.

"This is Elizabeth," he said, drawing the little girl to his side. "My name is Sebastian."

"I'm Serenity," she said. Then she added, "I think."

Elizabeth grinned, "You definitely are."

"Ready to go?" Sebastian asked her. Unsure of what other answer to give, she nodded.

He pulled them both into his arms again and she settled into the comfort of his strength. She wanted to know this man. To be held in his arms for even a second made up for the time she'd spent in the cold embrace of her master.

She lost track of time as he continued to run through the night, passing numerous towns and cities. Finally, the pinprick of lights of another big city grew brighter and she realized they weren't heading past this city but deeper into it.

Above them, huge white letters spelled out 'Hollywood', hanging as though suspended in the night sky. Had she seen these letters before? Had she been here with her master? She wasn't sure but the sight stirred something within her.

Within minutes, they'd stopped outside of a set of tall iron gates, a seven-foot wall stretching on either side. Carefully, the man lowered both her and the child to the ground, so they stood, flanking him. Through the bars of the gates she saw a beautiful house with a double-fronted door, gravel driveway and pillars around the porch.

The man took a set of keys from his pocket and pressed a button on a key-fob. In front of them the gates slowly opened.

The girl ran on ahead, skipping over the gravel.

His hand settled around her waist and he helped her toward the front steps of the building. Behind them, the gates automatically closed.

The house was more luxurious than anything she'd been inside before. She'd been living out in the open or buried beneath the earth and the thought of being enclosed within four walls and a roof made her insides tremor with uncertainty.

Her emotions were still tamped down and she was unable to react to her sudden case of nerves. Everything her master had subjected her to had left her as a shell and no matter what she suffered, it felt like only a hint of what she should be experiencing.

She didn't exactly have a whole lot of choices. This man, Sebastian, had told her that she didn't have a master. Without a master, what was she supposed to do with herself? She could hardly take off alone and build a new life. She was nothing but a ghost in her own world.

Perhaps she had a new master now. She glanced at the beautiful man beside her. Maybe he would be the one to help her remember. But what, she wondered, would he want in return?

Chapter Five

Sebastian allowed Elizabeth to run ahead, through the front door. He went to help Serenity up the couple of steps leading up to the entrance, but there was no strength in her legs. He scooped her up and her arms looped around his neck. Again the amount of weight loss she'd suffered struck him. Her wrists and forearms were skeletal, her thighs not much bigger than her arms. Her weight would never have meant anything to Sebastian, but right now she probably only weighed a fraction more than Elizabeth.

"You need to eat," he told her as he carried her through the front door. "You're wasting away."

She shook her head against him. "I can't."

"Yes, you can. I can get you whatever you want—pizza, Chinese, Mexican—anything you desire."

"Please... don't. Even the thought of putting something in my mouth makes me sick."

"Then I need to get you to a hospital. You need to be put on a drip."

She shook her head again. "No hospitals. I don't want to go anywhere else." She lifted her hand, inspecting it, as if suddenly noticing the thick grime wedged beneath her nail-beds, the filth covering her skin.

"I'm dirty," she said, pointing out the fact.

"Okay," said Sebastian, heading toward to huge curved staircase at the back of the house. "Let's get you cleaned up."

Elizabeth ran along behind them as he mounted the stairs, taking them two at a time. His big house in the Hollywood Hills was like a different place now that Elizabeth had moved in. Before, it had only looked like a place someone pretended to live in. Perfectly furnished and with a fridge full of food in case suspicions were aroused, the place had been more like a stage house. With Elizabeth, the house had become a home. Photographs of her were framed and hung on the wall or placed on the hall console. They were of important times—her first day at school, riding a bike, writing her first words.

All things Serenity had missed out on and would never get back.

He took her to Elizabeth's bedroom—the room both she and Elizabeth had used before she'd been taken. The adjoining bathroom contained a large tub and Sebastian took her directly into the en-suite, not wanting to put her on the bed. Jackson's stench still clung to her—as it probably did him—and he didn't want to taint Elizabeth's bed with the smell.

He set Serenity down on the tiled floor and Serenity took up her default position—sitting with her knees hunched up to her chest, her arms wrapped around her legs.

Sebastian leaned into the tub and turned on the faucet. Water thundered into the porcelain tub and Sebastian picked up a bottle sitting on the side and added a dash of floral-scented bubble bath.

He turned to their daughter, who hovered in the bathroom doorway. "Elizabeth, go and find your mommy some clean clothes."

After she'd gone missing, James had helped Sebastian take all the personal things from Serenity's small apartment. He'd kept a wardrobe of clothes for her the whole time.

I need to phone James, he thought. The other man had been Serenity's best friend and he deserved to know that she'd been found. Her disappearance had affected them all, and even though James Bently didn't live close by any more, he had a right to know about Serenity's safe return. Still, it would be a difficult conversation. The two males had never completely seen eye-to-eye and explaining Serenity's condition would be hard.

Later, he promised himself.

With the tub almost full, he turned to Serenity. "Are you ready? Do you need help?"

Serenity gave a brief nod and used the side of the bath to pull herself to her feet.

She stood beside the bath like a child; her arms huddled into her narrow chest, her shoulders curled.

"May I?" he offered and again she gave a nod.

With tenderness, he removed her clothes, tugging down the filthy jeans, pulling her crusty t-shirt over her head. Her skin was so pale it was almost blue, and bruises and scabs covered her body. Her once luscious, bouncy curls were knotted ropes that hung down, allowing her to hide behind the curtain.

When the tub was full, he lifted her in his arms again and settled her into the deep water. She moaned as the bubbles encased her skin, though Sebastian couldn't tell if the sound came from pleasure or pain.

With one arm, he supported her back, in the same way he would a newborn baby. Steam filled the room, condensing in a fine mist on the tiled walls. The scent of flowers filled his nostrils, masking Jackson's rotten odor.

He washed her hair with his free hand, his strong fingers massaging her scalp, creating a foaming lather. For the first time, he caught sight of the horrible scabs and scarring on her neck. Furious, he bit down on his emotions. He had no direction in which to vent them except at himself. Jackson was gone now and he was left to repair the damage the fiend had caused.

Sebastian forced himself to ask the question burning at his heart. He didn't want to give voice to the words, but there were things Serenity would have to come to terms with, and if these things happened, he didn't want her to keep them a secret from him. He wanted to support her every step of the way.

"Did he touch you, Serenity?"

She sniffed. "He bit me. Fed from me."

"I know, but did he touch you in any other way?" He forced the words out. "Did he rape you?"

She shook her head and the hard stone of fear at his core melted with relief. The idea of Jackson subjecting her to such a thing over and over again for the past two years had torn him up inside. He didn't want to admit it to himself, but the thought of Jackson touching her made his stomach turn. He wondered if her answer had been different, would he ever have been able to look at her again without seeing what Jackson had done.

He shouldn't even be thinking like that. This wasn't about him—none of this was. All of his focus needed to be on Serenity and what needed to happen to make her better again.

Elizabeth popped her head around the door. "I found some clothes," she said.

"Clever girl," said Sebastian. "Put them on the bed for me, okay?"

"Sure."

Sebastian used the shower attachment on the faucet and rinsed Serenity's hair out. He lifted her from the water and wrapped her in a thick, white fluffy towel.

A memory speared him; *Serenity kissing him hard, wrapping her legs around his waist. Tumbling together in a passionate mess of limbs. Making love on the bathroom floor, the towels a cushion beneath them.*

That passionate woman was nothing like the one he carried in his arms and he wanted her back. He'd missed her so desperately over the past couple of years. Two years ago he'd allowed himself to believe he had her back and when she'd been taken from him so abruptly, it felt as though someone had ripped out part of his heart.

Elizabeth stood by, patiently handing items of clothing to Sebastian as he needed them. She watched her mother with intense but wary eyes, offering Serenity small, shy smiles whenever her mother made eye contact.

Serenity's old clothes hung from her reduced frame; her breasts mere nubs beneath her t-shirt, her sweatpants hanging from her hips.

The three of them sat on the bed and Sebastian took a comb to Serenity's long hair—longer than he'd ever seen it—patiently working every knot from her mane.

"Everything will be all right," he said, though he didn't know who he was trying to comfort—himself, Serenity, Elizabeth, or perhaps all three. "Your memory will come back, I'm sure of it."

"How long?" she asked. "How long till I remember who I am?"

"Soon," he said, though his heart was troubled. He had no idea how long it would take—or if her memory would come back at all. The repetitive bloodletting Jackson had put her through had started to change her. That she didn't want to eat worried Sebastian the most. If a vampire fed time and time again from the same victim and something tipped the victim over the edge, then they would turn. He was concerned

Serenity was halfway there. The lack of appetite and memory might be because her change to an immortal was perilously close. He knew Serenity didn't want to become like him because she wanted to be human for Elizabeth, but what worried him most was that she wouldn't become like him...

She would become like Jackson.

He shook the thought from his head. He couldn't imagine Serenity being anything like the monster Jackson had become, yet the possibility was very real. He only hoped nursing her back to health would reverse the damage—both mentally and physically—that Jackson had caused.

"Done," he said, lifting his fingers through her restored curls, allowing the still-damp strands to fall back down her back.

"You look beautiful again, Mommy," said Elizabeth. Serenity gave a small smile, looking down at the ground. The little girl took her hand. "Come and see."

Sebastian almost went to stop her, worrying how Serenity would react to the sight of her reflection, but then he realized she might not even remember what she looked like. Perhaps seeing her own face would jog something in her memory?

He gave Elizabeth a slight nod of approval and she tugged her mother over to the large mahogany-framed mirror on the wall.

Serenity caught sight of her reflection in the mirror and stopped short. She stared at herself and lifted a hand to her face. She caught sight of the scabs and scars and winced.

"Is this who I am?" she asked.

Sebastian snatched up a photograph from the nightstand, one which showed Serenity and Elizabeth when Elizabeth was about three. Serenity had caught her daughter from behind, her arms wrapped around the little girl's body, their faces pressed close, side-by-side. He crossed the room in three long strides and pushed the photo into Serenity's hands.

"No," he told her. "This is who you are."

She studied the image for a long, hard minute and lifted her face. Tears trembled like liquid diamonds in the dark pools of her eyes.

"And this is you?" she asked, directing the question at Elizabeth.

Elizabeth gave a small smile and nodded.

Sebastian waited for Serenity to pull her into an embrace, but she didn't move. He glanced at her face to see tears spilling down her cheeks.

"I don't remember," she said. "I don't remember either of you."

He reached out and rubbed her back, feeling the nubs of her spine beneath the thin tee. "You will. It'll just take some time."

Elizabeth walked to Serenity's side and wrapped her arms around her waist. They stood there together in that way until Serenity's tears had subsided.

Beside them, Elizabeth yawned, wide and loud.

"Come on you," Sebastian said, ruffling her hair. "Time for bed."

Elizabeth nodded, hiding another yawn behind her hand.

"Where's Mommy going to sleep?" she asked.

Sebastian hadn't thought that far ahead. He'd not been sure they'd find her at all, never mind considered where she might sleep. Before she went missing, she'd slept with Elizabeth. While he didn't want to admit that he worried about her harming her own child, the truth was he didn't know anything about this new Serenity. Not putting Elizabeth in harm's way was the most important thing right now. If Serenity freaked out; he didn't want Elizabeth to be the person who'd have to deal with it.

Having her in the same room as him—the same bed as him—while she was like this was unthinkable.

"Your mommy can sleep in the guest room," he said. "She'll be right next door." He looked between Elizabeth and her mother. "Okay?"

They both nodded and Elizabeth headed toward her bed, shedding clothes as she went. He wanted to tell her to pick up her things, but didn't have the heart. What did it matter, tonight of all nights?

Elizabeth climbed onto her bed and slid beneath the sheets. Clearly exhausted, her eyes closed almost as soon as her head hit the pillow. Her usual demands for stories and songs didn't materialize.

"Goodnight," he whispered to her, before leading Serenity from the room and gently closing the door behind them.

Dawn was fast approaching. He felt the pull on his limbs like a current, the drag to a place of safety where the sun could not harm him.

The heavy clunk of the front door opening echoed up the stairs.

"Hello?" a voice called out.

Sebastian smiled. "Come on," he said, taking Serenity by the hand and then wrapping his arm around her waist, offering her support. "There's someone you need to meet. A new person. Someone you didn't know before."

"Someone I shouldn't need to try to remember?"

He heard the relief in her voice. "That's right," he said. "She's brand new."

He walked down the stairs to find Bridget standing at the bottom. Her long, white hair hung down to her waist, the ends fine and wispy. As usual, her slightly chubby wrists and neck were garnished with an excess of turquoise bangles and beads.

She saw Sebastian descending the staircase, his arm around Serenity, and her blue eyes widened.

"Oh my," she said, one hand clutched to her chest, making her beads jangle. "Is this who I think it is?"

"I thought we hadn't met?" hissed Serenity.

Sebastian grinned. "You haven't. She's just heard a hell of a lot about you."

Bridget bustled up to Serenity and placed a hand on each cheek. "You're too thin, girl," she said. "We need to fatten you up."

Serenity reared back from the embrace and Sebastian stepped in.

"Serenity doesn't remember anything, Bridget. She's been through a lot and she's going to need some time to recover."

"Oh, I'm sorry," she said, stepping back. "You mustn't mind me. I'm just happy to see you home. That little girl of yours has missed you something terrible." Her eyes flicked to Sebastian. "They both have."

"Thank you," Serenity mumbled. Sebastian sensed her awkwardness and shot Bridget a look.

"This must be very hard for you, dear," said Bridget, patting the back of Serenity's hand. "But you're in the right place now. Everyone here will take care of you."

Serenity gave her a tight smile, but remained silent.

"We need to sleep now, Bridget," Sebastian said. "I'm going to put Serenity in the guest room. I suspect both she and Elizabeth will sleep until nightfall, but should they wake, I trust you'll take care of them."

"Of course I will," Bridget smiled. "Don't I always?"

"I don't know where I'd be without you."

"Hey, enough of that sweet talk. You get to bed and I'll look after either Elizabeth or Serenity if they wake up."

He leaned forward and kissed the older woman on the cheek, causing a flush of heat to race up her throat into her cheeks.

"Now look what you've done," she said, fanning herself with her hand. "You've made an old lady blush."

"You're no old lady, Bridget," Sebastian said with a smile.

He helped Serenity back up the stairs and into the guest bedroom. It was as luxurious as Elizabeth's room—with a huge four-poster bed, thick velvet drapes and a soft wool carpet.

Sebastian tugged back the bedcovers, exposing the sheet-covered mattress; a small pocket for her to slip into.

"You'll be safe here," he told Serenity as he helped her out of her pants. She slid beneath the sheets in her tee and panties. He stroked her dark hair away from her face and she smiled, but it wasn't a happy smile. It was a smile, he realized, she used to fill in the gaps—one that said, "I don't know how else to react."

He bent down and kissed her forehead. He had her back, finally, after so long. He wished he could feel happier about it.

The sun was close to rising and he needed to get to his own room and sleep. Each of the bedrooms were fitted with black-out blinds so he would come to no harm in one of his own bedrooms, but he didn't want to impose himself on her. She didn't know him and sharing her bed felt like doing no better than Jackson had done.

He didn't ever want her to compare him to that monster again.

Chapter Six

Serenity didn't think she would be able to sleep. How strange to think, after all those nights at the mercy of her master, his cold body pressed against her, his revolting mouth attached to her throat, that she would somehow miss him now that he was gone. It wasn't that she wanted to be back with him—not at all—but at least then she understood her existence to a certain degree. She'd known the point in her being there—to allow him to feed, to dig his resting place. Now she had no clue as to her purpose; the reason she was in this big house or who the people were with her? They must want something from her, or why else would they have brought her here?

She wished she knew what she provided them with.

The man—or whatever he was—had shown her kindness and affection. He smiled and laughed with the older woman, but Serenity recognized his cold touch, the way he moved, his pale skin. So much of him reminded her of her master; she couldn't shake the idea that he'd want something from her eventually.

Despite her concerns, something about him drew her. When he was close, she restrained herself from reaching out and tracing her fingertips along the lines of his full lips, the square of his jaw. When he'd held her against him, she'd wanted to meld herself to his body, press herself against him and not let go. Somehow, she thought, when he held her, she could imagine not needing to remember her identity any more. In his arms, she could forget everything else entirely.

The intensity of his green eyes, how he looked at her, made her uncomfortable. It was as though he expected more from her than she knew how to be.

As though he were looking for someone else.

The girl, however, was different. The little girl looked at her with nothing but acceptance. Elizabeth seemed happy just to have her around. That the child with the dark ringlets and the wide, brown eyes meant no more to her than any other child, didn't seem to affect how the little girl viewed her.

Serenity's limbs slid against the smooth sheets, her head sank into the feather pillow. A sense of distrust surrounded her like a halo. She didn't understand the reason she'd been offered such comfort. That these people said they knew her meant little. If they'd spent time with her before, it must have been for a reason. What had they taken from her back then?

She closed her eyes and tried to wipe all thoughts from her mind. Being brought here was a gift. She needed to stop questioning everything and put trust in the people now in her life. They'd shown her more care and affection than her master ever had. Perhaps questioning that luck would only be asking for it to end.

Her thoughts grew foggy, sleep blanketing her consciousness.

A flash of memory speared through her: her lying curled up on her side on a bed, crying so hard every part of her hurt. The man who'd brought her here filled her thoughts, encompassing her in such deep, unfulfilled longing, she wanted to reach inside herself and tear out her own heart. But it seemed her heart had shattered like glass and now every shard pierced her insides, causing her pain.

Sebastian.

Serenity's eyes sprung open. A memory! A time from before. Yet the memory filled her with unease. Had he been the cause of so much pain?

The strong, compassionate man who'd carried her and the child through the night and had rid her of the horror of her master, conflicted with the recollection of such pain.

It didn't matter, she decided. She *had* been someone else once upon a time. She'd not been born on this earth in the arms of her now dead master.

Elizabeth ran through the dark, her small legs pumping beneath her, her bare feet slapping on a cold, smooth floor. Someone was chasing her, but she didn't know who. A small pinprick of light brightened up ahead, and it was to this she ran.

A man jumped out directly in her path. His long, dark hair swung down his back—almost as long as her mommy's. She'd never seen a man with such long hair. His black eyes sparkled with a hint of ferocity and she recognized the pale glow to his skin.

"Boo!" he yelled, as though they were playing a game.

But no part of Elizabeth felt as though this were a game. She shrieked and spun on her heels, sprinting off in the opposite direction.

She ran away from the light now, back to the darkness.

"Daddy!" she called out, starting to cry. "Help me!"

Though her legs pumped beneath her, she felt as though she wasn't getting anywhere. Running into the dark, she had no concept of anything moving past her. She might have just been running in place.

A cold hand reached out of the dark and touched her cheek. She screamed again and spun around, batting out into thin air. "Leave me alone," she cried. "Just go away!"

From somewhere behind came the sound of laughter.

Elizabeth woke up screaming, and bolted upright in bed. Salty tears wet her cheeks. Her damp bedcovers clung to her skin. She caught her breath, her heart hammering wildly in her chest.

The bedroom door opened and her light flicked on. She blinked in the sudden illumination and lifted her hand to shield her eyes.

Bridget hurried to her side. The nanny sat on the edge of the bed and stroked her hair with a gentle but firm touch.

"It's okay, Elizabeth. You just had a bad dream. Everything's all right."

Elizabeth shook her head. "No, I dreamed about a bad man chasing me."

"Hush, this whole thing is over now, Elizabeth. We've got your mommy home safe and no one else is going to hurt you."

"This was different," she said. "It was a different man."

"You being upset is only normal. You've been through so much. But I promise you, you had a nightmare. No one is trying to get you." She gave Elizabeth a pretend scowl. "And they'd have to get through me first."

Elizabeth sniffed but felt a bit better. "And Sebastian," she said.

Bridget pulled the sheets up around her shoulders and she settled back into the big bed. "You know your daddy would never let anything happen to you."

She wanted to agree with Bridget, but the memory of the dream lingered. Something bad had happened to her in the dream and she worried it wasn't just a dream but one of *those* dreams.

But everything Bridget said was true. They had her mommy back now and the bad man was dead. Sebastian killed him; she'd been there when it happened. She had no reason to believe someone else would be after her.

"Will you put the blue blanket over me?" Elizabeth asked.

Bridget smiled down at her. "Of course."

The blue blanket was Bridget's specialty and always made her feel better after she'd had a nightmare.

"Ready?" Bridget asked and Elizabeth nodded. Bridget rubbed the palms of her hands together and bent her forehead to the tips of her fingers. She closed her eyes and muttered in low tones, words Elizabeth couldn't make out.

After a few moments, she lifted her head and smiled down at Elizabeth, though her hands continued the rubbing motion, as though attempting to keep them warm.

"I'm creating a magical blue light in the palms of my hands," she said. "Can you see the glow?"

Elizabeth nodded, and for the briefest of moments, she thought perhaps she did get a glimpse of the magical light.

Bridget held her hands above Elizabeth, hovering in the air a couple of inches above her body. She began to stroke the air above her, as if smoothing down something Elizabeth couldn't see.

"I'm spreading out the blue light to cover every part of you," she continued. "And I'm smoothing it down so there are no creases or wrinkles. The blanket is a perfect blue light."

"You need to tuck it in," Elizabeth reminded her.

"Ah, yes, of course." She began to push Elizabeth's real blankets in snug around her and then proceeded to tuck the magic blue blanket right over the top of her head.

"Done," she said, sitting back as though to admire her work. "No bad dreams are getting past that beauty."

Elizabeth smiled. "So if I put my hand up, will my fingers go right through the blanket?"

"Nope. The blue light bends with your hand so you'll always be protected."

Satisfied, Elizabeth snuggled back into her pillow. "Thanks, Bridget."

Her nanny leaned over and kissed her forehead. "You're welcome, angel. Now get some more sleep. Your mommy's going to need you wide awake and fighting fit."

Bridget backed out of the room and flicked the light switch, plunging the room back into a darkness that was the result of the perfect fitting blinds. Outside of the window, the rest of the city was already several hours into morning.

Elizabeth shut her eyes again. She tried to picture the magical blue light surrounding her, the one that was supposed to keep out bad thoughts, but all she could make out on the backs of her eyelids was the face of the man from her dreams. The man with the long dark hair and black-as-midnight eyes.

Who are you? She threw the question out with her mind, as though the atmosphere could conjure up the answer. *Just leave us alone. Go away and leave us alone.*

Chapter Seven

Sebastian woke the moment the sun set below the horizon. He opened his eyes, as he always did, with none of the foggy sleepiness humans experienced. Instead, he was as awake as if he'd been up for hours.

Serenity.

The first thought on his mind. Closely followed by, *Elizabeth.*

He swung his legs off the bed and first made his way to Elizabeth's room. He poked his head around the door and his vampire eyes took in the sight of her small frame still curled beneath the bedcovers. Her heavy breathing, punctuated by soft snores, met his ears, signaling she was still in a deep sleep.

He backed out of the room and closed the door gently behind him. The poor girl must still be exhausted after yesterday's long journey. Children her age could easily sleep twelve hours or more, and despite Elizabeth's uncanny way of going without sleep, he wasn't worried about her having a lie-in.

Heading back down the hall, he stopped outside of Serenity's door and lightly knocked. He could tell she was awake by her breathing, but both that and the sound of her heart wasn't that of a healthy young woman. The slow, strained rate was more that of a man on his deathbed.

Serenity was far from healthy.

His knocked received no answer, so he pushed open the door. Serenity sat on the edge of the bed, her legs dangling over the side. Her long hair fell in sheets on either side of her face. The sight of her, so fragile and yet still so beautiful, despite everything she'd been through, made him want to weep.

She glanced up as he walked in.

"Hi," he said, offering her a smile. "Sleep well?"

Serenity smiled back, the one reserved for when she didn't know what to say. Then, taking him by surprise, she said, "I remembered something last night."

"That's great!" His heart lifted and he crossed the room to be closer to her. He sat on the bed beside her, but kept a respectful distance. "Perhaps it won't be long before your memory returns. Now you're away from Jackson and he's dead, the hold he had on you might be fading."

"The memory confused me," she said. "I remembered you, but I was crying because you'd hurt me somehow."

"I'd never hurt you," he said, an automatic response he'd given no thought to.

He was wrong; he had hurt her.

Sebastian paused, steeling himself for what he was about to admit to. "But I did let you down. Many years ago, after we'd first met and before either of us knew about Elizabeth, I left you. You begged me to take you with me, but I refused because I thought you'd go on to have a normal life and be happy. I didn't want you to become like me."

"So I was crying because I missed you."

He nodded. "I think so."

"I must have really loved you."

The use of the past tense stabbed like ice in his heart.

"I hope you will again," he said.

She paused, considering his words. "How is the little girl?"

"Elizabeth."

"Elizabeth," she repeated.

"She's your daughter, Serenity. She's *our* daughter."

"I don't know what that's supposed to mean. I don't understand how I'm supposed to feel."

"You don't need to feel anything right now, Serenity. Let's just get you better. Everything else will come back to you in time." He smiled, reassuring. "That you're already remembering is a good sign. Does anything else seem familiar to you? This house, perhaps?"

She shook her head, but didn't answer. Instead, she stared back down to where her hands rested in her lap, anxiously twisting around each other. Her hands expressed a worry and anxiety she'd not voiced, and Sebastian mentally chided himself. He needed to try to put himself in her place— she'd only known Jackson. He and Elizabeth were like strangers to her. He shouldn't be pushing her, however frustrating he found it not to have her back as her old self.

Sebastian longed for her to wrap her arms around his neck, hold him tight and tell him how much she had missed him and that she still loved him. His heart yearned for her so desperately it felt like a physical ache.

"Are you feeling stronger?" he asked, dragging his thoughts back to more practical matters. "Do you think you can eat something now?"

"I can try."

"That's good enough for me."

They made their way downstairs, Sebastian still supporting her. Bridget sat on one of the leather couches, her feet tucked under her, a paperback in hand. Her long white hair was wrapped around her neck like a scarf. She glanced up as they reached the ground floor and offered them both a smile.

"Hi, you two," she said. "All rested?"

"Yes, thanks Bridget," replied Sebastian.

"Where's the little one?"

"Still sleeping."

"Ah, well. She must have needed her rest."

Serenity stood awkwardly by Sebastian's side, making no attempt to join the conversation. Bridget gave a slight raise of her eyebrows; a gesture that said, 'Well? Any better?' Not wanting to discuss Serenity's recollection, especially not in front of Serenity herself, Sebastian gave a slight shrug of his shoulders.

"You can get home now, if you like," he said.

"You sure?" she said, already getting to her feet.

"Of course. Same time in the morning?"

"Always."

He saw Bridget out of the front door. Her small Prius sat parked in his driveway. She climbed in the car and started the vehicle up. She swung around, the tires crunching on the gravel driveway. He waved her off as she used her own key fob to open the big gates and drove off down the hill.

Sebastian stood and watched as the gates closed behind her and then closed the front door. Security was important to him. While he wasn't worried about someone causing him harm, the fragility of his little family always had him on high alert.

Happy the house was secure once more, he turned his attention back to Serenity. She stood exactly how he'd left her.

"Come on," he said, guiding her toward the kitchen. "I'm not a great cook, but I'm sure I can find something to tempt you."

"Please, something plain is fine," she said, finally speaking again. "I'm not sure I can stomach much more."

"Anything you want, I'll get you." Though she didn't realize, he was talking about more than just what she might want to eat. He'd do whatever it took to make her well again; he didn't care what sort of boundaries he needed to push.

The past two years living with Elizabeth had made him more at ease with preparing food. At first he'd found the idea strange—the act of cooking, cleaning, chopping. He had no idea how things were supposed to taste and much of what he'd learned had come from Elizabeth spitting out strange combinations he'd put together—ketchup and peanut butter, eggs and yogurt. He'd found it frustrating at first—to have so many capabilities but to have his culinary skills laughed at by a four-year-old. However, it had simply been part of the learning curve of becoming a father.

Serenity didn't need to be experimented upon with his cooking so his mind went to what people who'd been ill would eat: soup and toast. He was pretty sure he could crack open a can and toast some bread without making too much of a mess.

He helped Serenity onto one of the stools at the breakfast bar and turned to the job at hand. Within minutes, chicken soup simmered on the stove and bread popped out of the toaster, hot and crispy. He smiled at himself. To think a vampire could be so domesticated.

Feeling absurdly proud, he placed the meal in front of Serenity.

She picked up the toast and put the slice to her lips. He smiled at her, and she opened her mouth and took a bite. Serenity chewed, in slow, deliberate movements and swallowed. A strangled, painful sound came from her throat. She gagged, choking on the piece of toast.

He moved with his vampire's speed; at her back in an instant. Holding himself back, for fear of shattering her projecting spine, he gently (for him) banged her on the back, dislodging the bread from her throat.

Serenity pushed away from him and spat the lump of bread on the floor.

She sank to the ground. Her eyes filled with tears. "I'm sorry, I tried."

"It's okay. We'll try something different, and we'll keep trying."

She was able to take small sips of soup and Sebastian watched her with worried eyes. He didn't want to have to get any authorities involved. For many months following Serenity's disappearance he'd dealt with the interference of child support agencies and the police. It had been a hard juggling act; to be medically registered as suffering with a severe case of Xeroderma pigmentosum or XP, especially as his skin appeared to be so perfect, flawless even. Most people who suffered from the condition presented with patches of lightened or darkened skin, and those undiagnosed quickly developed cancerous growths. Nevertheless, money could buy almost anything, including a diagnosis from one of the most recognized physicians in the field.

After that, obtaining custody of Elizabeth had been much easier. With the employment of Bridget as her nanny, and the birth certificate naming Sebastian Bandores as the father, no one could object to Elizabeth coming to live with him.

Fending off all the busy-bodies who wanted to know what was going on in their lives long term proved to be more of a challenge. The authorities would always rather the girl went to live with an immediate family member—such as her father—than be put in state care, but that didn't stop social services making 'routine visits' to make sure Elizabeth was well-cared for and that her father's condition and night living hadn't affected her in any negative way.

"Done," Serenity declared, pushing the empty bowl out toward him. Then her face paled, and she turned to one side and vomited on the floor.

He darted to her side and rubbed her back, holding her hair out of her face as she retched again, bringing up only bile now.

"I'm so sorry," she said, lifting her head. Tears trembled in her eyes and tiny forks of red burst through the whites. "I'm so embarrassed."

"Don't be silly. You ate too much at once. We've just got to take things slow."

Moving as a blur before her eyes, he cleared the mess away. It didn't bother him. He'd cleared away much worse for Serenity after she'd killed Jackson, and if that was what was needed, he'd do it over and over again in order to bring her back to him.

She put her head in her hands. "I hate what I've become."

He circled her in his arms, unable to stay away. Her thin frame stiffened against him momentarily but then she relaxed. Her head settled against his broad chest and her warmth burned through his clothing. He lowered his face and allowed himself the moment to believe she felt the same way about him as he felt for her.

Sebastian wished he had the ability to take her pain from her. "None of this is your fault. I'll find a way to make you well again. Whatever it takes."

"What are you?" she asked. "Are you the same as my master?"

"Jackson," he corrected. "His name was Jackson and he wasn't your master, he was your husband. He beat and abused you for years. When you decided to leave him, he wouldn't let you go and you stabbed him."

Her eyes widened. "I stabbed him?"

"Yes, and he died. I thought I'd helped you to cover up the murder, but the woman who made me, Madeline, turned him into the monster you knew."

"But if he was my husband, how did you and I know each other?"

"We met by accident one day. I saw you running through the streets and I followed you."

"So what are you?"

"I'm a vampire, Serenity. I drink blood, like Jackson did. He and I shared the same strength and speed, but I'm not like him. I love you and I love Elizabeth."

"Elizabeth," she repeated the name as though practicing the feel of the word in her mouth. "Our daughter?"

He nodded. "Our daughter."

The padding of small, bare feet at the top of the stairs made him look up. Elizabeth stood in her pink nightdress, watching her parents.

"Are you feeling better now, Mommy?" she asked.

The name made Serenity glance up and she hesitated, unsure of how to answer. Concern and worry blanketed Elizabeth's small features and Serenity smiled brightly.

"I am feeling a little better," she said. "Are you okay?"

Elizabeth continued down the stairs as she spoke, "I had a bad dream."

"I have bad dreams too sometimes," Serenity admitted. "But they're only dreams, they can't hurt you."

"Sometimes dreams come true."

"Only the good ones," said Sebastian, smiling at her.

Elizabeth didn't return the smile. "That's not true."

Sebastian stepped in. "Elizabeth has dreams about things that happen. She also sometimes has visions, or if she touches someone, she can know things about them that she's never been told. She's had the ability since she was tiny. That's how we were able to find you."

"You dreamed about me? About where I was?"

Elizabeth nodded. "Most of the time I dreamed things, but the last time I was awake and it was like I was there with you."

"I think I felt you. Sometime, when I was with my—" she cut herself off, remembering. "When I was with Jackson, I sensed someone else with me. I thought I was crazy or it was just wishful thinking, but perhaps you were with me all along."

A new light had appeared in Serenity's face and Elizabeth glowed back at her. Finally, something had happened that allowed Serenity to tie her time with Jackson together with her life now. Something—however strange— she could make sense of.

"You were never alone, Serenity," said Sebastian. "Elizabeth stayed linked to you the whole time."

Tears filled her eyes once again, spilling down her cheeks. "To think all that time I only knew Jackson, yet I had you both searching for me. I never thought anyone would care for me."

"We never stopped caring and we never would have stopped looking."

"That's right, Mommy. We missed you."

She hung her head, her hair falling either side of her body. "Something always seemed to be missing, I just didn't know what."

Elizabeth reached her side and took her hand. "Of course you missed us, Mommy," she said, with the certainty of a child. "We're your family."

Chapter Eight

The days and nights passed at a frustratingly slow pace. Each evening Sebastian woke, hoping today would be the day a change would occur in Serenity's condition. But each day she stayed the same. She remained inside the big house, wandering from room to room, picking up photographs of Elizabeth and trying to jog her memory.

Other than the memory of Sebastian on that first night, no other recollections had come to her. She was getting to know Elizabeth and Sebastian again through the time she was spending with them, but so far, remembering the person she'd been before remained a mystery which left her frustrated.

Physically, she started to heal. Though she still struggled to eat, Sebastian forced her to drink calorie-rich protein shakes and she began to manage small pieces of toast and crackers. Her figure remained slender and waif-like, but she lost the half-starved appearance she had when they first brought her home. Her bruises faded and bite marks began to heal, though the scars would remain.

Sebastian decided the time had come to call James Bently. He'd been putting off the call, hoping he would be able to phone with better news. Since Serenity's disappearance, Sebastian knew James held him to blame. To be able to call James and tell him Serenity was home and well would have made the conversation a little easier.

Sebastian lifted the receiver and dialed James's home number. He answered on the third ring.

"James, it's Sebastian."

The other man didn't pause. "Hey. How's Elizabeth?"

"She's fine, great actually. Look, James, we've found Serenity."

A sharp intake of breath came down the line. "Where? How?"

"In Washington. Elizabeth had a vision about her—a clear one—and we left right away. We found her with Jackson in almost exactly the same place Elizabeth saw her."

"Jesus. How is she? Is she all right?"

"Physically, she's getting better. She was painfully thin when we found her, but she's putting on a bit of weight now." Sebastian paused. "The thing is, James, she can't remember anything. She doesn't know who she was before Jackson took her."

"So she doesn't remember us?"

"No, she doesn't remember anything. It might just be trauma, but Jackson fed from her this whole time. I think the constant feeding has changed who she is on a cellular level. If a vampire feeds numerous times from the same victim, they sometimes turn. I think Serenity may have been on her way to becoming like Jackson."

"My God," he said. "Can I talk to her?"

"There's no point, James. It will only confuse her and she doesn't have any idea who you are."

"I'd come out," he said. "But with Amy due any day..."

Amy was heavily pregnant with their second child.

"It's all right, James. We can manage. I just wanted you to know. I thought you had a right."

"Thanks, Sebastian. Keep me informed, okay?"

"Will do," he said and then hung up the phone.

The call had felt awkward. The two males had never completely seen eye-to-eye. Sebastian had always been slightly jealous of James's close relationship with Serenity, despite his marriage to Amy. He'd always wondered about James's motives for keeping her so close.

On the other side, James blamed Sebastian for Serenity's disappearance—not that he thought Sebastian caused it, more that he should have prevented what happened. He didn't thank Sebastian for either entering or returning to Serenity's life.

After Serenity first went missing, James had been wary about allowing Elizabeth to go to live with a vampire. But once he'd seen Sebastian's name on the birth certificate, he realized he had little control over the matter. Sebastian was Elizabeth's father and that would always take priority. In the end, Sebastian promised James that he and Amy would still be fully involved in Elizabeth's life. But Amy struggled to continue to live in the city after the attack on her son, Noah, so when James was offered a transfer to Savannah, they'd taken it.

James and Amy always kept in touch, sending birthday and Christmas presents for Elizabeth. Sebastian knew what a hard decision moving away had been, especially with Serenity still missing, but they'd needed to put their own family's well-being first.

It was early evening and Elizabeth had already been sent to bed. Serenity also slept. Her sleeping patterns worried Sebastian. While he'd not expected her to fall straight into a normal human's routine, he'd hoped she would have been more willing to try to adjust to Elizabeth's—and most of the rest of humanity's—habit of sleeping at night and being awake during the day. Instead, she slept only for a few hours at night and the same again in the day. She spent most of her waking hours lying in bed, staring at the wall or wandering aimlessly around the house. She tried to make conversation with him, Elizabeth, and Bridget when she was around, but it felt forced and difficult.

Hoping to get her up for a few hours, thinking the interaction would do her good, maybe even stir a few memories, he went through the unfamiliar process of making her coffee. Part of him yearned to just be near her, to keep her by his side and pretend everything was all right again. Naturally, they'd had no real physical contact since she'd been back and deep down he wanted to take her in his arms and bury himself deep inside her. Forget the past two years and the misery they were.

Sebastian made his way upstairs and knocked gently on the door, the cup of steaming coffee held in one hand. No answer came in response to his knock, but he knew she was there. Gentle sobs—those of someone crying but trying not to be heard—echoed from behind the door. Concerned, Sebastian pushed open the door and walked in to discover her bed empty.

"Serenity?"

The crying was coming from the corner of the room. Serenity sat on the floor, her arms wrapped around her legs, sobbing into her knees.

"Serenity, what's the matter? What's wrong?"

She lifted her head and her dark eyes fixed on his face, wide and wild. She put out both hands and tried to scrabble backward. With the wall directly behind her, she couldn't get any farther away.

"Please don't hurt me," she cried.

He stepped toward her, a frown marring his normally smooth forehead, and she shrank against the wall.

"Why would you think I'd hurt you? I'd never hurt you."

Had she remembered something else? Something that made her think I'd cause her pain?

"Who the hell are you?" she said, shaking her head, frantic. "Where am I? What did you do to me?"

Alarm fired through him. He set the coffee down on the dresser and raced over and crouched to her level. He put out a hand and lightly touched her knee, but she reared back, her eyes cavernous with alarm.

"How did you do that?" she whispered. "How did you move like that?"

He'd not realized he'd moved with his vampire's speed. "Because of what I am, Serenity. Do you not remember what I am?"

"I don't remember what *I* am."

She'd forgotten again! She'd forgotten who they were.

"You're human, Serenity. Human and a mother."

"Then why don't I feel human? Why do I feel like something else?" She raised her hand to her face and opened and closed her fist. "Like I could break things."

He closed his large hand over the top of hers and she looked up, her dark eyes penetrating his.

Slowly, she shook her head. "I don't know who you are."

"My name is Sebastian. We've known each other for a long time. We have a child together. Her name is Elizabeth. You've been through a trauma and that's why you can't remember, but we're working on getting you better again."

"How long have I been here?"

"Almost a week now. You were starting to get better, but now you've forgotten everything again."

Tears filled her eyes. "I remember something. I remember living in the dirt with someone else—a man, only he wasn't a man. He killed people—young girls—and he'd bring them back to the hole and feed on their blood!"

"He's dead," Sebastian said. "I killed him."

Relief melted onto her features. "He's dead?"

"I promise. I ripped his heart out myself."

She started to cry again. "Why can't I remember you?"

"I don't know, Serenity. I wish I did."

Frustration gripped him, but he forced his own emotions down. Hoping to offer her some comfort, he reached out and rubbed her back. Her body heaved with sobs beneath his palm.

To think he needed to start again. She'd finally started to connect to him again, finally started to accept him. Now they were back at the beginning. Would this keep happening? Would they teach her who she was only for her to forget again and cast them all back to the beginning? How long could they live like that? What sort of effect would it have on Elizabeth? For her mother not to remember her was bad enough, but to have Serenity forget Elizabeth over and over again while poor Elizabeth stood by and watched was just too much for a little girl to take.

For the first time, he wondered if Elizabeth would be better off without Serenity in her life. The problem was Elizabeth would always be attached to Serenity. Even when Serenity had been in Jackson's grip and had no recollection of them at all, Elizabeth still connected with her mother; still saw the things she did.

Only Serenity's death would ever truly free Elizabeth.

Immediately, he pushed the thought away, his heart cramping in such a sickening way he wanted to reach into his own chest and rip it from his ribcage. How could he think such a thing? He'd betrayed her by even allowing the thought to cross his mind.

But Serenity would never have wanted Elizabeth to suffer. When Serenity had been in her right mind, the thing that had been the most important to her was Elizabeth's well-being. Now, he realized, it was his too.

Serenity lifted her head. "What's going on, Sebastian? Why am I sitting on the floor, crying?"

He paused. "Because you can't remember who you are..."

"I don't remember how I got here."

"Elizabeth and I found you in Washington and we brought you back here."

She gave her head a slight shake and looked at him, her head titled to one side, a slight crease between her eyes. "Yes, I know. I meant I can't remember how I got on the floor."

He took her by the shoulders, forcing her to meet his eyes straight on. "Are you telling me you remember us bringing you here? You remember the last week happening?"

The alarm he felt sure had been so present on his own features transferred to hers. "Yes, of course I do. You're scaring me!"

He let her go. "I'm sorry, but a minute ago you didn't have any idea who I was. You couldn't remember the whole of the last week happening. It was as though I'd picked you up from Jackson's hole and dumped you right in this room."

"I forgot again?"

He nodded.

"That's not good, is it?"

Sebastian took her hand. "We'll figure this out, Serenity. I promise."

He helped her to her feet. "I think I'm going to go back to bed," she said. "I can't face any of this right now. It's all too much."

"Sure. You rest. I'm sure this is just a blip."

Depression radiated from her like a bad aura. He couldn't imagine how hard all of this was on her. He wished so badly that he could just get her back again. He needed to face facts—Serenity wasn't going to get better on her own. He needed to ask someone for help, someone who knew more than he did.

She climbed back into bed but didn't lie down. Instead, she sat in her customary position with her knees pulled up to her chest. As he watched, her whole body sagged and she hid her face in her hands.

"I'm not strong enough to handle this," she said, her voice mumbled behind her fingers.

He sat on the bed beside her and reached out. He touched her chin, tilting her face up to his.

"You are strong enough," he said. "And when you feel like you're not, we'll be your strength. Elizabeth and I. We'll be here to carry you when you feel like you can't go on."

Her eyes shone with fresh tears. "I don't know what I ever did to deserve you."

The thought about freeing Elizabeth speared guilt through his heart. She might think she didn't deserve him, but he would always wonder if he was good enough for her.

"Hush," he said, stroking her hair. "Lie down now. Get some rest."

Leaving Serenity curled up on her side, one hand beneath her face, the other clutching her bedcovers, he backed out of the room and quietly closed the door.

He went back down stairs and threw himself on the couch. He needed a drink, and not a stiff scotch. His time to feed was approaching and the need raised its head like a sleeping dragon and blew flames that fanned the desire.

The sound of Elizabeth creeping down the stairs caught his attention. He didn't have the heart to tell her to go back to bed. The little girl crossed the room and slid beside him on the couch. He lifted his arm and she tucked herself under it, resting her cheek against his chest. Sebastian kissed the top of her head.

"You're supposed to be asleep in bed," he chided.

"She's no better, is she, Sebastian?"

This time he was too distracted to correct her. "No, she's not."

"So what do we do?"

"We might need to ask for help."

"Who from?"

"I know an older vampire who might be able to help. He lives in New York. He's an ancient and might have knowledge about how to bring her back again."

Elizabeth scrambled to her knees, pulling away from him, her eyes shining bright. "Then we need to go! Right away!"

"You're not coming," he said. "The ancients are unpredictable and I don't know how they'll react to your mommy, never mind you."

"That's not fair!" she shouted, jumping to her feet. "I'm not missing out now. You both need me."

Sebastian shook his head. Sometimes he forgot she was only a six-year-old, then she'd throw a sulky temper tantrum and he was quickly reminded.

"I've not decided if I'm definitely going to go yet, but if I do, I'm not bringing you with me. I can protect you around most people—around most supernaturals—but not an ancient. He has hundreds of years on me and I don't even want him to know you exist."

Elizabeth's shoulders slumped and her lower lip stuck out, but she didn't argue with him. She settled back on the couch and took hold of Sebastian's hand. Her little hand looked tiny against Sebastian's large palm and she played with his fingers, folding them back and forth as she talked.

"Tell me about this ancient vampire," she said. "What is he like?"

"His name is Demitrios and he's originally from Greece. Do you know where that is?" She shook her head, her dark curls bouncing around her face. "Greece is in Europe and it's a very old country."

"Older than America?"

Sebastian laughed. "Much, much older. These older vampires have seen so much, so many changes in our world, it's no wonder many of them have not survived."

"I didn't think vampires could die," she said, immediately worried for Sebastian's own survival.

"For us to die is very difficult, but it is possible." He saw the alarm on her face. "But don't worry, I'm not going anywhere."

She snuggled back down into him again and his thoughts drifted. The truth was, though he'd not seen Demitrios for a long time, the other vampire was hard and cruel. Sebastian had no intention of telling this to Elizabeth. He had spent a brief period with him at the beginning of the twentieth century, but he'd not liked Demitrios's practice of bringing humans back and keeping them as slaves. He'd keep the same human for several weeks or more, holding them prisoner to be fed upon whenever he so desired. That wasn't Sebastian's style. While he couldn't deny his nature—he still fed from humans, despite having one as a child and being in love with another—he didn't believe in torture. He had no choice but to feed from people. Feeding from animals left him like them—animalistic—and not feeding at all left him not in his right mind. He'd never put Elizabeth at risk from his need for human blood and the only way he ensured such a thing happening was by feeding regularly and on time. He hated that it meant he picked another human life above his child's, but in the end Elizabeth and Serenity were more important to him than any other human.

He'd not seen Demitrios for over a hundred years and had no idea about the other vampire's frame of mind. He was sure of one thing; he didn't want Elizabeth anywhere near him.

Serenity, however, she would be a different matter. He had no choice but to expose Serenity to Demitrios. Sebastian couldn't simply explain Serenity's situation to Demitrios. He had no comparisons. Jackson had been one of a kind—neither vampire nor human—and he didn't know if Demitrios would be able to judge the situation if he didn't see her for himself. Taking her to him would be risky, but he didn't think he had a choice. If Serenity's memory continued to deteriorate, he might be left with nothing but a shell of a person.

Sebastian glanced down to find Elizabeth asleep, her dark head rested against his chest. He stroked her hair with a gentle touch. He couldn't imagine how all of this was affecting her. Elizabeth's resilience didn't prevent her from hurting. Just like Serenity years before, he only wanted her to have a normal, happy life.

With Elizabeth in his arms, Sebastian got to his feet. Careful not to wake the sleeping child, he carried her back up the stairs and into her bedroom. He settled her beneath the covers and flicked off her nightlight. He doubted she'd wake again before morning.

As he made his way back down the hallway, Sebastian paused outside of Serenity's door. From her slow, steady breathing and heartbeat, he knew she too, had fallen back to sleep.

Satisfied his family was at peace, at least for the moment, he headed back downstairs.

He needed to feed; even more so if he intended on seeking out his old 'friend'. His strength would never match Demitrios's, but he still intending on being as sharp as possible.

For the second time that evening, Sebastian picked up the phone.

This time a female voice answered.

Sebastian leaned his cheek into the handset. "Hey, Bridget, it's me. Sorry to call so late, but I need a favor."

"Sure," her voice came back. "Name it."

"I'm going to need to go away for a couple of days. Do you think you could come and stay here with Elizabeth? I'm talking twenty-four hours a day, instead of your usual daylight hours only."

"Of course," she said. "Does this have something to do with Serenity?"

He sighed, his heart like solid lead in his chest. "She's taken a turn for the worse. I went into her room and she didn't recognize me or know where she was. She forgot the whole of this last week and went right back to the beginning. I'm scared if I do nothing things will get worse and her mind will continue to deteriorate."

"I'm so sorry, Sebastian. Do you need me to come over right away?"

"Yes. Thank you. We won't be leaving until tomorrow night, but I need to do something else first."

Although Bridget was perfectly aware of his nature, he didn't want to voice his need to feed out loud. The act felt too personal and he didn't want to put either of them in an awkward position considering he would basically be telling her that he was going out to kill.

"No problem. Give me an hour."

His shoulders sagged in relief. *Where would I be without her?* "Thanks, Bridget. See you soon."

Chapter Nine

Within the hour, Sebastian heard the low thrum of a car engine and the metallic creak of his front gate opening, followed by tires crunching on gravel. He'd opened the front door and was standing on the porch before she even pulled the car to a halt.

Bridget switched off the engine and climbed from the vehicle. Her white hair hung in a braid down the center of her back, and she pulled the fabric of a long, red skirt around her legs, lifting it as she walked.

"The way you always hear me coming unnerves me," she said as she walked up the steps toward him, an exasperated frown marking her face. "One of these days I might just want to sneak up on you."

"And why would you want to do that?"

"You never know. Maybe I'll surprise you one day."

Sebastian smiled, brushing off her comment. He stepped to one side and allowed her through the front door.

"How is Serenity?" she asked, her features straightening. "How's Elizabeth?"

"They're both sleeping for the moment."

"Good, they need their rest." With Sebastian following, Bridget headed into the kitchen and placed her purse on the breakfast bar. She turned to him, her blue eyes serious.

"Listen, Sebastian. There's something I need to talk to you about. I think I may be able to help Serenity without you needing to take her away. I've practiced some magic in my past and though I don't practice any more for personal reasons, I might be able to find a spell to help her."

Sebastian's heart sank. He didn't want to be rude to Bridget, but he'd heard of plenty of occasions when humans had played at Wiccan magic. The act was somewhat laughed upon in the vampire world. He'd not yet met a single 'witch' who could do much more than whatever natural properties already lay present in the roots and herbs they used.

"No offense, Bridget, but she needs more than a few roots and chanted words to bring back her memory."

"There's more to it. The magic comes from the earth, and yes, herbs are used, but that's because they're part of our planet. Mother Nature is a very powerful thing, Sebastian. She shouldn't be sniffed at."

"I'm sorry, I don't mean to belittle whatever spells you learned when you were younger, but whatever they are won't be enough to beat the sort of effect a vampire bite has on a human. I may not believe in herbs and special words, but the physiological effects repetitive feeding has on a person changes them at a cellular level."

Her lips thinned and she shook her head. "Is that not a type of magic? Isn't the effect a vampire has on a human magic? And what about what you are? Your heart isn't beating. You have ferocious strength and an ability to heal. Are they all not a magic of sorts?"

"What I am goes against nature, not with it."

"Your existence in this world proves you are a part of nature. Have you forgotten my own child is like you now? I refuse to believe my son is something unnatural."

He bristled. "What you believe or don't believe is irrelevant. I need to get Serenity proper help from someone who knows what they're talking about. Most vampire's aren't good, Bridget. They're killers and the vast majority have little or no respect for humanity."

She shook her head again, a brisk, sharp movement. "They're not all like that. The type of vampire they become must be linked with the person they were as a human. My son was a good boy and I'm sure he's not some bloodthirsty murderer. Besides," she glared at him, her blue eyes as sharp as glacial ice. "What about you? You love your human family. How can you describe yourself as an unnatural killer?"

"Because that is what I am."

"No, you're not. I know you're so much more. You have a heart, a soul. How can that be unnatural?"

"You might be trying to convince yourself what happened to your boy is all fine, and he's happy and normal. But it's not like he told you he's gay. He's a vampire and that means he kills. If he was human and told you he murdered people, would you be quite so accepting?"

"How can you say such a thing? You're not just insulting me and my son, you're putting yourself down as well. I won't hear you talk like that!"

Sebastian clenched his teeth. Her outburst made him uncomfortable. "I'm not your son, Bridget," he said. "I'm your employer."

She flinched as though he had slapped her. "I know you're upset right now, Sebastian, so I'm going to let this go. I was only trying to help you—all of you—but if that's how you want to think, then I'll keep my mouth shut and concentrate on what you pay me for—taking care of your family when you can't."

With his anger, the need for blood crept beneath his skin like a thousand scuttling insects. It was always this way. Any strong emotion instigated a desire to feed. He couldn't afford for Bridget to be the one who walked out. However much he might not like it, right now he needed Bridget a damn sight more than Bridget needed him.

Sebastian turned away from her, fists bunched at his sides. He stalked from the house, banging through the front door, not giving her a chance to leave before him. Bridget was too responsible to leave Elizabeth without a guardian and even if she hated his guts right now, she wouldn't take out her anger on the little girl.

Sebastian fled into the night, only one thought encompassing his soul: blood. He didn't often feel like this— the addiction making him think he needed to feed immediately or he was going to start tearing up the people around him. The stress of the last week must have affected him worse than he'd realized and now only one thing would make it all go away.

He crossed the city at a run, flying with the wind. He never felt more free than when he moved like this, except, perhaps, when he had Serenity's naked body moving beneath his. When he lost himself within her depths.

The memory brought a pang of pain and he roared at the night, needing blood more than ever. He raced past traffic on the freeway, leaping from car roof to car roof, his feet barely leaving a dent in the metal as he propelled himself from one to the next. For once, he had no plan as to where he was headed. He moved on instinct, wanting only to put distance between him and the house.

Was this what happened to other vampires who tried to 'domesticate' themselves. Did they eventually lose it? Did they end up hurting the humans they'd come to love?

No, he couldn't think like that. These weren't normal circumstances. He'd never hurt Serenity or Elizabeth, or even Bridget. He'd never fought with Bridget before but her bringing up the subject of a few spells she'd done in her youth as being a possible solution to Serenity's problems would be laughable if it wasn't so sad. A few bits of mumbo-jumbo she'd read from a book many years ago weren't going to have any effect on something as powerful as a vampire's bite.

Sebastian mentally shook himself. He kept thinking of Jackson as being a vampire, but he hadn't been, not fully. That he was some kind of half-breed made this whole thing even more dangerous and unpredictable. Perhaps the ancient vampire he intended on visiting would know a precedent to Serenity's case.

Sebastian crossed the Century Freeway, easily darting between traffic, and entered the outskirts of Compton. Now late at night, the streets were quiet with most people safely tucked in bed.

An elderly man pushed a cart along the side of the street. He walked with a stooped back and hunched shoulders. A dirty, beige overcoat hung from his shoulders. A thick mass of beard covered half of his face and from this, a bulbous nose protruded, spider-webbed with broken red-capillaries.

He didn't hear Sebastian's approach, just continued to shuffle, muttering to himself under his breath.

Focused upon his prey, Sebastian's body adjusted for the kill. His jaw structure changed, his fangs elongated, pushing the canines to the front of his mouth. Strength built in his muscles, burning with unreleased energy.

Sebastian lunged, catching the man from behind. His arm wrapped around the hobo's neck, clasping his beard-covered jaw in the palm of his hand. He wrenched his head backward and exposed his throat. Stale alcohol, cigarette smoke and body odor filled Sebastian's nostrils, but the scent of blood overpowered all those repellents.

His fangs pressed upon the man's rough skin, puncturing it with a pop. Hot blood flowed down his throat; iron and life. He sucked hard, ferocious, drawing the blood over his tongue and down his throat, draining his victim. The old man beat at Sebastian's arm with his fists, but he was powerless to do anything in the vampire's grasp. The man had probably been too out of it to even realize what was happening.

Heat spread from Sebastian's center, flooding to his extremities, filling him with a power only fresh blood could give. Never did he feel more alive than when he thrummed with the life-force of human blood.

Sebastian dropped the body to the sidewalk, needing to concentrate on the immediate rush in the same way a drug addict focuses on the sensations of a hit.

He felt better now, calmer and stronger. He would need to go back home and make things right with Bridget. If he was going to take Serenity to visit Demitrios in New York, he needed to be sure Bridget was still willing to take care of Elizabeth.

He glanced down at the dead man at his feet. Before he could deal with anything else, he first needed to dispose of the body.

Chapter Ten

Serenity woke with the certainty something had happened, yet had no idea what it was. The niggling feeling worked away at her so she sat up in bed and swung her legs over the side. She remembered Sebastian being here, but little else.

She climbed out of bed and pulled on her jeans. A cup of coffee sat on the dresser and she placed her hand against the outside of the mug. The cup was stone cold. Serenity frowned. He must have brought her the coffee, but then why didn't she drink it?

Perhaps she'd still been asleep? She slept little and in small catnaps, so it was a possibility. Yet she felt sure she'd spoken to him. Maybe she'd been sleepwalking or at least still been half asleep?

Her sleeping habits had been strange over the past week, since she'd been brought to the house. When she'd been with Jackson, she'd slept when he slept. Now, the freedom to sleep when she pleased had left her body clock confused. She caught a couple of hours during the day, and then another three or four during the night. At least her erratic sleeping habits meant she got to spend time with both Elizabeth and Sebastian alone. During her time alone with either one, she found it easier to connect with them. But for those couple of hours in the evening, when they were all together, she felt like even more of an outsider as she watched the natural connection between father and daughter, the way they laughed and joked together.

If she thought back to her past, she only knew Jackson and the hell she'd been living in. Before Sebastian and Elizabeth found her, she'd not fully understood the nightmare her life embodied. She'd never known anything other than pain and cold and violence. That someone could show her such affection and compassion at first surprised her and made her question their reasons, but then she finally accepted their attention for what it was—love. She only wished she could return the affection they showered on her. How could she love someone else when she didn't even know who she was?

Serenity left the bedroom and stepped out into the hallway. The house seemed quiet, but what else did she expect in the middle of the night? Elizabeth should be fast asleep and she guessed Sebastian would be out doing whatever vampires did in the dead of night.

Unable to sleep anymore, she headed down the stairs. To her surprise, the nanny, Bridget, sat on one of the leather couches, a book held in one hand. She stopped short and Bridget glanced up. "Sebastian asked me to watch over you while he went out."

"Okay," she said, unsure of what sort of reaction this should evoke. Despite being told she was the girl's mother, Sebastian clearly didn't trust her to be left alone with Elizabeth.

Serenity didn't blame him. She wouldn't trust herself either.

Bridget placed her paperback on the empty space beside her. "How are you feeling?"

Serenity rubbed her palm over hot, gritty eyes. "The same. Confused, sad, frustrated."

"Sebastian told me you forgot coming here. He said you'd forgotten him again."

Serenity frowned. "He did? I guess I forgot that as well." She sighed, the sound coming from the bottom of her lungs. "I don't know how I'm supposed to remember things. I try to think back and there's nothing but the time I spent with my master... I mean Jackson. Sebastian and Elizabeth are both treating me with such kindness, I feel as though I'm letting them down by not remembering who they are. They both look at me as though they're expecting someone else and I'm trying to be that person, but I simply don't know how."

Bridget moved her book and patted the empty seat beside her. Serenity sank into the spot.

"It will happen," said Bridget. "Sebastian loves you and he's passionate about making you better again. He won't let anything stand in his way."

"I'm sure you're right. It's just hard to believe in someone I don't even know."

The older woman's soft, warm palm covered the back of her hand. "He believes in you enough for both of you."

Serenity forced a smile. She wished Bridget's words touched the part of her she thought they should, but everything at the moment left her cold.

"How are you so understanding about all of this, Bridget? Isn't it strange for you?"

"My son was turned when he was twenty-eight. He didn't run from me, but came to me and told me what he was."

"That must have taken a lot for you to adapt."

"I used to wear a lot of silver," she laughed. "But then I discovered it was no good for their kind. I'd give my son a hug when he came to visit and leave burn marks around his neck. Of course they healed right away but it's still not how I want my son to remember his mother's embrace."

"Where is he now?"

Bridget's eyes flicked to the floor and she gave a slight, dismissive shake of her head.

"Oh, ran off to France with some other vampire he met. It's typical. I brought him to America from England when he was only a baby, trying to offer him a new life, and then he grows up and runs off back to Europe again."

"Weren't you tempted to go with him?"

"He's got his own life now," she said, her words sharp. "Or perhaps I should simply say existence. This is my home, has been for the past thirty years. I don't intend on going anywhere."

Serenity got the impression the older woman struggled to talk about what had happened. More than anyone, Serenity understood how it felt to not want to talk about something.

They settled into silence.

Bridget rose from the couch and headed toward the kitchen.

"You're still so thin," she called out over her shoulder. "I'll make you something to eat and drink."

Her appetite had not returned, but she realized one of the things required for her to do in order to fit in with what people expected of her was eat.

"Thank you. You're very kind."

"Nah." She threw Serenity a wink. "I'm paid to do it."

Bridget bustled into the kitchen and began to open cupboard doors, pulling a pan from the rack and a plate from the shelf.

"Don't go to too much trouble," Serenity called out, hoping Bridget wasn't planning on making a full meal. She hated to sit, forcing herself to eat while the people who wanted her to watched with encouraging smiles and eagle eyes, counting every mouthful.

A sharp pain speared through Serenity's right temple. She sucked air between her teeth and clutched the side of her head. The pain stabbed deep behind her eye and suddenly the whole room seemed to sway to one side. Something in her head jerked; a mental realigning. Her heart picked up a notch, panic firing adrenaline through her sluggish heart and veins.

She squeezed her eyes shut, willing the intense agony in her head to go away. The dizziness made her feel sick and she kept her eyes closed to prevent the room spinning. Gradually, the pain subsided and the strange sense of vertigo passed.

What had happened? Had her master hit her again?

Serenity opened her eyes to find herself in a strange room, sitting on a dark brown leather couch. Panicked and confused, she pulled her legs up onto the couch, scrabbling to the back. She tucked her knees into her chest, as though making herself physically smaller might make her disappear. She twisted her head from side to side, trying to figure out where she was, trying to recognize *something*.

A woman with long white hair and floaty clothing approached her holding a grilled cheese sandwich on a plate. The strange woman smiled at her but must immediately have realized something was wrong. Her head tilted to one side, the smile disappearing from her face, replaced by a slight frown.

"Serenity? Are you all right? What's happened?"

Serenity put out a hand to ward her off. The cleanliness of her nails didn't escape her; they'd lost the usual cake of mud.

"Who the hell are you? What am I doing here?"

The woman put the plate down on an occasional table and mirrored Serenity's body language, placing her hands out in front. Steadying her.

"You've been having periods of memory loss, Serenity. That's why you can't remember getting here. You and I were sitting on the couch together only a few minutes ago, talking. No one here is going to cause you any harm."

Serenity looked around again, her head darting from side to side. Her voice was little more than a whisper. "Where's my master."

"He's dead, Serenity. Sebastian killed him."

"Dead!" She shook her head. "I don't believe you."

"If he wasn't dead, Serenity, do you think he'd have let us bring you here?"

She didn't want to believe what this woman was telling her. Surely her master wasn't dead. She'd never allowed herself to imagine a time when she might be free of him.

"Who's Sebastian?"

But the woman didn't get a chance to answer. Movement behind her caught her attention and she glanced over her shoulder. Serenity followed her gaze.

A small girl with dark, bouncing curls slowly made her way down the stairs. "What's wrong with Mommy?"

The name set off alarms in her head. This was all too much. The walls of the big house pressed down around her, the space she occupied shrinking. Her heart clambered up her throat, its thumping resonating in her ears.

Unable to take it anymore, she bolted over the back of the couch and ran for the door.

"Serenity, wait," the woman called after her, but she paid no attention. She yanked open the heavy double door and ran down the couple of step leading down to the driveway. Her bare feet crunched against gravel as she ran toward the gate. The moon hung high above, but the stars were not visible behind the glaring city lights. A sharp piece of stone cut into the sole of her foot and she cried out, bending to make sure the offending object was not still piercing her skin.

As she bent, pain spiked through her temple. Her legs gave out beneath her and she fell to her knees. The injured foot forgotten, the world swayed around her until it became no more than a blur.

Elizabeth started toward her mother, now kneeling on the driveway, but Bridget's hands grabbed her shoulders and held her back.

"Let go!" she cried, struggling. "Something's wrong with Mommy."

"You stay here, I'll go to her."

She didn't want to be told to wait. If Mommy needed her, she wanted to be there. She'd missed her so much over the last couple of years. Just because she was different now, just because she didn't put her to bed anymore, or read her stories, or laugh and tickle her under the ribs like she used to, didn't mean Elizabeth loved her any less.

Elizabeth didn't like to get in trouble, it made her sad if people yelled at her, but for once she wasn't going to do as she was told.

With a burst of speed, she broke out of Bridget's hold. Her nanny gave chase but Elizabeth reached Serenity first.

She touched her arm. "Mommy?"

A flash of a man's face filled Elizabeth's mind. Long, dark hair and black eyes. She felt a strange sucking sensation and then she was with him, standing before him in a cavernous room.

'*Let's see what you can do*,' the man said.

Mentally she screamed and stumbled back, but the man caught her in a vice-like grip. His fingers were ice-cold and straight away she knew the man was another vampire.

Elizabeth gasped and snatched her hand away. In her mind, she was pulling away from the dark-haired vampire, but, in reality, the movement broke the contact with her mother's skin. The vision vanished.

Tears sprang in her eyes and her face crumpled. Bridget must have noticed the change in Elizabeth, for her attention switched from Serenity.

"What's the matter, Elizabeth? What's happened?"

"I saw something," she whispered. "Something that's going to happen."

101

Her mommy raised her head, a frown creasing her brow. "What's going on? How did I get outside?"

Bridget stepped forward. "Do you remember where you are, Serenity?"

"Well… I'm at the house, but I don't remember coming out here. My foot hurts and…" She trailed off, noticing Elizabeth's pale face. "What's happened to Elizabeth?"

"She saw something when she touched you—a vision of some kind."

Serenity turned to Elizabeth. "What did you see?"

Elizabeth spoke, trying to contain her sniffles. "Another vampire, the same one from my dream. I don't think he's a good vampire."

"According to Sebastian, none of them are," said Bridget. She sighed, her face grim. "Let's get you both back inside. He'll be home soon, I'm sure, and then you can tell him what you saw, Elizabeth. Maybe he needs to rethink his plans."

"What plans?" Serenity asked as Bridget helped her to her feet.

Elizabeth looked between the faces of the grown-ups, trying to read their reactions.

"He wants to take you to visit an elder vampire," said Bridget. "He thinks the other vampire might be able to help you remember who you were."

Serenity's face lightened, the corners of her lips twitching. "Really?"

Bridget didn't return the smile.

Chapter Eleven

Sebastian walked through the front door. Turning the corner to the living area, he found everyone sitting on the couch, waiting for him. Serenity and Bridget sat side by side, Elizabeth squashed in between them.

They looked up as he walked in and Elizabeth squealed, "Sebastian!" before jumping up and running to his side. She collided with his legs, wrapping her small arms around his thighs and giving him a hug. He reached down and messed up her dark hair.

"Hey, kiddo. What's going on?"

"Lots of stuff," she said, her eyes wide as she craned her neck to look up at him.

The man's blood still burned through his veins, firing every nerve. To appear normal—as normal as he could be— he restrained himself, holding himself back when he wanted to run, jump and ravage. Just before and immediately after a feeding were the times he struggled hardest not to give into his basest instincts.

Those were the times he felt every bit the monster he was.

But he needed to act normal for Elizabeth's sake. He'd never want for her to be frightened of him. That would break his heart.

Serenity didn't meet his eye. She sat hunched over, her skinny arms wrapped around her knees.

Bridget spoke for her. "Serenity had another period of memory loss. She tried to run away, but we chased after her. Elizabeth touched her and saw… something."

Sebastian glanced down at his daughter. "You had a vision?"

Elizabeth nodded. "I dreamed about him too."

"About who?"

"A bad man. A vampire like you.

All Sebastian heard was 'bad…a vampire…like you'. How long would he be able to protect her from the horror of what he was? One day she'd learn that he killed people, fed from them. Such knowledge would mean she'd never look at him in the same way, with such total trust.

One day, he thought, with a sadness that made his heart drop to his stomach, *she'll hate me*.

"Was the bad man Jackson?" he asked, crouching to her level. "Are you sure you didn't pick up on some of your mommy's memories?"

Her small face crumpled in a frown as she tried to think. "I don't think it was him. He looked different and I'm sure he was talking to me, not Mommy."

Damn it!

He didn't need any more complications.

"Well, we don't know who this man is at the moment, and until we do, there is nothing we can do about what Elizabeth has seen."

Bridget got to her feet. "Aren't you missing something, Sebastian? Don't you think Elizabeth seeing another vampire has something to do with your plans to take Serenity to an elder?"

"We don't know that."

"So it's coincidence?"

He narrowed his eyes, rage flaring up inside him. Heat burned behind his eyes and he knew his pupils flashed yellow for the briefest of moments.

Sebastian tightened his jaw. "I don't have any other choice, Bridget." He lowered his voice in vain hope that Elizabeth, who was right beside him, somehow wouldn't hear what was being said. "She's deteriorating. What would you have me do, risk losing her forever? Elizabeth will be safe. She'll stay here with you. I won't take her anywhere near the ancient one."

"My offer to help is still open, Sebastian. I know you don't believe in the craft, but it's not just herbs—"

He raised a hand, cutting her off. "Let's not speak of this again, Bridget. My mind is made up. I'll be taking Serenity to New York as soon as dusk arrives tomorrow."

Bridget stalked to the kitchen counter where she'd left her purse. "I guess you won't be needing me for the rest of the night then."

"Bridget, please don't—"

"Don't what? Try to help fix this mess without putting your family in danger yet again? Jesus, Sebastian, sometimes I think you enjoy the pain."

Her words struck a chord somewhere deep inside him. He, too, had wondered if he sabotaged himself, that he punished himself for what he was. But he'd never purposefully put his family in harm's way purely so he could suffer with them, would he?

Bridget snatched up her purse. "Don't worry. I'll be back before daylight."

She slammed out of the door, leaving him to mull over her words. The sound of her car's engine hummed to life and the vehicle crunched back down the driveway.

A hand squeezed his and he glanced down to find Elizabeth looking up at him. "I don't like it when you and Bridget fight," she said.

"Me neither, sweetheart, but sometimes grown-ups don't agree on everything."

"Should I stop telling you and Bridget about the things I see?"

His heart clenched. "No! Never think you can't tell us. I'm so sorry we made you think that you shouldn't."

"But if it makes you and Bridget fight..." She trailed off, uncertainly.

"Sometimes adults need to argue in order to work things out. It doesn't mean we're not friends anymore, okay? The things you see are very important and I don't want you to ever feel like you have to keep things from us. Bridget's just worried about your visions."

"Do they mean I'm in danger?"

"No, I'm sure they don't. You're going to be perfectly safe right here. No one even knows about you."

"Okay, Sebastian."

He gently cuffed her around the head. "It's Daddy to you. Now come on. You shouldn't even be up. Let's get you back to bed."

She reached up to him. "Carry me upside down!"

Sebastian grinned. With a quick flip, he hoisted her up and spun her around so he had hold of her by her legs, her hair trailing on the floor. He shot a look at Serenity, who still sat on the couch, and she gave him a weak smile.

Elizabeth giggled and laughed as he carried her that way up the stairs and into her room. He threw her on the bed and she bounced a couple of times before scrambling to her knees. "Again, again!"

"No, get into bed. I shouldn't be getting you over excited when you should be asleep anyway."

"Awww…" she whined, but Sebastian lifted the blankets for her and she climbed beneath.

He kissed her on the head. "Go to sleep."

Leaving her snuggled in bed, he made his way back down the stairs to Serenity.

"Hey," she said, brushing her hair away from her face with one hand. "How's she doing?"

"She's fine. She's more resilient than any other six-year-old in the world."

"Being half vampire?"

He shrugged. "That and everything else she's been through. I hope when all of this is over, we can give her as normal a life as possible."

Serenity nodded, but continued to stare down at her hands in her lap. Sebastian realized how strange it must be for her, with him referring to their life together and how he wanted them to live in the future, when both he and Elizabeth were little more than strangers.

"Did you hear what I said to Bridget about wanting to take you to see another vampire?"

"I only caught the gist of it, but I think I understand. He's an older vampire, right? You think he might know how to get my memory back."

"That's right. He's an ancient from Greece. His name is Demitrios of Savos and he lives in New York now, where he runs a downtown nightclub. He's been around much longer than I have. If anyone has seen your situation before—or at least something similar—it will be him."

"Is he dangerous?"

"I don't believe he's any more dangerous than any other vampire," said Sebastian. He felt a twinge of guilt at not really answering her question.

She lifted her dark eyes to meet his, her interest evident. "How did you meet him?"

"I come from Europe myself," he said. "Spain, to be exact. After I was first turned, I wandered for years, only staying in one place for a brief period before moving to the next. I met him on my travels through Greece, in an ancient place called Delphi."

"Are all of your kind from Europe?"

"The ancient ones are," he said. "It's the place of our origin."

"But why? And how?"

"How did vampires start?"

She nodded.

"I wish I had the answer. I believe we're simply another branch of evolution. Some of our ancestors might have had an ability to regenerate—maybe tapped into a dark source of magic and harnessed the capability. They passed on the secrets, generation after generation, and evolution happened as it always does. Those who were the most powerful survived. Those who allowed themselves to be exposed to others were—like witches—hunted down and killed. In the end, we became what we are—solitary beings who live with a curse."

"But the ability wasn't seen as a curse back then?" she persisted. "If what you believe is true, people tried to harness the power because they thought it would bring them great things."

Sebastian shook his head. "The power was always bad. The whole reason we exist centers around human blood. The way we evolved must have involved human sacrifice or bloodletting. That's magic—black magic. It was never intended for good, and whatever magic those ancient rituals harnessed is now passed on when we take our victims to the point of death and then fill them with a vampire's blood. It's always about the ritual."

Serenity opened her mouth to speak, then seemed to change her mind and closed it again.

He reached out and touched the back of her hand. Whatever was going on in her head, he wanted to know. "What is it?"

"I can't help wondering if being like you would be a better way to exist. You seem so in control of yourself, so strong and self-assured. Why am I struggling to remember who I am when I could be like you?"

"Serenity…"

"I *could* be like you." She nodded, the small motion filled with urgency. "It's possible, isn't it?"

"I'm not sure. If I went through the motions to turn you, you might end up like me, but there's a chance you might end up like Jackson. What would we do if that happened? You might hurt Elizabeth."

Her face fell. "I'd never want to hurt her."

"Which is why we need to try this other option first."

Serenity took a deep, shaky breath. "I want to trust you. It's just, after everything that's happened, I'm not sure I even know how to anymore."

He reached out and clasped both of her hands within the shell of his own. "I want you to trust me again, but I also need to earn that trust."

"Did I ever trust you?"

"Once upon a time. Though, now I wonder if that trust was unfounded."

She tilted her head toward him, her eyes slightly narrowed. "Why?"

"I let you down. Twice, I've let you down."

"Yet you think I should trust you again." She paused. "How did you let me down?"

"I left you alone when I shouldn't have."

"But the second time you left me was to save Elizabeth's life."

He nodded but didn't meet her eye. "How did you know that?"

"Elizabeth told me a couple of days ago, while you slept." She pulled one of her hands from his and reached out, touching his jaw. The contact caused a flash of heat to race through his skin. "If you saved her life, it was worth the sacrifice."

"I should never have taken you to the mine. What happened was my fault."

"It was my master's... Jackson's fault," she corrected.

They sat in silence for a moment.

"I want to go to this ancient vampire," she said. "I'll do anything I can to be normal again. I can't stand living like this. I'm scared all the time, but that's the only real emotion I feel."

"I'll find out how to make you well again, Serenity. I swear I will, if it's the last thing I do."

She studied his face. When she spoke, she did so in hushed tones. "Why do you care so much? I'm nothing and yet you act as though I'm the most important thing in the world."

He gave a small smile. "Next to Elizabeth, of course."

She smiled back and this time the expression reflected in her eyes. "Of course."

He shook his head. "You're not nothing."

"You haven't answered my question."

"When you and I first met, we were both lost. I'd been alone for so long I'd forgotten how to feel for anyone else. I saw something in you that I recognized in myself—a loneliness, a sadness. I wanted to help you and in return you helped me to live again." He paused. "How you feel now— that emptiness, with nothing anchoring you to the world, no connection with anyone—that's how I'd lived for centuries. It wasn't until we met that I learned how to live... and love again."

Her eyes welled with tears. "I can't believe you're talking about me."

He lifted a hand and touched her cheek, brushing away a tear with the back of his fingers. "Believe it. Why else would I still be here?"

She nodded, her lips pressed into a thin line. "When do we leave?"

"Tomorrow, as soon as night falls."

When Sebastian rose at dusk the following evening, everyone else in the house was already up and waiting for him. Serenity sat at the kitchen counter, a mug of almost-cold coffee clutched between her hands. She twisted the mug around, staring into its depths. Dressed in her old clothes, her jeans hung from her non-existent hips, and she'd tried to cinch them with a belt. Her previously form-fitting t-shirt hung loosely, as though she wore one of his shirts instead of one of her own. She'd pulled her long hair into a ponytail, exposing her long neck and the myriad of still-pink scars and healing skin. "Been up long?" he asked, entering the room.

She nodded. "A while. Couldn't sleep."

He never suffered from such a problem as his body was programmed to sleep from dawn to dusk. Only if his life were immediately threatened would his body ever wake during that time.

In the living room, Elizabeth sat on the couch, Bridget beside her. They were both engrossed in a Disney movie, something involving a girl with very long hair and a prince. They weren't even aware of his arrival.

Sebastian turned back to Serenity. "Are you ready?"

She nodded. "I guess so."

He reached out and she took his hand. Her fingers were fragile, her grip slight. Her skin still held the coolness he'd experienced when he'd first found her, but compared to him, she was warm.

Sebastian headed into the living area, Serenity following close behind. Elizabeth turned her head with a ready smile, but Bridget ignored him.

"We need to go now, Elizabeth," Sebastian said. "You'll be a good girl for Bridget, won't you?"

"Yeah, of course. Will Mommy be all better when you get back?"

"I hope so, kiddo, but I can't promise anything. Just remember that I'll do my best, okay?"

She nodded. "Okay, Sebastian." Elizabeth looked at Serenity and gave her a small smile. "Bye, Mommy. I hope you can remember us all when you get back."

Serenity returned the smile. "I hope so too."

Elizabeth opened her arms and Serenity leaned down, allowing the little girl to embrace her. She hugged Elizabeth back, but there was no display of the emotion one would expect from a mother saying goodbye to her child.

"We need to go now," said Sebastian. "We've got a long journey and every hour is important."

"Good luck," said Bridget with a strained smile. Sebastian knew, whatever their differences, she only wanted what was best for Elizabeth.

"Thanks, Bridget. We may be more than one night, so don't be alarmed if we're not back by morning. It's a long way and we don't know what we'll come up against when we get there."

"Be careful."

"We will."

Sebastian caught Elizabeth up and squeezed her tight.

"Hey! You're squishing me," the little girl laughed.

"Sorry, sweetheart. I'll miss you." He kissed the top of her head, Elizabeth's familiar scent filling his sensitive nose. "Love you."

"Love you too, Sebastian."

He narrowed his eyes in mock annoyance and wrinkled his nose at her. She gave an over-exaggerated sigh. "Daddy."

"That's better. We'll see you very soon."

Sebastian and Serenity left the house. Sebastian stepped through the big gates of the property and held his arms out to

Serenity. With one of the only memories she had being of traveling with Jackson, she knew exactly what was required of her. With her diminished, almost child-like size, she wrapped herself around him, her legs hooked around his waist and her arms around his neck.

He would need to run that way for several hours to reach New York. Even with his supernatural speed, they had thousands of miles to cover, a task which would not drain his inexhaustible strength, but would exhaust Serenity.

He needed to get her in front of Demitrios before she lost who she was completely and irrevocably. Flying would be better for Serenity's sake, physically, but they couldn't risk it. The thought alone instilled him with terror. A delayed flight—especially one caught circling above a city—might risk him being exposed to daylight. He'd never taken the risk before.

Sebastian ran, taking comfort in the touch of the woman in his arms. He held her close, protected in the circle of his embrace. Her face was buried in his neck and her breath warmed his skin. The touch of her lips distracted him. Too much time had passed since he'd kissed her and had her return that kiss with passion. If Demitrios didn't have the answer, he might never get Serenity back. To live with this shell of a woman was almost as bad as not having her at all.

They crossed the country, skirting the big cities. He crossed forest and desert, leaping raging rivers. Where he could, he stuck to the highways, the surface easier to negotiate.

After an hour, Serenity's grip on him began to loosen and he knew she needed to rest. He leapt up onto the roof of a large truck and allowed the vehicle to take the brunt of the travel for a few miles until she felt stronger again. He hadn't thought to bring any kind of sustenance for her, something he inwardly cursed himself for. She still wasn't eating as she should be. Though she thought he wasn't aware, he'd seen her throw food in the trash and then sit back down with a half-empty plate, trying to convince the people around her that she'd eaten. If she continued to starve herself like this, it wouldn't be just her mind he needed to worry about.

Her body simply wouldn't survive.

Chapter Twelve

Even in the middle of the night, New York thronged with people and traffic. Yellow cabs sat bumper to bumper, ferrying late night business people and small groups of clubbers across the city. All night cafés housed party-goers, serving coffee and pie in equal measure. The city had a different feel than Los Angeles. While it still had the designer, metropolitan atmosphere, it was somehow less manufactured than L.A.; it was grimier, more *real*.

Demitrios's club, *The Danger Zone*, was located downtown, hidden down a dark alley. Nightclub owning was popular amongst vampires for obvious reasons—they could live almost as a human would in the same situation, awake at night to run the business and asleep during the day. Though the club was frequented by humans, Sebastian noticed right away the two people guarding the entrance—a man, a burly creature with thick arms and a shaved head, and woman with short, spiky blonde hair and killer heels—were vampires. Both wore white button-down shirts, black pants and black bowties. Above the door, a red, neon 'DZ' sign glowed. The vibration of a low, fast bass traveled up through the soles of his feet.

Sebastian stopped short of the entrance. He'd hoped—and expected—to find Demetrios unaccompanied. Vampires were not known for their sociability. Like most other large predators, they preferred to hunt and live alone. Seeing Demitrios with two minions put Sebastian on edge

He wasn't worried for Serenity's safety—not yet anyway. These vampires were clearly used to mingling with and passing themselves off as humans. If something did happen, a group of vamps would always prove to be more of a challenge than one alone. Demitrios's decision to have other vampires around meant one of two things: he either thought he was in danger from others and would be paranoid, or his opinion of himself was over-inflated.

A row of party-goers lined up, waiting to be allowed entry to the club, unaware of the lethal creatures standing in such close proximity. The vampires didn't smile as they checked I.D.'s and granted patrons access past the velvet rope, allowing them into the cavernous depths.

The two immortals noticed Sebastian standing aside from the rest of the crowd. They turned simultaneously, two sets of eyes flashing yellow at the sight of him, but they couldn't do anything about him for the moment. They had a job to do and clearly had been instructed not to cause trouble and to act as human as possible. Sebastian could wait, and the two vamps continued to allow the remaining clubbers onto the premises.

As the door opened, the bass grew louder, the music thumping. A few more people trickled up, ignoring the dark, brooding man with the waif-like woman on his arm. They laughed and chatted as they gained entry to the club.

Finally, the two vampires closed the doors.

Instantly, both were in Sebastian's face, eyes glowing in the dark, the deadly glint of white fangs drawn.

"What are you doing here, stranger?" said the male. "This is our patch."

Sebastian stood his ground. "I'm here to see Demitrios."

"He doesn't see just anyone."

"I know Demitrios from the turn of the nineteen hundreds—before you were even created. He'll want to see me. Now run along like good little pets and tell him."

The blonde got in his face. "We work for Demitrios. We're not his pets!"

"Is that why he's got you both trussed up like turkeys?"

The male vamp leapt at Sebastian, snarling, his fang exposed. Sebastian shoved him away with one hand. The much younger vampire flew away, landing on the ground. The blonde paused, indecisive as to whether she should risk continuing the attack or simply do as Sebastian asked.

She made up her mind. "Who shall I say is visiting?"

"Sebastian Bandores."

She disappeared and it was only a matter of seconds before she was back again.

"Follow me."

The blonde pulled open the doors to the club, music blasting out at them, and slipped inside, the male vampire close behind. Sebastian followed, holding Serenity close. They entered a windowless corridor before the space opened up into the depths of the club and the volume of the dance music increased a notch. With Sebastian's sensitive hearing it felt as though someone pounded a drum inside his head. He wondered how the other two vampires could stand being around this volume all the time; it would drive him crazy.

People danced; hot, sweaty bodies jammed side by side. The two young vampires pushed their way between the dancers and then finally ducked through a door marked 'private'.

117

Once again, Sebastian followed, his arm still around Serenity's waist. The clubbers ignored them as they moved between them, allowing him and Serenity through. The floor of the long corridor they now walked through had a distinct slant, leading them below ground. A number of other corridors branched off the main one; a labyrinth beneath the club.

They turned several corners and reached the end of the passage, another set of black, double doors blocking the way. The two vampires paused briefly and then pushed the doors open, holding them ajar to allow Sebastian and Serenity through.

With every nerve on edge and Serenity hugged close to his side, Sebastian passed between them.

They walked into a huge room. Polished, dark wood floors stretched out before them and wood paneling covered the walls. Above their heads, an intricately painted ceiling curved into the center. Murals depicting beautiful, violent, and somewhat erotic scenes of sensual, half-naked women feasting on men and other women filled every part of the ceiling.

Only two items of furniture were in the room, positioned at the far end—a huge mahogany desk and an even larger, black leather chair. Seated in the chair, behind the desk, was Demitrios.

His appearance had changed little since Sebastian had last seen him. With the exception of a change in dress-style from the era of the nineteen hundreds—he now wore an expensive, black, three-piece suit—Demitrios looked the same. His long, raven hair hung in a sheet, the light above his head catching the sheen. His eyes were also black but around the edges were circles of yellow glow, like the sun during a total eclipse. His nose was large but strong, his lips full.

He rose from his chair as Sebastian walked in. "Well, well, Sebastian Bandores. How many years has it been?"

Sebastian smiled, trying to ignore the two younger vampires who now stood either side of the door, guarding the only way out. "Too many, Demitrios."

"Please, it's Demitri now. I found the shorter version fits in better in these modern times."

"Very well. Demitri it is."

His dark eyes turned to Serenity. "And who have you brought me? A present?"

Sebastian pulled Serenity closer to his side. "Serenity is mine."

Demitri raised his thick, black eyebrows. "I see. So why are you here?"

"I need your advice. You've been around for hundreds of years and you've seen everything."

He sat back in his leather chair and steepled his fingers. "That is true."

"Did you hear of the creature who could walk in the light?"

"Yes, of course. It was interesting but not unheard of."

"The creature used to be Serenity's husband. Another vampire raised him from the dead and made him what he was. The creature took Serenity from me and fed from her repeatedly. I found them and killed the monster, but now she has no memory of her life before she was taken and her condition is getting worse."

Demitri lowered his chin, his eyes flicking between Sebastian and Serenity.

"And what do want from me?"

"I want you to tell me how to bring her back again."

He smiled and nodded. "First, we shall feed together, like old times?"

Sebastian stiffened, his grip around Serenity's waist tightening. "I'm fine, Demitri. I fed only a day ago."

"But you still love to feed, do you not, Sebastian? I mean, you come here with a human companion asking for my help. I don't believe it's polite to turn down a meal when it's offered. The Sebastian I once knew enjoyed the taste of human blood. Are you even that same vampire anymore?"

"Of course I am. Who else would I be?"

"Excellent. In that case, we will feed together and then I will tell you what I know. Natasha, Vincent," he addressed his two minions. "Bring us something to eat. Make them young and fresh."

The two younger vampires each gave a brief nod and disappeared from the room. Seconds later, they were back again. In Natasha's grip, a woman in her early twenties struggled helplessly. Vincent had hold of a slightly older woman who had her blonde hair tied up in a knot, wearing a skin-tight leopard print dress. Their eyes darted between Sebastian and Demitri. The older woman's eyes locked on Sebastian's handsome face, perhaps thinking someone so beautiful would be incapable of causing harm.

"Help me," she begged him. "Please, don't hurt me. I'll do whatever you want."

The other girl gave up her struggles and sobbed, limp in Natasha's grip.

Demitri rose from his seat and shot over to the girls. The younger one screamed, only seeing him vanish from one place to reappear directly in front of her. He put out a hand, his fingernails long and perfectly manicured. He touched the girl's chin, raising her face to him. She cried, her eyes squeezed shut, her breasts heaving in time with her sobs. Demitri leaned in and smelled along the line of her throat as though he were taking in the scent of a fine wine.

The older woman watched with wide, terrified eyes. The muscles of her neck stood out, her skin strained white. Demitri turned his attention to her. He grabbed her by the jaw, wrenching her face so it was only inches from his. More defiant, she pressed her lips together and dared to stare him in the eye.

Demitri laughed and released his grip on her jaw. "Yes, I think this one will do me. I like them with a bit of spirit."

Sebastian was in turmoil. He didn't kill the young, especially not women, but if he didn't do as Demitri wanted, he may never get Serenity back. A war raged within him. How could he place this young girl's life above Serenity's? But then he thought of Elizabeth back home and how she needed her mommy back.

The fresh scent of the women spoke to something deep inside him, the thing he kept under wraps most of the time. Deep down he wanted nothing more than to sink his teeth into their sweet-smelling, succulent, young flesh. His forced diet of drug-dealers, pimps and hobos did little for the sensory arousal of feeding. In truth, feeding should be like any other kind of intimate connection. To desire the one he fed from was a natural instinct he'd kept under control for centuries.

"Natasha?" Demitri said, nodding in Sebastian's direction.

Sensing his awkwardness, Natasha flashed a grin and shoved the young woman over to Sebastian. He let go of Serenity to catch the girl and immediately he changed. His eyes burned, his fangs elongating and protruding. He wanted to fight it, to fight Demitri, but in the back of his head, a voice spoke. *You have to do this to save Serenity.* He didn't want to admit it, but the voice spoke to the part of him that wanted nothing more than to sink his teeth into the young woman's luscious throat.

Sebastian felt Serenity's eyes upon him. If it had been the old Serenity, he might have held himself back. She surely would have begged for this girl's life herself, but the woman watching him had lived with Jackson as her master and she'd seen more death than he could imagine. Serenity watched the scene unfolding around her with dull, impassive eyes.

Demitri gestured at the woman in Sebastian's arms. "Please, after you."

"I can't," he said, fighting his instincts, his voice hoarse. "I don't kill the young and innocent."

121

Demitri's eyes flared and he raised his upper lip, exposing the fangs that had killed hundreds of thousands over the years. "You will kill who I tell you to, or your human companion will remain a shell."

The woman he held saw his face—now bone white, his eyes bright yellow, his jaw and fangs protruding from his face—and screamed. She renewed her struggles, but they were pointless. She was no more than a rabbit caught in a fox's jaw. The girl in Sebastian's arms glanced up and caught sight of Sebastian's own face. He had changed in the same way Demitri had, ready for the kill, his normally smooth and calm features now the mask of a killer.

I'm doing this for Serenity; for her and Elizabeth.

Demitri roared, unwilling to wait for Sebastian to change his mind. He lunged down at the woman, his teeth puncturing the soft skin of her throat. The heady aroma of blood filled the room and Sebastian could hold himself back no longer. Roaring his own frustrations, he lowered his face, the girl's soft hair brushing against his cheek, and bit.

Warm, sweet blood flowed and Sebastian moaned with pleasure, even as the girl screamed. So much time had passed he'd forgotten how much of a delicacy the blood of the innocent was.

Even as the sweet nectar flowed down his throat and spread through his veins, he couldn't block out his inner turmoil.

This wasn't who he was. He didn't do this.

Sebastian wrenched himself away and the girl dropped to the ground. She scrabbled away, terrified, clutching her still bleeding neck, tears streaming down her face.

"No, I won't do it! I won't kill her!"

Demitri's woman was already dead. He let her fall and the body slumped in a heap. The girl caught sight of her dead friend and her screams increased in volume.

Demitri snarled. "Damn you!"

The elder vampire launched himself at the girl, flying through the air to land directly on top of her. She didn't get the chance to utter another scream. The vampire sank his fangs into her neck and tore. Blood gushed from the wound.

Demitri stood. "Your turn," he said to Natasha and Vincent.

The two youngsters didn't need any encouragement. They were on the wound in a flash, licking and slurping as the last of the life drained from the girl. Sickened at his part in this, Sebastian looked away. His eyes flicked to Serenity, still standing to the side, but she stared at the ground and didn't meet his gaze.

With both girls dead, Demitri settled back in his chair. "Take the bodies away."

Natasha and Vincent did as they were told, removing the bodies to dispose of in whatever fashion Demitri had previously instructed.

"So, Sebastian. You've gone soft on me."

"I'm simply more selective in who I kill."

"Why? Because you've fallen in love with a human?"

"I chose not to kill the young long before meeting Serenity. But I did as you instructed. You asked me to feed with you, not kill with you, and I did as you asked."

Demitri waved a hand. "Semantics," he sighed. "If I share with you the secret, Sebastian, you will be indebted to me. Should I want something from you, you will be obliged to give it to me."

"Whatever I have is yours as long as you can help her."

He gave a sly smile. "Are you sure about that?"

"Of course," Sebastian snarled. "I'd give up everything I own to make her well again."

"Very well." Demitri rose to his feet and paced back and forth. "All you need to do to make, and keep, her well is feed her your blood."

"What?" Sebastian reared back in shock. "I can't!"

Demitri laughed. "Of course you can. It doesn't have to be much, just a few drops. She'll heal again quickly—become whole again—and remember who she was. You'll need to continue to allow her to take your blood, a few drops at least once a month. If you don't, you may find she goes back to the way she is now."

"Serenity doesn't want to become like us."

"She won't," he said. "Your blood alone would not turn her because she hasn't been drained. However, should something happen to her, should she reach the point of death and you feed her your blood, well then yes, she will turn. As long as she stays alive, she will stay human. She will, however, experience side effects from your blood—the aging process will slow, she'll heal faster, she'll be stronger. But if you want to keep her alive, she'll be tied to you forever."

He glanced her way. "As long as she wants me, I'll always be there for her."

Demitri jerked his head at Serenity. "Go on, then. I want to watch."

"You mean I should do it now?"

"No time like the present," Demitri grinned, flashing his lethal canines.

Sebastian studied Serenity's face. "Do you understand what's about to happen? I'm going to need to feed you my blood and it should make you well again, but I won't do anything unless you're absolutely certain this is what you want. You'll be tied to me for the rest of your life."

She gave a weak smile. "I can't think of anywhere I'd rather be."

A snort of laughter came from Demitri's direction, but Sebastian ignored him. "Ready?" he asked.

She nodded.

Sebastian felt his face change once again—the muscle building in his jaw, his fangs protruding. Serenity's eyes were trained on his and they widened as his face took on that of a predator. He lifted his arm to his mouth and bit into his wrist.

His fangs punctured the skin in two perfect circles of beading blood.

His held his wrist out to her. "Quickly, Serenity. Before they heal."

Her slim fingers wrapped around his arm and she lowered her mouth, her warm lips encircling the wound, her hot tongue licking the flesh in a way he found to be almost erotic.

She dropped his wrist and stepped back, drawing in a long, rattling breath.

"Serenity!" Sebastian stepped forward in alarm, catching hold of her. "Are you all right?"

Struggling to breathe, she couldn't answer him.

He turned and saw Demitri watching with intense, fascinated eyes. "What did you do to her?"

Demitri grinned. "It's not what I did to her. *You* were the one who fed her your blood."

"Because you told me to!"

"Oh, pshh. If I told you to walk off a bridge, would you do it?" He laughed. "Actually, I suppose you would. It's not like you'd be harmed."

"If she dies, I'll kill you."

"Hush, now. Stop talking nonsense. Your little girlfriend will be just fine. Look."

He turned back in time to see Serenity straighten. Before his eyes, her hair softened and sprang in loose curls around her face. Color flooded the pale orbs of her cheeks. Her flesh filled out—the curves of her breasts and hips rounded again. The remaining scabs and cuts on her throat melted away, the scars disappearing, leaving smooth, perfect skin.

She raised her dark eyes to his and there was a light behind them again, a recognition. The sad, vacant expression that had been present for so long had disappeared.

Chapter Thirteen

Sebastian barely believed what he'd seen. He'd witnessed the birth of a new vampire before, but he'd never seen such a transformation occur in someone who remained human.

Pleasure at finding him standing before her flashed across her face, but was quickly replaced by a frown.

"Sebastian?"

"It's me. I'm right here."

She spun around, suddenly wide-eyed. "Where am I? Where's Jackson?"

"It's okay. He can't harm you anymore. Jackson is dead—forever dead."

She stared at him, as though she didn't want to believe him but hoped it was true. "He's dead?"

"I promise."

"I can't believe it's you." She stepped forward and lifted her hand to touch his cheek. Her warm fingers grazed his skin and he caught her hand, pressing her fingers to his lips in a kiss.

She burst into tears and flung herself into his arms. "I was so scared," she said, burying her face into his neck. "I thought Jackson would kill me."

"I'd never let that happen," he said, though he was only too aware Jackson could have killed Serenity at any time. Only Jackson's sadistic desire to keep her as his slave kept her alive.

She broke away. "Elizabeth? Where's Elizabeth?"

"She's safe. She's at home with Bridget."

"Who the hell is Bridget?"

"Don't you remember anything about the past week?"

Serenity frowned and shook her head. "No… I remember being in the mine and Jackson taking me. I remember him biting me…" She raised her hand to her throat.

"It's okay, you're healed now."

"How long have I been gone?"

"It's been two years."

"Two years!" Her eyes filled with tears. "I've missed out on two years of Elizabeth's life?"

"She's been with you every step of the way. She's thought about you every day, talked about you every day. You both have a lot of catching up to do. Do you not remember anything about the last two years?"

"Nothing! I don't know how we got here or even where 'here' is." She caught sight of the other vampire, still sitting in his chair. Instinctively, she pressed closer to Sebastian's side. "And I certainly don't know who that is."

Demitri got to his feet and gave a mock bow. "Demitrios of Samos. Pleased to make your acquaintance."

"Demitri helped us," said Sebastian. "He told me how to make you well again." He turned to the other vampire. "Thank you. Thank you so much. We'll leave you in peace now."

He started to back out of the room, when Demitri stopped him with a theatrical clearing of his throat. "Aren't you forgetting something?"

"Such as?"

"We agreed you should give me something of yours, did we not."

"Oh," Sebastian stuttered, caught off guard. His mind whirred, trying to figure out what Demitri could possibly want. "I didn't realize you meant right away."

"Of course!" he exclaimed, flashing his white, elongated canines. "I'd say life's too short, but I guess that doesn't apply here, does it? Now, tell me all about the child."

Alarm raced through him and Serenity's hand tightened on his. "What child?"

"Now, now, Sebastian. Don't play games with me. I hear you have a half-vampire child and the girl possesses somewhat predictive tendencies, does she not?"

"I don't know what you're talking about."

The vampire shot from his seat and slammed into him, knocking Sebastian backward. Beside him, Serenity screamed. Demitri's long fingers wrapped around Sebastian's throat, his eyes burning yellow.

"Don't fucking lie to me, Sebastian. Do you think I can't tell when a younger vampire is lying?"

"The girl is not up for exchange," he said, tearing Demitri's hands from his throat. "She's a little girl, not a thing to be bartered with."

"No, but she can always be a meal."

Sebastian snarled and leapt at the other vampire. Demitri put out a hand and pushed Sebastian away. The impact felt like a concrete block hitting him in the chest. He slid across the polished floor, smashing into the far wall.

In an instant, he was back on his feet.

Serenity stepped forward, terrified and out of her depth, but determined to fight for her child. "Elizabeth's only a little girl. Take me if you want something in exchange. I can do more for you than a child ever could."

He looked her up and down with scorn. "Is that what you think I want? I'm not interested in the physical. I want the girl for what her mind can do. Can you imagine the fun I'd have if I could predict what was going to happen in the future?"

"She only gets glimpses of things. Parts of the lives of people who are important to her. She couldn't tell you when an earthquake was about to happen, or if someone was about to shoot the president. She'd only be able to tell you about the people closest to her."

Demitri grinned. "That might be true at the moment, but imagine what will happen when she hits puberty. We both know her powers may escalate and I'm sure a regular feeding of blood will help to make her stronger."

"You'll have to kill us first," Sebastian snarled.

"Now, now. You know perfectly well I can make that happen. I'll allow you to go home and say goodbye to the child, and then you shall bring her to me."

Sebastian stood, glaring, his fists clenched, his jaw so tight he thought his teeth might shatter. He couldn't kill the other vampire—he was too old and in vampire years that made him stronger and faster. Even if he hadn't been an ancient, Sebastian still wouldn't have been able to kill him. One vampire couldn't kill another. Serenity had been the one who killed Madeline, Sebastian's maker, in the end. Only his lack of knowledge about the act allowed him to play the small part in her death that he had.

He needed to take Serenity away from here, get her home to Elizabeth and allow them to be reunited. Then he'd come up with a plan about what to do about Demitri. He had to. He refused to allow Demitri to take Elizabeth. The very idea called to something dark and fierce at his core.

He took Serenity's hand. "This isn't over, Demitri. Don't think for a moment I'll let you take her without a fight."

The other vampire wrinkled his nose and gave a shrug. "I wouldn't expect it any other way."

Sebastian stared at him. "Why would you even want to know the future? What possible benefit could you take from such knowledge?"

"Entertainment, my dear Sebastian. Life gets so dull, century after century with nothing new or exciting to look forward to. You can only travel the world so many times or lust over and kill so many beautiful women before everything becomes so tedious. Even killing loses its thrill. I know you understand me. Why else would you fall in love with a human, if not to try to capture some excitement back in your existence? Do you think I've not realized that you've spent the last few years living vicariously through her? Her trauma and problems have become your own. By loving her, you're attempting to be human again. Of course you and I both know such a thing is impossible. Eventually you'll grow bored of her, or her of you."

His hand tightened on Serenity's. "Never."

Demitri huffed air through his nose. "We'll see. Forever is a long time, Sebastian. Who can tell how many changes both you and the rest of the world will go through?"

"I still don't understand how Elizabeth can help you?"

"What?" He feigned astonishment. "You mean you don't think being able to predict world events be entertaining? Imagine being able to immerse yourself in all the great tragedies humanity succumbs to—the plane wrecks, the earthquakes, the mass shootings. With Elizabeth's help I can be there to witness it all first hand."

Serenity tried to step forward, but Sebastian held her back. "She can't predict those sorts of things," he said. "She only sees what happens to the people around her and even then they're mere glimpses."

"Ah, for the moment, anyway. But how old is she now? Six, seven? In a few years, she will hit puberty and her powers will increase. That's only a few years from now. I've been around for thousands; I can wait a few more."

"So, leave her with us until then. She's only a child. She needs her parents."

Demitri tilted his head to one side, as though considering the option. "I can't promise that long, but I will allow you to go home to her. I realize the mother won't have seen her child in a long time."

"Not that she can remember."

"Then you are free to go. But remember, you owe me payment, Sebastian. As soon as I decide I can't wait any longer, I will take what is owed to me."

Sebastian bristled with anger. "If you try to take her, you'll need to go through me."

The older vampire shrugged. "Very well. Now, I suggest you leave before I decide to make a meal of your little girlfriend."

Sebastian hated feeling as though he'd been bested, but he also knew better than to stay and try and fight. He couldn't take on the elder vampire, not on his own, and he wouldn't place Serenity in harm's way again. He'd just gotten her back and someone would need to tear off both his arms before he allowed her to be taken from him again.

He tugged on her hand. "Come on, Serenity. Time to go."

"Wait." She turned back to Demitri. "I thank you for bringing me back, but if you ever go near my daughter… I swear to God…"

He laughed. "Empty threats don't bother me and I won't hurt your child. Now, run along before I change my mind."

"Serenity," Sebastian said, his tone firm.

Serenity glared at Demitri, but Sebastian wrapped an arm around her and left the building with a burst of speed.

Back on the street, Sebastian took Serenity in his arms. Her arms snaked around his waist, her face pressed against the

131

breadth of his chest. Sebastian buried his face in her hair, breathing in the citrus scent of her shampoo.

"I can't tell you how much it means to me to have you back," he said. "I won't let anything hurt you ever again."

"You heard what he said. I need your blood now to keep me well."

"I'd give you every last drop if it means you and I are together."

"But what about Elizabeth? Do you think he means what he said about wanting Elizabeth?"

Sebastian chewed at his lower lip. "I've never known Demitri to not mean what he says, but right now we can't think about that. He said himself he'll give us time to say goodbye to her…"

Serenity's eyes filled with tears. "I don't want to say goodbye! I've already missed two years of her life. I won't let him come and take her away. We must be able to do something."

"Shhh," he rubbed her back. "There will be something we can do. I just need some time to figure out how to stop him, how to make him want something else, or come to some kind of compromise."

She looked up, her eyes wide and horrified. "There is no compromise! I won't let him anywhere near Elizabeth. And if you're actually considering handing her over, then you're not the man I thought you were."

"I'm not a man, Serenity."

She yanked away from him. "You may not be a man, but you *are* a father."

"Hey, wait. I love Elizabeth as much as you do. I'll die before I let Demitri harm her, but we need to think about this rationally and being over-emotional about the situation won't help us figure things out."

"I guess it's easier for you to not be affected by your emotions."

"I can shut them down if I need to, but never for you or Elizabeth."

He gently tugged her back to him and this time she let him. "We'll figure this out. Let's go home. You'll feel better with Elizabeth at your side."

Sebastian glanced at the sky. Though the city's illumination dulled the brilliance of the stars, his internal clock told him dawn wasn't far away. Going home right away wasn't an option.

"We're not going to make it back tonight," he said. "We need to find a place to stay."

"What about Elizabeth? I want to see her." She paused, her brow furrowing in anxiety. "Who's taking care of her?"

"Her nanny—a woman named Bridget. She knows all about my kind. Her son was turned several years ago."

"So Elizabeth is safe?"

"Perfectly."

Her shoulders relaxed. "So where are we going to stay? What about the sunlight?"

"A hotel will be fine. As long as the room's got a large closet, I can sleep in there."

"It'll be weird to think of you asleep in the closet."

"You won't need to think. You've been through so much I expect you'll sleep right through the day."

Serenity's hand slipped into his and, they walked away from Demitri's club and out to the main street. Up ahead, a white sign protruded from a wall of a building, the word 'HOTEL' in big, black lettering. They didn't have time to be fussy.

They entered the small, but tidy lobby and a woman behind the reception desk smiled at them.

Sebastian reached into his jacket pocket and took out his wallet. "We need a room." He laid a credit card and driver's license on the reception desk.

"Just for the one night?" the woman inquired.

"Make it two. And we've been traveling all night. Can you please ensure we're not disturbed?"

"Of course, Sir."

The receptionist handed Sebastian the keycard and pointed them toward the elevator. Hand in hand, they made their way up to the room.

Chapter Fourteen

How had she missed the last two years?

Serenity was struggling to come to terms with the reality that she was missing two years of both her and Elizabeth's life. Sebastian, of course, still looked as he always had, and she'd yet to see Elizabeth. Her heart broke for both herself and her daughter. How awful for Elizabeth, to have to grow up without her mommy.

As Sebastian led her down the hotel corridor, toward their room, she lifted her free hand to her cheek. Had she aged? Would the years be apparent on her face when she looked in the mirror?

She felt different, but not in a bad way. Her senses were heightened. The soft snores and deep breathing of other guests sleeping behind the bedroom doors filtered to her ears as they passed. A waft of gone-off milk made her turn her face away from the source of the smell, but the carpet had been long cleaned, she'd simply picked up on a slight residue. She was also incredibly aware of Sebastian beside her, of the relation of his body to hers. Despite the insane circumstances, her physical desire for him had not changed—if anything, she wanted him more than ever. She glanced at his profile as they walked—his straight nose, full lips, cut jaw and cheekbones, and fierce eyes. Her heart fluttered, something catching tight in her chest. He'd always been beautiful to her, but right now the urge to immerse herself in him felt like a physical addiction. His familiar scent filled her nostrils and she clamped her jaw together, restraining herself from throwing herself at him right here in the corridor.

They reached their room and barely made it through the door.

"Serenity…" Sebastian started as he closed the door behind them. He turned, his green eyes locking on hers. Her want for him notched up a level—an urgent, desperate need.

"Don't speak," she said. "Not yet." She stepped toward him, closing the gap so only an inch of air remained between them. The tiny space seemed charged and she was almost surprised she couldn't see electricity dancing between their bodies. Her hands found the buttons of his shirt and his eyes lit when he realized exactly what she had in mind.

"Are you sure?" he said. "So soon?"

"It doesn't feel soon for me."

His fingers laced in the back of her hair and he drew her mouth to his. The sensation of his soft, cool lips made her moan. She stood on tiptoe, pressing herself into him as he kissed her, long and slow and deep.

Sebastian broke the kiss, looking into her face. "I've thought of this every night since Jackson took you. It's been as though a piece of my heart was missing."

His words brought tears to her eyes but she placed her fingertips against his lips. "No talking. Not yet."

Their lips met again, hungry and passionate. With fervor, she popped the buttons of his shirt apart and tugged the material from his broad frame. Her palms sought the smooth curves of his chest, skirting over his skin. Sebastian pulled her t-shirt over her head, his lips finding her throat... her collarbone... her shoulder.

They matched each other's urgency, stroke for stroke, kiss for kiss, lick for lick. Within moments, their remaining clothes had been cast to the floor, leaving them naked in each other's embrace. She was stronger now and she could take his ferocity. Sebastian lifted her and slammed her against the door, the sound ricocheting down the corridor behind. He reached between her thighs and stroked her open, and with a nudge of his hips, filled her.

Serenity lifted her head and they locked eyes as he moved inside her. Had she ever experienced such a connection to another being before—a total sense of oneness?

They maintained eye contact even as their motions grew more frantic, almost challenging each other. Pleasure built deep at her center and she could look at him no more. She cried out and buried her face against the cool skin of his neck. Her fingers clawed into the hard muscles of his back, her thighs locked around his hips, drawing him deeper.

They were regaining each other again, each one claiming the other.

Even as her climax spilled over her, her only thoughts were, *'I love you, I love you, I love you.'* She didn't need to say them out loud; with their blood connection, he'd heard them anyway.

Afterward, they lay in bed, Sebastian on his back, Serenity curled against him, her head on his chest.

Sebastian kissed the top of her head. "It's almost morning."

"Is it too early to call the house?" she asked, anxiety in her voice. "I want to speak to Elizabeth, but I don't want to wake her."

He gave a small laugh. "She probably already knows you're about to call. I expect she's sitting by the phone."

She picked up the phone, sitting on the nightstand, and handed the receiver to Sebastian, nerves suddenly jangling in her stomach. "You call. Just in case the other woman—Bridget—picks up."

He nodded. "Sure."

Serenity picked at the skin around her nails as he dialed the number. Someone picked up on the first ring and Serenity leaned in close to hear who answered.

"Mommy?" Elizabeth's small voice echoed through the handset and Serenity snatched the phone from Sebastian's fingers.

"Elizabeth, honey? I'm here. It's Mommy!"

"Mommy! You're all better again."

"Yes, sweetheart. Your daddy made me well."

"So you remember us? Just like you used to?"

"Yes, and I'll never forget you again. Your daddy told me you went and got big without me." Tears flooded her eyes and her voice broke as she struggled to speak past the hard, painful lump clogging her throat."

"I did, Mommy! I got real big. I'm six years old already."

Her hand clamped over her mouth, trying to stop the sob threatening to burst from her mouth. She didn't want Elizabeth to hear.

"I've missed you so much, Mommy. I can't wait for you to come home."

"Me too, baby. I'll be there real soon, okay. I'll be with you tonight, I promise."

"Okay, Mommy. See you tonight. I love you."

"I love you too, baby. So, so much."

Serenity hung up the phone and burst into tears. "She sounds so grown up."

Sebastian pulled her against his chest and she clung to him as she cried.

"I can't believe Jackson stole two years of her life from me. Out of everything he did, I think that's the worst."

"He's dead now, Serenity. Dead and gone for good. I tore out his heart and watched as he turned to dust and blew into the wind. There is no coming back from that."

"Thank you," she said, kissing him. "And thank you for never giving up on me."

"Never." He glanced at the drape covered window.

"You need to sleep now?"

He nodded. "Yeah. And you should get some rest too."

The closet was more than long enough for him to lie down on its floor. He grabbed a pillow and kissed her again, his strong hand brushing through her hair. "Everything will be all right again. One more day, and we'll all be back together."

She nodded. "I love you."

He kissed her. "I love you."

Then he was gone, the closet door closed.

Serenity woke early the next evening, ravenous and anxious to get home to Elizabeth. The thought of seeing her daughter again made her nervous. Would Elizabeth still look like the same girl? Would Elizabeth even still remember her as her mother, or had the other woman—Bridget—taken her place?

A flash of jealousy clutched at her heart. To think another woman had replaced her in the lives of the people she cared most about in this world hurt deep down. She wondered what the woman was like and again jealously blazed through her, hot and bright. Serenity shook herself, trying to dislodge the pain and uncertainty. It was normal for her to have concerns. After all, she'd been missing for two years and that was a long time, even if she couldn't remember the time passing.

Remembering her desire to find out if the years had marked her own face, Serenity wrapped the bed sheet around her nakedness and stood. She crossed to the dresser with its mirror hung above. With a thumping heart, she leaned in, studying herself. She breathed a sigh of relief. Sebastian's blood had affected more than just her memory and senses. Her skin was smooth and clear, her dark eyes bright, her lips full. No crow's lines marked her eyes, no cracks above her upper-lip. Her forehead was as line-free as it had been in her early twenties. Curious, she opened the sheet and looked down at her body. The faint silvery stretch marks left from her pregnancy had all but vanished, only the widest ones still left the faintest trace on her skin. Her breasts were full and high, like those of a twenty-year old, her stomach perfectly flat.

Serenity smiled and tugged the sheet back around her body. No wonder Sebastian's body was always so perfect—clearly vampire blood was good for the physique.

The thought of Sebastian made her squeeze her thighs together, pleasure racing through her at the memory of their time together earlier. She glanced at the closet. How strange to think he was behind those doors. She got no sense of a presence, no sounds normally associated with a sleeping man.

She made her way over to the window and pulled back the drape enough so she could peer out. The light had grown dim. Traffic raced below, some of the headlights of the cars illuminating the road. Street lights started to flicker to life. It wouldn't be long before Sebastian would awaken.

Arms encircled her waist and Serenity jumped. She twisted around to find Sebastian fully dressed. "I was just thinking you'd be awake soon."

"The sun already set. Did you sleep?"

She grinned. "Like the dead. I want to get home though. What Demitri said worries me."

"I know. Me too. We'll go right away."

"Give me a minute." She stood on tiptoe and planted a quick kiss on his mouth before disappearing inside the bathroom. She used the toilet and washed, using the toiletries the hotel provided to brush her teeth and comb her hair. She reemerged feeling less like a tramp.

"Are you ready to travel with me? Do you remember what it was like? It can be quite a strain on you, physically, over such a huge distance."

"I remember and I'll be fine. I'm stronger than I've ever been."

"That would be the vampire blood."

"I could do with something to eat though," she added, almost apologetically.

"Of course. I forget you need to eat."

They left the hotel room and headed down through the lobby and out onto the street. Sebastian had paid for two days in advance so they simply left the key in the room and walked away.

Out on the street, the world carried on, unaware of the secrets that walked among them.

Serenity's stomach grumbled and Sebastian grinned down at her, his sensitive hearing easily picking up on the sound.

She flushed. "Sorry."

"Don't be silly. You're still human, remember. You need to eat."

A bagel shop made up the corner spot of the street and they headed inside. Serenity ordered a cream cheese bagel and a large coffee. They took a seat near the window while she ate with urgent bites and slurped down the drink, despite it still being too hot.

She glanced up at him, suddenly self-conscious about her gluttony. "I feel bad sitting here when we should be getting back to Elizabeth, especially considering what Demitri threatened."

"Well don't. You need your strength. We've got to cross thousands of miles. Demitri won't go anywhere near her. First he'd need to find out where we live and then he'd still have to make the same journey."

141

"I'm just scared."

He reached out and took her hand. "We might not see Demitri again for years. Maybe even not at all. He might lose interest and find something else to provide his 'entertainment'. But whatever happens, we'll find some way to hide Elizabeth from him, even if it means traveling to the other side of the world and starting over somewhere new."

"I don't care where I am, as long as I have both of you."

"I feel the same way."

He looked down at the bagel wrapper, now containing only crumbs, and the empty cup. "Ready?"

Serenity nodded, and they stood and left the shop. Night had now completely fallen. Headlights of cars swept across the road before them. Streetlamps shone like spotlights onto the sidewalk. People walked with their heads down, hands shoved in pockets or talking on cell phones. Everyone rushed by and no one noticed when the striking man picked up the woman with the long, dark hair and then seemed to vanish into the night.

Chapter Fifteen

Serenity stood outside Sebastian's front door, her heart hammering. Perhaps she was crazy for being so nervous about facing her own daughter but she couldn't change the way she felt. Seeing Elizabeth would be the first real confirmation that she'd completely lost the last two years; Sebastian didn't change, and ingesting those few drops of his blood had wiped out the past ten years on her face—never mind two.

Beside her, Sebastian reached down, his cool fingers lacing through her own. He squeezed her hand in reassurance. "There's a little girl behind that door who is dying to see you."

She took a deep breath. "I'm desperate to see her too. I'm just scared it'll be weird, like I won't know who she is anymore."

"She's exactly the same—only taller."

Serenity turned her face up to his and kissed him. His lips pressed firm against hers. His mouth was soft and moist, and she forced herself to break away.

"Thank you," she said.

She climbed the steps, turned the handle and pushed open the front door. Immediately, the sound of feet rushed toward them and Elizabeth rounded the corner, her dark hair flying and her eyes bright.

"Mommy, Mommy, Mommy!" She slammed into Serenity's legs and Serenity lifted her up, squeezing her tight. Elizabeth's small arms wound around Serenity's neck, and her soft cheek pressed against hers. "I missed you so much, Mommy."

Serenity kissed her daughter's hair, breathing in the scent of her shampoo. She bit back tears, trying not to think of all the things she'd missed out on.

"I missed you too, baby. I'm so sorry I've not been here for you."

"It's okay, Mommy. I know it wasn't your fault and Sebastian took real good care of me."

"My goodness, you got so big!" Serenity untangled Elizabeth's arms from around her neck and set her down. "Let me look at you."

Elizabeth stood, her hands held out either of her body, a self-conscious smile on her face. Sebastian had been right—she did look the same as she always had, only taller! Perhaps, Serenity thought, her face was a little slimmer and she'd lost some of her baby fat. Otherwise, she was still the same Elizabeth.

She became aware of another person standing in the background and she forced her attention away from her daughter. A woman in her fifties stood watching them with bright blue eyes. Her hair was as long as Serenity's, trailing down to her hip.

Bridget.

Serenity pushed all her doubts aside and walked up to Bridget. She put her arms around the older woman and hugged her. "Thank you for looking after my baby."

Bridget froze for a moment, taken by surprise, and then returned the embrace. "You're more than welcome. She's an absolute joy."

Elizabeth grinned with pride.

Bridget peered around Serenity at Sebastian. "So everything went well, then? No problems?"

Sebastian's gaze flicked to Serenity and the words passed between them without being spoken out loud; *not in front of Elizabeth*. Bridget must have picked up on the look, for her eyes darted between them and her lips thinned.

"Are you talking about the man with long hair?" said Elizabeth.

Serenity gave a wry smile. She'd forgotten how hard it was to keep anything from Elizabeth. "Everything is fine, sweetheart. He was just interested in how you know things before other people do."

"Do I need to go see him?"

"No, Elizabeth," said Sebastian. "It's nothing for you to worry about."

Elizabeth looked between her parents, not seeming entirely convinced. Neither, for that matter, did Bridget.

"Is there anything I can help with?" she asked. "My offer is still open."

Sebastian shook his head. "You've done enough, Bridget. I don't know where we'd be without you."

"And you're sure nothing happened?"

"Demitri was most accommodating to us. He asked a few questions about Elizabeth and her abilities, but we left on good terms."

Her blue eyes flicked between them, but Sebastian held his tongue. Serenity wasn't sure why he didn't want to tell Bridget what happened. She assumed he simply didn't want to discuss things in front of Elizabeth.

"So what now," Bridget said. "Do you still need me to come back at daylight? I mean… with Serenity back now, am I still needed?"

"If you're asking if you're out of job, Bridget, of course you're not. Elizabeth loves you and I'm sure Serenity can use the help."

Serenity smiled, though she was still unsure how she felt about having someone else in her home, so close to her family. But she wasn't going to push the other woman out and she didn't want to hurt Elizabeth—especially when the two of them were clearly so close.

"Sure," she said.

Bridget let out a sigh, her hand on her chest. "Phew, I was worried."

"You didn't need to be, but you can go home now and get some rest yourself. We've got a lot of catching up to do." Sebastian guided her to the front door and Serenity watched as he leaned in and kissed Bridget on the cheek.

"I'm so happy you're all back together again," said Bridget. "Everything is going to be all right now, isn't it?"

"I hope so, Bridget."

Serenity tried to ignore the coil of anxiety winding tight in the pit of her stomach. The big house was well protected against humans trying to gain access, but twice she'd been here when something paranormal had scaled the tall walls and broken in through a door or window—first Madeline and then Jackson. The memory made her shiver. She wanted this all to be over with. She wanted things to be normal—for her to be able to wake in the morning and have breakfast with Elizabeth, take her to school, perhaps sleep some in the day, and spend her evenings wrapped up in Sebastian's arms.

She didn't want any more drama.

With Bridget gone, the three of them curled up on the couch together.

Elizabeth chattered non-stop. "I'm going to big school now. And I've got loads of friends, haven't I, Sebastian?"

"More than anyone else I know," he said with a grin.

Serenity laughed. "You're hardly the most sociable person I know."

"I'm good at reading now," Elizabeth continued, "and I can write lots of words too."

Serenity kissed the top of her head. "I'm so proud of you."

"I'm proud of you too, Mommy. You were really brave."

"Well I needed to be brave so I could come home to you."

Elizabeth snuggled up to Serenity's side, and Serenity leaned into Sebastian. For the first time, Serenity had a real family around her.

"How are James and Amy?" Serenity asked. "What about baby Noah?" She realized something and clapped a hand to her mouth. "Oh, he won't be a baby any more, will he?"

Sebastian shook his head. "No. He's three years old now. And James and Amy are fine. Amy is pregnant with their second child. Her baby is due in a few weeks."

Serenity's face broke into a smile. "That's wonderful. I'm so happy for them. Can I go and visit them?"

"They don't live in Los Angeles any more. James was offered a transfer to Savannah and he took it. I think it's a different pace of life, but it's what they wanted. After everything that happened, Amy just couldn't stay."

Serenity lowered her eyes to her hands, twisting her fingers. It was a double blow to hear they'd left. Not only would she miss them, but Elizabeth had been without their nurture for the past two years on top of her own absence.

"I understand," she said. "They needed to do what was best for them." Despite knowing that, a part of her still felt hurt. They'd left her. They'd left Elizabeth. All at a time when she'd needed them the most. "I'd still like to talk to them though."

"We'll call tomorrow. They'll love to hear from you."

"Does Amy know what she's having?"

"It's a baby girl. I think since you've returned, they may have to re-think their name choice."

"Really?" her heart lifted at hearing her old friends thought highly enough of her to name their daughter after her. "They'd have named the baby after me?"

He laughed, his Adams' apple bobbing in his broad throat. "They were thinking about it, but I'm sure they'll be happy not to need to now."

Elizabeth stifled a yawn behind her hand and Serenity glanced at the wall mounted clock. It was almost one in the morning—no wonder she was tired. Though she didn't want to let Elizabeth go, she hadn't slept all day like Serenity had and she needed her rest.

"Come on, you. Time for bed."

"Aww, Mom. Can't I stay up just a little bit longer?" She put her palms together in a prayer position. "Please."

"It's the middle of the night. You shouldn't even be awake. How about I tuck you in and tell you a story or sing you a song."

Elizabeth yawned again and relented. "Okay." She scrambled over the top of Serenity and planted a rough kiss on Sebastian's cheek.

Hand in hand, Elizabeth led Serenity up the wide staircase and up onto the landing. Elizabeth's bedroom door was shut and Serenity noted the hand-carved, painted wooden plaque of her daughter's name that had been fixed to the door. She smiled. Knowing some effort had been made to make the house a home eased the pain in her heart a little.

Elizabeth pushed open the bedroom door and Serenity laughed out loud. The big room had been transformed into a myriad of pinks and whites—a pink rug lay atop the thick cream carpet, a flowery bedspread covered the bed and more floral designs were in the wall paper. The room looked completely different from the stark and formal place she'd slept in before.

"Do you like my room, Mommy?" asked Elizabeth, racing over to her bed to bounce. "I chose loads of stuff myself."

"Your room is beautiful."

Elizabeth beamed and then quickly hid another yawn.

Serenity spotted the yawn. "Come on. You can show me more in the morning."

Elizabeth didn't put up any more of a fight. She stripped off her clothes and then pulled a set of pink pajamas from beneath her pillow. Serenity helped her into the nightclothes, marveling at how long and slim her daughter had become. The little pot belly and chubby thighs she'd had at the age of four had vanished.

Serenity pulled the covers up over her daughter's shoulders and sat on the edge of the bed. Elizabeth reached under her pillow and pulled out her comfort rag—the same one she'd had before.

The sight stirred a conflict of emotions in Serenity. Part of her was pleased Elizabeth still maintained this tiny bit of her babyhood, but, at the same time, the thought Elizabeth hadn't felt secure enough to get rid of the comforter filled her with sadness. She knew her absence for the past two years had a lot do to with that.

"Will you do the blue blanket?" Elizabeth asked.

Serenity shook her head, confused. "Do what?"

"The blue blanket. It's a magic blanket Bridget puts over me. She rubs her hands together and says special words and this blue light comes out of her hands. Then she spreads the light all over me—even over my head—and tucks it all in around me."

"Why does she do that?"

"To stop the bad dreams getting in."

Serenity smiled. "I don't know if I'll do it exactly as Bridget does, but I can try."

Elizabeth wriggled back down in bed and lay with her hands at her side.

Feeling faintly ridiculous, Serenity rubbed her hands together. "Hubba-mubba... Jubba wubba..."

Elizabeth burst into laughter. "Mommy! That's not how she does it and I can't see the light."

"But it's an imaginary light. Can't you close your eyes and imagine the magic blanket?"

"No, Mommy. The light's real." She nodded her head in earnest. "It is, honest."

"I'm sorry, sweetie," she said, crushed. "I don't know how to make the light."

In some ways, she guessed Bridget had taken her place. All those bedtimes she'd missed; Elizabeth and Bridget had created their own nighttime routine which now Serenity was unable to mimic. "Do you think you'll be able to sleep without it tonight? Maybe I can ask Bridget how to make the magic blanket in the morning."

Elizabeth snuggled back under her blanket. She forced a smile and Serenity knew it was only to make her feel better. "Okay, Mommy."

Feeling as though she'd already let her daughter down, Serenity kissed her forehead. "Love you."

"Love you too, Mommy."

Serenity was about to leave the room when Elizabeth said, "I'm really happy you're home."

"Me too, baby. Goodnight."

Serenity left the room backward, pulling the door closed behind her. She turned and collided with Sebastian's solid chest.

"Hey," she smacked his shoulder, playfully. "You made me jump."

"Sorry, just wanted to check how it was going."

Serenity sniffed, not wanting to cry yet again. "She wanted me to do this pretend thing Bridget does—make a protective, magic blanket or something. I told her it was pretend and she needed to use her imagination, but she insisted Bridget's blanket was real and that light really does come out of her hands."

A flicker of an expression crossed Sebastian's face.

"What?" she asked.

"It's nothing, just something Bridget said. Don't worry about it."

His green eyes smoldered down at her, one corner of his full lips turned upward in a lopsided grin. "She's gone straight to sleep. We've got the house to ourselves."

Losing herself in Sebastian would temporarily make her forget the pain of missing out on two years of Elizabeth's life. It would push down the sickening sensation that part of her daughter's heart had been taken by someone else.

Sensing her need, he reached down, caught hold of her hand and tugged her toward a different bedroom door.

They burst into the room and Serenity flung herself against him. Her mouth sought his and she kissed him with hunger and ferocity. His hands trailed down her back, crushing her body to his. Serenity hooked her legs around his body, winding herself around him like a snake.

Her tongue pushed into his mouth and his lips parted, welcoming her in. Urgently, she tugged at his clothing, opening his shirt and pulling the item from his shoulders. He carried her across the room to the huge, four-poster bed and laid her back on the soft surface, his body pressed hard against hers. Her breasts crushed against him, her nipples hard against the thin material of her tee.

Sebastian lifted himself from her for a moment, looking down at her. "I've missed you so much."

"Don't tell me," she said, pulling his mouth back down toward hers, her fingers lacing in the soft, dark hair at the back of his neck. "Show me."

He smiled, a wicked glint to his green eyes. His lips found hers once more and his tongue searched every inch of her mouth, teasing and flicking in a kiss that went beyond sexy.

It felt so good to be back in his strong arms. Emotions welled up inside her, tightening into a painful knot at the base of her throat. But she wasn't going to allow herself to cry; she'd done enough of that over the years. Right now, she only wanted to drown herself in the sensations coursing through her body. She wanted him so badly.

She sat halfway up and Sebastian tugged her shirt over her head. Her hair fell down her back in soft curls. His cool mouth kissed the delicate and now flawless skin of her throat, pausing above the steady trip of her pulse. He nipped the skin with his lips before continuing down her body. Level with her lace-covered breasts, his mouth covered the hard nub of her nipple. His cool tongue laved moisture, leaving a wet mark on her bra, before moving to the other breast and repeating the action.

Serenity moaned and arched her back, pressing herself into him. His mouth on her hot skin sensitized every nerve ending in her body and the sparks seemed to converge deep at her core. Taking Sebastian's blood had heightened all of her senses, making every single lick, stroke, and nibble one hundred times more powerful. The blood had also served another purpose; it bound her to Sebastian in a way she'd never experienced before. It was as though the edges of their beings were now enmeshed—she could almost pick up on his emotions, taste her own skin. The sensation was strange, but not unpleasant, and only served to make her feel closer to him than any other person she'd known. Even her relationship with Elizabeth didn't come near this level of intimacy.

Sebastian reached behind her and unclipped her bra, freeing her breasts. They rose to meet his eager mouth and he feasted upon them once again, this time with no fabric to hinder the way.

Serenity pulled at his clothing, wanting to rid him of the offending items. She wanted his skin naked against hers, to wrap every inch of herself around him and make them one.

Sebastian's lips trailed down her stomach and she sucked in a breath as his tongue left a cool, wet trail on her midriff. His fingers worked the button of her jeans and he slipped them from her hips and pulled them down over her legs, dropping them on the floor at the foot of the bed.

She smiled up at him. "I hope I'm not going to be the only one naked."

He stripped off his shirt, exposing the curves and lines of muscle making up his chest and abs. His pale skin only served to define the shape of the muscle just beneath the skin and she knew when she touched him he would feel as hard as he looked.

Sebastian kicked off his shoes and shed himself of his pants. She held out a hand toward him and, with his vampire speed, he launched at the bed, catching her in his arms, pulling her with him. She squealed with laughter as she discovered herself now on top of him, though the movement had been little more than a flash.

Her hair tickled his chest as he held her on top. "Are you trying to show off?" she said, smiling.

Before she knew what was happened, he'd flipped her to her back. Now he was on top of her. His eyes had taken on that yellow glow they got when his emotions ran high. He looked intense and dangerous, and a thrill ran through her.

She laced her hands in the back of his hair. "Enough playing around."

Their lips met once again, a kiss so deep she thought she might drown in it. With only underwear between them, her breasts crushed against his hard chest and the thick ridge of him pressed against her. She wrapped her legs around his hips, her heels digging into the hard muscles of his ass.

He used his speed once again, this time ridding them both of their underwear. And then he filled her. Perfectly. She gasped and held him close as he moved above and inside her. Her palms stroked the length of his strong back, his taut muscles flexing beneath his skin.

153

Pleasure soared through her, like nothing she'd ever experienced before. Joined to Sebastian both physically and through his blood created an intimacy unlike any other. Even as he moved within her, she experienced every touch, sound, and texture.

They tipped over the edge together, plummeting into the depths of pleasure, the intensity washing over them and carrying them away. Spent, he dropped to his side next to her and gathered her up against him.

"I can hardly believe I'm holding you again," he said, his face buried against her neck.

She turned her face, her lips brushing his smooth forehead. "It feels like only yesterday you and I were in the bathroom, up against the wall, on the floor..." She tailed off, grinning at the memory.

"I'm so happy you can't remember what happened with Jackson."

"Shhh." She pulled back and placed her finger on his full lips. "Don't even speak of him. I want to forget he ever existed."

"I hope you can. I hope we both can."

"What about Demitri? Will he keep his word and come after Elizabeth?" Terror clutched her heart. She couldn't stand the idea of anyone, much less another vampire, threatening her family.

"He said he'll give us some time. We'll work something out. Everything will be okay."

She shook her head. "You've said that before, Sebastian. They always have a way of tracking us down. We can't pretend his threat wasn't real. Even if he's not coming right away, he'll still come. And we need to consider the fact that he knew about Elizabeth and what she can do. That must mean word of her has spread around your kind. I don't know how, because I'm sure you wouldn't talk to others about her abilities."

He frowned. "Of course not. But different vampires have different strengths. Another vampire may have picked up on Elizabeth's powers telepathically and reported back to Demitri."

"I can't tell you how much this all scares me."

He held her close. "Me too, but I don't think Demitri will just take her. He enjoys the drama too much. He'll make sure I fight him for her."

Her hold on him tightened. She wanted Sebastian to go up against Demitri almost as much as she wanted Demitri to take Elizabeth. "You're not making me feel any better."

"Sorry. I just want this to be all right again. I want you and Elizabeth to be safe. I hate that what I am always seems to put you both in harm's way."

"It's not because of what you are that's put Elizabeth in Demitri's path. It's because of what *she* is."

"She's half vampire, Serenity. If it wasn't for me, she'd be fully human."

She twisted to face him and caught his chin between her fingers, focusing his eyes on hers. "If it wasn't for you, she wouldn't be here at all. I had multiple pregnancies with Jackson, but lost the babies; my body simply couldn't nurture them. Elizabeth was so strong. She survived despite my body's weaknesses. I believe she survived when the others didn't because of her genetics—because she is half vampire."

He shook his head slightly, his eyes downcast, lips pressed together. "I hate that you've been through so much pain in your life."

"I'd go through it all again as long as it ended up with me being here with you, our daughter asleep in the room next door."

He touched her face and she pressed her cheek into the cool cup of his palm, and kissed the inside of his wrist.

"Nothing else matters but you and Elizabeth," she said. "I'm home.

Chapter Sixteen

Elizabeth's eyes sprang open with the certainty she was not alone. The looming dark shadow of a man stood over her. His long hair fell on either side of his face. His pale skin had an eerie glow in the low light. Shadows cast by her nightlight made his features appear even darker—as though his eye sockets were no more than holes in his face.

She wasn't surprised to find him standing in her bedroom; she'd just been dreaming of him.

Elizabeth sat herself up in bed. "I'm not dreaming anymore, am I?"

A smile played on his lips. "Not this time, child."

"Are you going to take me away?"

"Yes, I am. I made your mother well again and you are my payment."

"My mommy and Sebastian would never give me away."

"Do you want your mommy to get sick again? I could take away her memory like that!" He snapped his fingers, the click cutting through the silent night.

Elizabeth's lower lip trembled. "I don't want you to do that."

"Then I suggest you come with me and not make a fuss," he said, holding out his hand. "I've no intention of hurting you, child. In fact, I'd like us to grow to love each other. With your clever abilities, I'm sure we will have so much fun."

"But I don't want to." Her lower lip started to wobble.

"You have no choice." He caught her up in his arms, fast and strong. Elizabeth opened her mouth to shout for help, but before she'd got the chance, his cold hand clamped over her lips, preventing her cry.

"Shhh," he spoke in her ear. "You wouldn't want me to hurt your mommy, would you?"

Elizabeth forced herself to push her fear deep inside her. She believed the man when he said he wouldn't hurt her, but she still didn't want to go anywhere with him. She'd only just got her mommy back. She wanted to stay with Mommy and Sebastian.

Though she was used to traveling with Sebastian, this journey was different. This creature moved so quickly, Elizabeth didn't even sense the motion. One moment they stood in her bedroom, the next in the city, the next out in the countryside. Elizabeth didn't feel the wind rushing past her face, as she did when Sebastian carried her. Instead, there was a strange lurching motion and, in the next moment, they were somewhere else.

She closed her eyes and tried to push her thoughts ahead, tried to see this person's intentions, but her mind remained blank. She didn't have enough control yet to be able to choose a precise time and location to look into. Instead, the visions came to her randomly and suddenly. She might be able to see what was going to happen to her, but she couldn't force the vision to happen.

The strange movement of this man was unlike any she'd experienced before. It made her head spin and her stomach started to churn the way it did when she'd eaten too much cake, or sometimes when Bridget took her out in the car.

He stopped barely long enough for her to get the briefest glimpse of her surroundings—a forest, a city, an empty highway—before he took off again, a sudden flash of almost unnoticeable movement, interjected with a brief stop.

She wished Sebastian carried her now. The thought made her want to cry. He always stopped and asked her if she was okay. Her daddy would have cared if she felt sick.

Her resolve broke down and she sobbed, keeping her face turned from the vampire's shoulder. Eventually she dropped into a light, exhausted sleep, despite her fear.

Only when the vampire came to a standstill did Elizabeth fully rouse herself. They were in a new city now; a place she didn't recognize. The city rushed around her, people brushing past them with their heads down, music blaring from car stereos as they drove by. Oil shimmered on the road. Meat hissed on the grill of a hotdog vendor. All the commotion was almost as confusing and disorientating to Elizabeth as the race through the night. She wished she was at home, safe and comfortable in her bed.

The vampire put her down on the sidewalk. Her bare feet met with the cold pavement and she shivered. He'd not thought to get her dressed or grab a coat for her—the cold was never a consideration for a vampire—and the chill on the night air had worked its way into her bones. He reached down and took hold of her hand. She knew trying to run or shout for help would be pointless. He'd snatch her up and run before anyone even turned their heads. Even if they did notice her, another human could do nothing to help.

The vampire ducked down an alley and, in a flash, his name came to her, written on her brain in big, neon letters. *Demitri.*

Of course it was; hadn't her father told her already? Only Sebastian had said something slightly different, she just couldn't remember what.

Up ahead were more neon words; each letter a couple of feet high and attached to the wall above a door. Somehow those letters had got twisted around in her brain, revealing his name to her. Quickly, she read the sign; *The Danger Zone.* She didn't know what 'zone' meant, but she understood the meaning of 'danger' all too well. At least now she knew her location should she get the chance to call for help.

People wearing revealing outfits stood in a line in front of the painted black doors. Elizabeth and Demitri passed them on one side, but none of them paid any attention to the strange pale man and the small girl dressed in only her pajamas; they purposefully averted their gazes.

A big man and a lady with short blonde hair stood at the front of the line, letting some people in and turning others away.

No, not a man and a woman, Elizabeth realized—*two more vampires.*

Demitri breezed past. "Natasha," he snapped at the blonde. The female vampire, needing no other instruction, followed them as they walked through the black doors.

Walls enclosed around them, loud music thumping in her ears. It was dark but lights flashed and swooped. They walked through a short corridor and then out into a huge room. People danced, heat and the scent of sweat filling the air. Elizabeth cowered at Demitri's side, wanting to disappear. Demitri whisked through the people and exited via another door. They walked down a passage, taking a number of twists and turns, until the sounds of music grew faint. Eventually, they entered a huge room with shiny wooden floors and a curved ceiling covered in paintings. At the far end of the room sat a massive desk made of a dark wood.

Demitri dropped Elizabeth's hand and rounded the table to take his place in a big leather chair behind the desk. He swung his legs up onto the desk's polished surface and leaned back, his fingertips touching.

Elizabeth was only too aware of the blonde vampire—Natasha—standing behind her. Danger radiated from the female, burning into Elizabeth's narrow back.

"Is this what all the fuss is about?" Natasha asked. "Doesn't look like anything special to me."

"It's not what she looks like," Demitri smiled. "Smell her."

Natasha's eyes narrowed but she took a couple of steps until she stood beside Elizabeth. She bent and inhaled through her nose and a smile played on her lips.

"She's not human."

"Not fully. To drink from her would be like feeding from another vampire."

Natasha wrinkled her nose. "Ugh." She reached out and grabbed Elizabeth, her cold fingers wrapping around Elizabeth's tiny upper-arm.

"Get off me," said Elizabeth, wanting to seem bigger and older than she was but knowing she failed miserably.

The blonde ignored her and addressed her master. "So she can predict the future?"

"Yes. Not well yet, but I believe if I can strengthen her vampire side, her powers will also increase."

Natasha raised her eyebrows. "Sounds interesting."

"I hope so, though I am expecting some interference from her father. He may have to be dealt with."

"Vincent and I can take care of him."

Demitri laughed. "Don't be a fool. He's stronger than both of you put together."

Natasha cowered at the rebuke and Elizabeth experienced a brief burst of satisfaction. Sebastian *was* stronger. She resisted the urge to stick her tongue out at the blonde.

The words burst from her lips, an almost joyous elation building inside her. "Sebastian is going to be real mad when he finds out I'm gone. He'll come after me and you'll be sorry when he does."

The long-haired vampire laughed. In an instant he was out of his chair and standing directly in front of her. His finger touched her chin, tilting her face to him. Elizabeth set her small jaw and forced herself to stare him back.

"So feisty," he said. "I like that! You and I are going to get along just fine."

"My daddy, Sebastian, will come and get me real soon."

"Sure, child, sure. You tell yourself that if it makes you feel better." He crouched in front of her. "Now, close your eyes and tell me what you see?"

She frowned, her lower lip protruding. "I don't understand."

"Now, now, don't give me that. I want to know what you can see in the future."

Her frown deepened. "I can't see anything."

The creature before her growled in response and his eyes flashed a bright yellow. Elizabeth gave a cry of surprise and stumbled back, but his hand shot out and caught her upper arm, his grip like a band of ice around her skin.

She tried to tug away but he held her firm.

"I don't see anything!" she cried. "It doesn't work like that. I can't make it happen."

All her reserve gone, she started to cry. She wanted to be brave, knew Mommy and Sebastian would be telling her to be strong, be brave—but she was scared and she wanted to go home. The bad man hadn't even let her pick up her comfort blanket before he took her, and she couldn't sleep without it.

The vampire addressed the blonde. "Go and get our little child a drink from the special fridge. You know the one I mean…"

Her eyes widened. "Are you sure?"

"Don't question me. Now go."

The female spun on her heels and vanished, the door slamming in her wake.

Demitri crouched in front of Elizabeth. "You know what you are, don't you?"

Elizabeth didn't answer. More tears sprung in her eyes. "I just want to go home."

"You are a Dhampyre, Elizabeth. A child of a human mother and a vampire father. Your kind is rare, very rare indeed. And for you to have such extraordinary powers when you're still so young is most exciting. Your parents thought I should wait until you are a young woman before I tried to use your visions for my own benefit, but then I started thinking about the one thing that intertwines your becoming a young woman and being a vampire. Blood."

Elizabeth had no idea what he was talking about, his words lost in her fear and panic. She put her hands over her face and sobbed, "I want my Mommy."

"Hush now, child. I'm sure you do. But you're going to have to learn to live without her. I'm sure both she and you're father will be here soon to try to reclaim you and I will be forced to deal with them. But, in time, you will forget them and come to think of me as your father. That is the beauty of your youth—in time, you will forget."

"I won't forget them. I won't!"

He let out a theatrical sigh. "I guess time will tell." He clapped twice in quick secession and the door behind her opened. Natasha strode back in, a black marble, long-stemmed cup in her hands. Her eyes were locked on the cup, her fangs protruding. She looked at Elizabeth and snarled.

Elizabeth didn't like her; the blonde frightened her.

"Have you ever tried blood, child?"

Elizabeth wrinkled her nose. "That's disgusting."

But the drink held beneath her nose didn't smell disgusting. In fact, the aroma was heavenly—like liquid chocolate, only richer. Saliva flooded her mouth, and, at the same time, all the moisture sapped from her throat. She tried to swallow but the action hurt. Her throat had constricted, as though she'd swallowed red-hot, burning sand. Somehow she knew only the thick, dark fluid held before her would make her throat better.

Elizabeth had never wanted anything more in her life. With the typical self-control of a six year old, she snatched the cup from Natasha's hands. Without another thought, she brought the heavy drinking vessel to her lips.

Heat sparked at her center, like a little nugget of hot coal. She took a sip and its warmth flared within her. The smooth liquid soothed her ravaged throat and she gulped it down.

Energy pulsed through her limbs, a trippy beat that matched her racing heart, but once again her throat was painfully dry. She tried to swallow and discovered she couldn't.

Elizabeth held out the drained cup. "More."

Demitri gave a bark of laughter. "Really? I never imagined this would be so easy."

"I'm thirsty," she whispered, but even as she spoke the words an unimaginable guilt fell over her. Mommy and Sebastian wouldn't want her to be taking things from this man, yet she couldn't help herself. Her whole body raged for the fluid in the cup. She wanted it like she'd never wanted anything before.

"Please?" she said, more tears filling her eyes. "Please, can I have some more?"

He made a sound close to a chuckle and pried the cup from her hands

"Natasha, you heard our little guest." He held out the empty cup. The blonde took it from him and spun from the room, the door banging in her wake.

Within seconds she was back again, the cup refilled.

Elizabeth drank the liquid down, a trickle slipping down her chin. She wiped the fluid away with the back of her hand

and was surprised to see red smeared across her pale skin. Had she known what she was drinking? Yes, she had known. After all, Demitri had told her. She'd just chosen to ignore the fact because she'd wanted the drink so badly.

A thin whine of despair escaped her throat.

"There, there," said Demitri. He reached down and ruffled the top of her hair, smiling down on her like a proud father. "You and I are going to get along just fine."

Chapter Seventeen

Before Serenity even woke fully, her hand strayed to the other side of the bed, hoping to find Sebastian beside her. Her fingers met with nothing but the cool sheets and she opened her eyes, disappointed.

Serenity sighed and rolled over, her hand tucked beneath her head. Would they ever be able to sleep together in an actual sense? She knew Sebastian felt awkward about sleeping in front of her, and truthfully, the thought weirded her out a little as well. When awake, Sebastian positively thrummed with energy and strength. To see him lying so still and cold seemed a bit too unsettling.

She lifted her gaze to the blind covering the windows. From the slight shift in color from total black to an almost dark gray, she realized morning had come. Sebastian would be back in his own room, she assumed in his bed, or possibly under it. He didn't need to worry about exposure to daylight in his own home—he'd made sure blackout blinds had been fitted in all of the upstairs windows.

There was no clock in the room to tell her the time, but she guessed it was mid-morning at least. They'd not fallen asleep until the early hours so sleeping late was only to be expected. Elizabeth must still be in bed or Serenity was sure she'd have come charging into the room by now.

Serenity sat up, swinging her legs off the side of the bed. She'd go and wake Elizabeth. She wanted to see the joy in her daughter's eyes when she woke up to find her mommy looking down at her.

She stood and then bent to retrieve her clothes from the floor. A smile played on her lips as she pulled her jeans and tee back on, remembering how they'd ended up on the floor in the first place. Whatever happened, she'd never grow tired of Sebastian touching her in such a way. The memory took her breath away and made her heart skip a beat.

A pang of need gripped her, a desire to have him with her right there and then. She didn't want to spend another minute without him by her side and being forced to wait for nightfall was frustrating.

Pushing her thoughts to one side, she left the room and padded down the hall to Elizabeth's bedroom. The door stood slightly ajar, so she pushed it open and poked her head around the corner.

Serenity frowned. The bed was empty, the sheets ruffled. She crossed the room. Elizabeth's comforter still lay half tucked beneath her pillow and her favorite bear was on the floor. She picked up the toy and held the soft fur against her chest.

"Elizabeth?"

Serenity made her way to the adjoining bathroom. The small space was empty. Her breath caught and her heart started to race. She was probably just being paranoid. Elizabeth had probably woken up ages ago and was downstairs, eating breakfast and watching television.

Her eyes flicked to the clock hung on Elizabeth's wall. Only eight-fifteen—not as late as she'd assumed. If Elizabeth was up, she'd not have been up for long.

With her free hand, she reached out and ran her hand across the mattress. The whole thing was cool; she couldn't find a single spot that remained warm from her daughter's body.

The teddy fell from her arms, landing face-down on the floor.

Serenity spun around and raced from the room, trying stem the panic now rising from her core.

Please don't let it be Demitri... please don't let him have taken her.

She raced down the hall to the top of the huge staircase.

"Elizabeth," she called again, this time loudly, not caring if she disturbed Sebastian. If such a thing was even possible. "Elizabeth? Where are you?"

She received no answer. The house remained painfully silent.

"Elizabeth!" she yelled, tears burning the backs of her eyes like fire. "Please answer me!"

She almost stumbled down the stairs in her haste. The television screen was black. No breakfast bowls or milk sat on the counter. No cereal packets spilled on the surface.

"Oh, no, no, no." Her words came out as a moan.

A click from the front door made her jump, her heart lurching in her throat. She spun around to see Bridget walking in and she almost hit herself on the head for her stupidity. Of course, Bridget had taken Elizabeth out. She must have arrived earlier and decided to let Serenity sleep so took Elizabeth out to keep the noise down.

She let out a sigh of relief, her shoulders sagging.

But Bridget walked in and closed the door behind her. There was no sign of her daughter.

"Please tell me you know where Elizabeth is." Serenity couldn't help the begging tone in her voice.

At first Bridget's face crumpled in a frown, but she must have seen the panic in Serenity face for her eyes widened in alarm. "No. I've not seen her since last night. Why, what's happened?"

"Oh God." Her hands clamped to her mouth. "I can't find her. She's not anywhere and her bed is cold, like she's been gone awhile. For a moment I thought she was with you…"

Realization dawned on the older woman. "It's the other vampire, isn't it? The one Sebastian took you to see."

Serenity nodded, hot tears finally rolling down her face. "He said he wanted Elizabeth as payment for making me well again."

"What?!" she said, shocked. "And Sebastian agreed?"

She shook her head. "No, but it was too late. Demitri had already told Sebastian how to get my memory back. He said he wouldn't come for her right away, that he'd give us some time back together as a family."

"How heartwarming. And now the son-of-a-bitch has plucked a defenseless little girl out of her bed in the middle of the night." She thought of something. "How come Sebastian didn't hear him? Surely he should sense another vampire in the house?"

Serenity remembered what they were doing the previous night and heat rose to her cheeks. "Demitri is so much older," she said in a rush. "Perhaps he's quieter than Sebastian."

She felt sick. To think they'd been doing *that* while their daughter was being abducted in the next room.

Bridget pressed her lips together and shook her head. "Damn Sebastian! I told him something like this would happen. He should know by now to listen to Elizabeth's dreams. When are vampires going to learn that being immortal does not make you omnipotent? In some ways, I think male vampires are no different than any other man."

Serenity felt a rush of protective love toward Sebastian, despite her anger at them both for not protecting Elizabeth better. She folded her arms across her chest.

"This isn't his fault, Bridget. He only wanted to make me better again. He couldn't have predicted this was going to happen."

"Yes, he could, Serenity." Her voice was sharp, her blue eyes hard. "I told him this would end badly and he refused to listen."

"Demitri told us he'd give us some time. He went against his word. How was Sebastian supposed to know what was going to happen?"

"Well I suggest we go and tell him now."

"But he's..." she sought for the right word to describe the state of stasis Sebastian entered during the day. "Sleeping."

Bridget placed her hands on her hips. "Then it's about time he woke up."

Together, the two women headed upstairs, Serenity drying the tears from her face with the back of her hand.

They stood outside of his bedroom, no sign of life coming from behind the solid wood. Serenity's heart pounded. This would be the first time seeing him in this state and she didn't want to think about what he'd look like.

Taking a deep breath, Serenity pushed open his door and entered the room,

Sebastian lay on the bed, motionless. He still wore his suit and his arms were folded over his chest, his hands clasped together. His pale face was expressionless, his features smooth. He looked exactly as she had feared—like he was dead.

Pushing her fears to the bottom of her gut, she stepped forward. She needed to wake him—Elizabeth needed her to wake him.

She reached out and took hold of his shoulder. It felt like granite beneath her hand, as though she was trying to wake a stone statue.

"Sebastian," she hissed, "You have to wake up. Demitri's taken Elizabeth." She glanced back over her shoulder and Bridget gave her a nod of encouragement.

"Louder," she said. "You're trying to wake him, remember?"

Serenity gave a brisk nod and turned back. She shook him as hard as she could, but it made no difference. He remained immobile.

"Sebastian!" she yelled in his face. "Wake up! We need you!" Still she gained no response and she drew back her hand slapped him across the face. Pain stung her palm but Sebastian didn't flinch.

"This is hopeless," she said, turning back to Bridget. "He's not going to wake until nightfall. He's told me before that only being in immediate danger will wake him."

"So put him in danger," she said. "Draw back the blind."

Sebastian blackout blind had also been taped down—extra protection against the murderous sun.

"I can't do that." Her voice was barely a whisper. She couldn't stand the thought of watching his beautiful face sizzle, smoke and burn. "It'll hurt him."

Bridget marched over to the window. "Then I will."

"No, Bridget, wait! You don't know how he'll react. He might kill the both of us purely by instinct and then where would Elizabeth be? And think about how he'd feel if he hurt us. This isn't fair." She thought of something else. "And what can he do anyway? It's not like he can go outside."

Bridget's hand hovered above the blind and then dropped to her side. "We could bundle him up and put him in the trunk of the car. By the time we drove to New York, it would be well into night time."

"By the time we drove to New York, it would be tomorrow night and Elizabeth would have spent forty-eight hours with Demitri." She shook her head, her mind racing. "No. He's faster on his own. And anyway, look at the size of him. We'd never be able to move him."

She was right. Sebastian was six foot two, two-hundred pounds of solid muscle, and inert as stone. Even if he'd been human, they'd never budge him.

"Okay," said Bridget. "So what do you suggest? We wait for Sebastian to wake up?"

"No, we have to do something! I won't just sit around the house all day knowing that son-of-a-bitch has Elizabeth."

Bridget fixed her gaze. "Too damn right. We'll fly to New York and leave Sebastian a note telling him what's happened. When Sebastian wakes at sunset, he'll have to make the trip back across the country himself. This vampire—Demitri—will be sleeping like Sebastian during the day. Maybe he's got some human watch-dogs, but I can deal with them."

"What do you mean?"

"I've got my own powers, Serenity. I tried to tell Sebastian but he dismissed me. I'm a witch and I come from a long line of witches. That's why it was so easy for me to accept what happened to my son. I've known about vampires for years. I grew up learning the craft from my mother, but she passed away and I was left with my grandmother. She was very powerful indeed and taught me how to release my own powers. I might not be strong or fast like a vampire, but I've got some tricks up my sleeve."

Serenity stared at her. "Are you serious?"

"I wouldn't say such a thing if I wasn't."

"But what sort of things can you do? Pull rabbits out of hats and make things disappear?"

She laughed. "Not so much with the rabbit, but I can make things appear to disappear. In truth, they're still there, but I cast a spell around them—like a magic veil—and the spell hides the object or person."

She wanted to believe Bridget, but she'd been born with a healthy dose of skepticism. Even so, a sense of hope wrapped around her. She held the feeling at bay, not wanting to be let down if Bridget's claims went unfounded.

Something else occurred to her and a tiny part of her heart lifted. "So the blue blanket you did with Elizabeth was real?"

"The light, you mean?"

"Yes. She wanted me to recreate it for her, but of course I couldn't."

"I'm sorry. I didn't mean to make you feel bad."

"I know you didn't. Honestly, I feel better knowing the blanket was real. I was worried Elizabeth had replaced you as a mother figure in her life—and she has in a way—but at least I know that's something I genuinely couldn't do, not that Elizabeth would rather have had you doing it instead."

"No one will ever replace you in her heart. You'll always be the only mother she has."

Serenity smiled to hide the tears threatening to break through. She needed to focus on more immediate issues than self-pity.

"Can you wake Sebastian using magic?"

Bridget shook her head. "No, I can't interfere with his sleep, it's too much a part of who he is, and besides, the magic is harder to work on supernaturals."

"Show me something else then?"

"We don't have time right now. You're going to need to trust me. I promise, as soon as I can, I'll show you what I can do."

Serenity swallowed her doubts and crossed the room to hug the older woman tight. "Thank you so much, Bridget. I don't know what I'd do right now if you weren't here."

"Yes, you do. You'd be heading off to New York and probably getting yourself killed."

The world trembled before her as tears flooded her eyes. "You might be right," she admitted. "And Sebastian is going to think exactly the same thing."

"Screw what Sebastian thinks."

"I just hate for him to be scared for all of us when he wakes up."

"We can't do anything about that."

Bridget took hold of her arm and pulled her from the room. Serenity sent Sebastian one last longing glance, wishing for him to be awake to help her deal with this. She'd feel so much better with him by her side.

"Do you have identification?" Bridget asked. "Enough to catch a flight?"

Serenity sniffed and wiped her eyes, pulling herself together. "I've got a driver's license." She felt a brief stab of panic. "I hope it's not expired!"

"Well, go check."

Serenity ran to her room. Sebastian had brought in all of her belongings from her apartment. Her clothes hung in the closets and more were neatly folded in drawers, though she had no idea where to find anything.

She started to pull open drawers, searching through her clothes and underwear. In the nightstand, her fingers closed around the stiff rectangle of her driver's license.

Thank God, she still had twelve months left on the document.

"Got it!" she shouted to Bridget. Serenity paused just long enough to pull on some socks and her sneakers. She grabbed a sweater off the back of an occasional chair and then went back to the closet and pulled out a jacket. Los Angeles was warm almost all year round, but at this time of year, New York would be ready for snow. She hoped Elizabeth had warm clothes with her. She hated to think of Elizabeth shivering, cold and frightened somewhere. The vampire wouldn't think to give her a blanket or something to keep her warm—the temperature didn't affect him.

As an afterthought, she ran into Elizabeth's room and grabbed her small rucksack. She pulled open the drawers and shoved in a couple of items of warm clothes. The teddy bear still lay on the floor where she'd dropped it, so she bent and scooped the toy up, and stuffed it in the bag. Somehow, Elizabeth not having her comforter hurt worst of all. Elizabeth couldn't sleep without the blanket. That she'd been denied such a small comfort made Serenity want to cry all over again.

She burst from the bedroom and found Bridget waiting impatiently at the bottom of the stairs.

"What were you doing?"

Serenity held up the bag. "Some of Elizabeth's things. She's going to need them when we get her back."

Bridget smiled. "That's the spirit. Now come on, we'll take my car."

"Wait a minute. I still need to write Sebastian a note." She paused for a moment. "How will he even know where to find us?"

"Is there a place Sebastian will recognize?"

The hotel, of course.

"Yes," she said with relief. "We stayed in a hotel near Demitri's club during the first day after I got my memory back."

"Can you remember the name? Would you know how to find it again?"

She wracked her memory, trying to think of the name. In her mind's eye, she saw the sign hanging from the side of the building—one with the big back letters that read 'HOTEL'. But what had been written above in a smaller, italic font? Serenity put her hand over her eyes. What had it been? She knew she'd seen and read the name...

"The Metropolitan Hotel!" she blurted. "That's what the place was called. We'll go back to the hotel to wait for him."

A notepad and pen sat beside the phone on the hall console. With a trembling hand, Serenity picked up the pen and poised the tip against the white paper. She pressed too hard as she wrote, the nib leaving deep indentions that would surely go several sheets deep.

Serenity tore the sheet from the pad and raced to the kitchen. She placed the note in the middle of the kitchen counter. Though no breeze stirred the air, she was still paranoid the note would somehow be blown away so she weighed it down with a saltshaker.

"Okay, done," she said to Bridget.

Bridget was already heading toward the front door. "Then let's go."

The drive to the airport seemed to take forever. Serenity sat in the passenger seat as they drove through Beverly Hills, looking out the window and chewing on her already non-existent nails. When they came to the slightest bit of traffic, her stomach clenched in anxiety. They didn't even know if seats would be available on the next flight to New York and every minute felt like torture. She found herself leaning forward every time they slowed, as though her body could propel them forward.

Finally, on the freeway, they started to gain some ground. When they turned off San Diego Freeway and onto West Century Boulevard, she saw the metallic letters of the LAX sign rising into the sky.

How strange to think she was back here again. Sometimes she felt as though her life kept echoing itself. Not far away stood the hotel Madeline had abducted her from and then the hanger the vampire had kept her in. Four years later, Jackson had attacked Amy here. Now she was back, chasing another vampire. One who had her daughter.

Bridget pulled up to the curb in front of the terminal and jumped out. "Come on."

Serenity climbed out and glanced at the abandoned Prius. "You can't leave it here. You'll get towed."

"Who cares? We'll pay to get the car back later. In the grand scheme of things, it's really not important."

Serenity wasn't going to argue. Every minute felt precious. She imagined the gates closing for the flight, missing it by mere minutes—minutes they'd spent fussing about parking the car.

"You're right."

Together they raced into the terminal. A number of airlines flew to New York, but only a couple flew direct. Serenity didn't think she could stand a stopover in Phoenix, knowing the hours were ticking by with Elizabeth still in the hands of Demitri. She only hoped that the daylight meant Demitri would be forced to leave Elizabeth alone.

"There!" said Bridget, pointing at the departures board. "Virgin America has a direct flight leaving in just over an hour."

They ran to the counter and waited as a couple of people ahead of them checked in, chatting and weighing in luggage as though they had all the time in the world. Serenity hopped from foot to foot, resisting the urge to push them out of the way.

At last, they moved on and Serenity and Bridget both slammed against the counter. The pretty brunette manning the desk reared back at their sudden arrival.

"Please tell me you have two seats available on the next flight to JFK," Serenity blurted. "I'm sorry, but it's an emergency," she added, not wanting to make the woman think they were some kind of danger.

The brunette gave them a nervous smile and tapped her keyboard. "You're in luck. We do have seats."

"Thank you, thank you, thank you," said Serenity, resisting the urge to lean over the counter and hug the woman.

Bridget handed her credit card over and Serenity's heart sank. "Oh Bridget, I didn't even think about how we'd pay!"

"Don't be silly. Elizabeth's like my daughter as well. I don't care about the money."

"How long's the flight?" Serenity asked, directing her question to the brunette behind the counter.

"A little over five hours," the woman said, almost apologetically.

Inwardly, Serenity groaned. What the hell would she do for five hours? It wasn't like she'd just be able to lose herself in a book or magazine, and she certainly wouldn't be able to sleep. This would be the longest five hours of her life.

"Okay, thanks. We'll take two round-trip tickets," she said, handing over her identification. She noted the damp marks her fingers had left on the card and self-consciously wiped her palms on her jeans. She needed to calm down. At this rate, she would get pulled aside by airport security and detained for her frantic behavior. What would she say? 'Sorry, my daughter's been kidnapped by a vampire.' That would only land her a stint in a psychiatric ward. If she even mentioned her daughter being kidnapped, the police would get involved and that would be no good for anyone. If they busted Demitri's lair, the cops would probably end up dead, and so would Elizabeth. Either that or Demitri would vanish with her forever.

The thought of police made her thoughts drift to James Bently and his family. She hoped he was doing well. She wondered if Amy had given birth to their second child yet. She was relieved they were both well away from this whole mess. James had done the right thing by moving them away. If only she and Sebastian had that option as a family. But they couldn't run away from what they were.

With tickets in hand, they went through security and toward the departure gates. Everyone seemed relaxed and friendly, the total opposite of Serenity's mood. She had to stop herself grabbing people and shoving them out of the way, yelling, 'My daughter's in danger, why isn't anyone doing anything?'

Bridget placed a steady hand on her arm. "It'll be all right. You need to calm down."

"Sorry."

Serenity paced around until their flight was called. They boarded the airplane and, once they were in the air, Bridget ordered them two large brandies.

"Here, drink this."

Serenity stared at the plastic cup of amber liquid. "Are you serious?"

She pressed the flimsy cup into Serenity's hand. "You need it. It'll calm you down."

Serenity nodded and knocked the drink back. It burned her throat and she coughed. She'd never been a big drinker and immediately the alcohol loosened her limbs.

"Better?" Bridget inquired.

"Yes, thank you."

"Now try to relax. We can't do anything until we get to New York. Giving yourself a heart attack before then isn't going to help anyone."

"I know. You're right."

Even so, the rest of the flight passed painfully slow. Serenity fidgeted and made multiple excuses to go to the bathroom, partly to break up the time, but also to be alone for a few minutes. She stared at herself in the tiny mirror, wondering why she didn't look as bad as she felt. Then she remembered Sebastian's blood. It seemed, even in a crisis, when the whole world seemed to be falling down around her, she still had perfect curls and skin.

A pang of longing almost doubled her over. She wished Sebastian was with her. Even though he'd been wrong about Demitri, she'd still feel better with his solid, indomitable strength beside her.

The plane touched down and, luggage free, they passed right through the terminal and out to where a line of people waited for cabs. The vehicles pulled up and whisked people away. The process was slow, but they moved forward until it was their turn.

"Where you headed?" the driver asked as they slid in the back.

"The Metropolitan Hotel," Serenity said, thankful she'd remembered the name.

"You know what part of the city that's in?" he asked, his New York accent strong.

"No. I…" Tears threatened once again. "I didn't think to check."

"No problem," he said, pulling out a smart phone and keying in the name of the hotel. "Here you go. Midtown East."

For the second time that day, she resisted the urge to hug a complete stranger.

The day was getting late. Now heading into late afternoon, the sky had taken on a gray shade of blue, the sun low in the sky. The air had a distinct bite and Serenity was thankful for her sweater. Would Elizabeth be cold? Was anyone taking care of her?

A lump formed in her throat.

Please let her be all right. Oh God, please let her be safe.

At least the vampires would also be asleep during the day. She hoped that meant they'd leave Elizabeth alone. Demitri may have humans he used to keep watch during the daytime hours, but he didn't seem the type to trust the living.

Bridget's warm, soft hand closed over her own and gave a reassuring squeeze. Serenity looked up and Bridget smiled.

"Not far now."

Despite the reassurance, Serenity fidgeted through the thirty-minute drive. The vehicle crept through traffic—traffic that seemed to build up around them the deeper they got into the city and the closer they got to rush hour. Eventually, Serenity recognized the bagel shop she'd eaten at and the cab pulled over and deposited them on the sidewalk outside the hotel. The sun was finally dropping in the sky and Serenity watched its progress. Never had nightfall meant so much. It meant dangerous vampires would once again surround Elizabeth, and Sebastian would wake to discover his family gone.

Chapter Eighteen

Sebastian's eyes shot open. He lay motionless on the bed, his arms folded across his chest, his ears straining.

The house was quiet—too quiet. He couldn't hear a single heartbeat thudding within its walls, not a breath, no talking or laughter.

The house was empty.

Sebastian sat up. Where was everyone? Dusk had fallen and he felt sure Serenity and Bridget wouldn't take Elizabeth out at night.

They've probably just gone to get some take-out for dinner...

Uncertainty buzzed at his nerve endings. Something wasn't right. Serenity would have wanted to be with him when he woke. He didn't think she'd want to miss even a minute of them being a family again.

Using his speed, he darted in and out of their bedrooms. In both Serenity and Elizabeth's room, the dresser drawers hung open, clothes spilling from the insides. The closet doors stood ajar, another little jumble of clothes on the bottom, as though items had been torn from the hangers with no intent of picking them back up.

His sense of unease increased.

He left the first floor and raced around the house. On the kitchen counter, a sheet of paper had been weighted down with a saltshaker. Sebastian snatched up the note, the paper crisp in his fingers. His eyes scoured the lines, a combination of fear and rage creeping in as his brain processed the words:

Sebastian,

Demitri came in the night and took Elizabeth. We tried to wake you, but we couldn't. Bridget and I have flown to New York. Please, come as soon as you can. I'll be at the hotel, or if I'm not there, you'll know I've already encountered Demitri.

I love you. Come as fast as you can.

Serenity.

Fury erupted from his core and he lifted his head and roared, the sound echoing around the big house. His fingers hooked beneath the kitchen countertop and he lifted, wrenching the huge piece of marble from the solid wood units beneath. The wood creaked and split in protest and tore apart. Enraged, Sebastian flung the huge slab to the floor. The marble hit with a resounding crack and shattered into several pieces, breaking the tiles that made up the kitchen flooring. But Sebastian wasn't done. With anger controlling him, he yelled again and swung his arm, sending all of the kitchen appliances—kettle, coffee machine, microwave—hurtling across the room, smashing into the opposite wall with a clanging crash. He punched the wall behind where the counter had been, his fist crunching through plasterboard and finally brick.

Goddamn what he was! What good was so much strength when, once again, someone had hurt his family while he lay helpless? He hated to think of Serenity trying to wake him, begging for his help, while he lay motionless on the bed—to her eyes, for all purposes, dead.

She deserves better than me. They both do.

He hated himself, but didn't have the time to wallow in self-pity or smash up any more of his house. He needed to make the journey back across the country again, and fast. He dreaded to think what sort of situation Serenity had already gotten herself into. The possibility of her waiting, sitting on her hands at the hotel, was remote. Knowing Demitri held Elizabeth only a couple of blocks away, Serenity wouldn't just do nothing.

Elizabeth.

His heart contracted with pain. If Demitri had hurt her in any way, Sebastian would find a way to destroy him.

He knew the thoughts were hollow threats. The elder vampire had made it into the house without Sebastian even being aware of his presence. He'd been so caught up in Serenity, in losing himself in the pleasures of her body, he hadn't noticed a thing outside of her arms.

He wished he could be wakened during the day, but only threatening his existence would break through his unnatural sleep. If Serenity tried to harm him—expose him to light, cut off his head, stake his heart—he would slaughter her without even realizing what he was doing. His body would simply react, even if they'd previously come to an agreement that she needed to take such actions to get through to him.

Damn it! He'd never thought Demitri would come already; he'd promised them time to be together again. Surely one night didn't amount to 'time'? Sebastian growled, a low rumble deep within his chest. He was always making mistakes—so many mistakes. Would a time ever come when he wouldn't let his family down?

How could someone so strong also be so weak?

At least this journey across the country would be made alone. He wouldn't have to worry if the person he carried was comfortable or needed to rest. He would be faster on his own and he wouldn't tire.

Sebastian cast a glance at the mess he'd created. Serenity would go nuts at him for smashing up the house. Understandably, after living for so many years under Jackson's violent hand, she would hate if he showed any kind of anger toward something not immediately threatening their lives. This kind of loss of control was what she feared most.

Still, he didn't have time to start making repairs right now. He just hoped that a destroyed kitchen would be the worst of their worries by the time they got home.

Ignoring the mess, Sebastian stormed out of the house, shoving through the double fronted doors. They slammed open, hitting the walls behind. Mortar crumbled and a large crack appeared down the center of one of the panels. Sebastian kept going, running at breathtaking speed along the gravel, his feet touching the ground so lightly they barely made a sound. He lowered to a crouch, centering his strength, and sprung over the high walls.

He ran across the city, leaping over highways and the roofs of buildings when it was quicker to do so. He took more risks than he ever had when he traveled with Serenity or Elizabeth; bigger, longer jumps that made him feel like he was flying, soaring through the air until he hit the ground, light on his feet.

He left the city far behind, crossing through miles of forest. Gradually, the forests gave way to the drier, scrubbier land of the Mohave National Preserve. Huge sandstone mesas rose from the ground and he negotiated canyons to cut across the country.

Long distance vampire, he thought and would have smiled to himself if not for the gravity of the circumstances. As his legs ate away the hundreds of miles, his thoughts remained with Elizabeth. He hoped she wasn't too frightened and Demitri hadn't hurt her.

Sebastian crossed through the corner of Colorado and a pang of hunger hit him. Running back and forth across the country may not tire him out, but it sure as hell made him hungry. The previous night, the young woman's blood had been racing through his veins. The night before, the blood of the hobo. He'd killed more in the past three days than in the last couple of months. But if he were to be any kind of force against Demitri, he needed to feed.

Sebastian paused for a moment, taking stock of his surroundings. Though only dense forest stretched in every direction, his keen hearing picked up the definitive high-pitched roar of a motorbike. A bike meant a road and people. He would take down whoever rode the bike if he needed to, leaping from the forest like a wildcat, colliding with it with enough speed and force to knock the rider to the ground while the bike spun away in the opposite direction.

He followed the roar. As he got closer, he picked up the sound of music playing, voices and laughter. Heat flooded through the trees, carrying with it the distinctive scent of blood. The engine of the bike cut out, but he no longer needed the constant drone as something to follow.

Sebastian broke through the trees and found himself standing on the side of an almost deserted highway. No vehicles passed, but he understood the reason for the silenced bike. On the other side of the road was a bar. Twenty or so bikes were parked up outside.

A biker stop.

One guy, a huge brick of a man complete with leather, long scraggly hair and an even longer beard, stood to one side of the building, sheltered in the bushes. The fizz and acrid stink of hot urine hitting the earth filled the air.

Moving quickly, Sebastian crossed the road. He passed the bikes and entrance of the bar, coming to rest only feet behind the big man. Though Sebastian was big, this guy stood at least two inches taller and was easily twice as wide.

Sebastian stood, silent, at least offering the man the opportunity to zip his fly.

He didn't, however, give him a chance to turn around. He launched onto the biker's back, teeth snapping into the thick throat. Cigarette smoke, beer and fresh urine filled his nostrils. Stale sweat pressed against the flat of his tongue. The biker was strong, but nowhere near as strong as Sebastian. He yelled out and teetered backward, but Sebastian clung to him, his fingers digging into the man's thick shoulders. He growled and sank his teeth deeper. The man's neck crunched and he slumped to the floor.

Sebastian drank with speed and intensity. Urgency didn't allow him to take pleasure in the act or dispose of the body as he normally would. This was one he'd have to take the risk of coming back. Sometimes, if the bodies weren't trapped beneath the earth in some way, they reanimated, becoming almost zombie-like. Unlike in the movies, the need to eat human flesh didn't compel them. Instead they simply wandered around. Eventually the body ran out of steam and dropped wherever it stood.

He didn't have time to bury the body, but he didn't intend to leave it in the parking lot. More bikers might be here any minute. Discovering the drained body, with obvious puncture wounds, would cause chaos.

Two men left the bar, the door swinging open in a blast of music and chatter. Sebastian lifted his head, blood smeared across his chin. Not wanting to be seen, he scooped up the body. From a crouch, he sprang to the roof of the bar, the body in his arms. Voices drifted up to him like smoke, and a low snort of laughter rumbled in the night.

Sebastian moved with silent steps to the back of the roof. The bar backed onto miles of forestry, the road it served being the only one in the area. Sebastian leaped from the roof, landing deep within the branches and tree trunks with no more than a rustle of foliage.

He dumped the body out in the middle of the forest as he ran. The corpse may reanimate, but wouldn't get anywhere near other humans before it fell down forever.

With the man's fresh blood rushing through his veins, Sebastian picked up speed. The world flew by in a blur of color, light and sound. He passed big cities, sirens and traffic blaring past his ears as he moved. His mind stayed focused, seeing only Elizabeth and Serenity's faces, trying not to think of them hurt or possibly dead.

No, Demitri wouldn't kill Elizabeth—she had too much value to him. But Serenity... If Serenity got in his way, the vampire may well envisage her as no more than a good meal.

The thought made Sebastian's stomach tighten in rage and fear. He couldn't lose her now; not after everything they'd been through together. They deserved their happy ending. He wouldn't let one of his own kind be the one to put an end to that. If Serenity died, he'd always want to raise Elizabeth, but he'd never be whole again. A piece of his heart would die with her.

Sebastian remembered how Elizabeth had seen herself in Serenity's place, seen where she was and what was around her. If only that talent could be reversed, so that she projected her own thoughts and the things she saw around her into his head. At least then he'd have more to go on. At the moment, however, he would be going in blind.

Don't do anything stupid, Serenity, he thought to himself, remembering the time she'd taken on his maker, Madeline, single-handedly. Okay, that time her plan had worked, but she'd still come too close to getting herself killed.

At least Bridget was with her. Surely sensible, steadfast Bridget would rein her in if she tried to rush headfirst into Demitri's lair.

He tried to push away the niggling uncertainty that Bridget might try to attempt something herself—that she really believed all her talk about magic potions and spells.

CAPTURED

They'll wait for me. He reassured himself. *The two humans would have to be insane to think they could take on a den of vampires.*

Chapter Nineteen

The moment they had sensed the approach of daylight, the female vampire, Natasha, had locked Elizabeth in a storeroom. When Natasha pulled the door shut behind her, Elizabeth heard a click. She'd understood the meaning of the sound but that didn't stop her from trying the door. Sure, she might only be a six-year-old, but since her thirst had been awoken, she felt like a *strong* six-year-old. She'd grabbed the handle and twisted, pulled and shoved, but the door didn't budge. This place had been designed with vampires in mind. A child didn't stand a chance of escaping.

Boxes of bottles surrounded her, some stacked several high, and big steel cylinders stood in one corner. A single, dimly lit bulb dangled from a frayed wire in the ceiling. A chill clutched the dank air, though her captors had thought to give her a blanket and several cushions to sleep on. The acrid tang of something she didn't recognize and rusted metal filled the room. At first, the smell filling her senses was all she could focus on but then she grew used to it and the stink became less noticeable.

Elizabeth had spent most of the day asleep. She'd curled up on top of the cushions, though she struggled with the blanket. Her legs poked from the bottom and if she sat up to try to rearrange it, the material fell off her body. Eventually she gave up, deciding the comfort meant little in relation to the craving still clutching her throat. Her only escape was sleep and, exhausted, sleep mercifully claimed her.

In the brief periods where she roused, a terrible thirst gripped her. She fought to go back to sleep, desperate to escape the discomfort. But even in her slumber, the hunger plagued her. Her mouth remained dry, her throat painful. Her dreams were of drinking down long, tall glasses of the delicious liquid, but still her thirst—even in her sleep—was never quenched.

She woke to the sound of the lock clicking again and lifted her head, blinking away the sleep. Demitri—the longhaired vampire—smiled down at her. Dusk must have come.

"I'm thirsty," she said, her voice raspy, and unlike her own.

He crouched to her level. "I know, child. I have what you want but, first, I want you to do something for me. Can you do that?"

Elizabeth nodded. She'd do whatever he wanted if it meant she'd get some more, something to ease the pain in her throat and the way her tongue stuck to the roof of her mouth. When she moved her lips to speak, the inside of her lips stuck to her gums, exposing her small teeth.

"Good. You know how you sometimes see things that haven't happened yet?" She nodded again. "I want you to try to do it now for me, okay?"

"I'll try." Elizabeth closed her eyes, plunging herself into darkness. The vampire could ask all he wanted, but she wouldn't be able to visualize something just because she'd been told to. Sometimes it happened when she wanted, but usually the visions happened by accident.

A flash of something burst in her mind: Sebastian standing in front of Demitri as she sat on her captor's lap. Though she wasn't able to hear what was being said, she understood from the vampires' expressions they were arguing.

Elizabeth gasped and her eyes sprung open. Only rarely had she been able to call a sighting to mind like that. Her talent suddenly seemed nearer, more within reach.

"Tell me what you saw," the vampire demanded.

She agonized. She didn't want to tell him, but she couldn't stand the thought of not being fed. Her thirst overshadowed everything else—even her loyalty to her family. "I saw you and my daddy, Sebastian. You were fighting."

"Hmm," Demitri said, one hand rubbing his lips. "I thought he'd come." He flashed a bright, white smile, exposing his canines. "But did you see anything else? Anything... more important."

Stubborn anger lodged inside her and she pouted. "My daddy *is* important. Can I get my drink now?"

Demitri paused, seeming to decide if he should punish the outburst, then erupted into laughter. He reached out and ruffled her hair, but Elizabeth jerked away from his touch.

"There's my good little half-breed. Who knew the vampire side was so close beneath the surface?"

"I want my drink," she repeated, her throat scorching. "I'm thirsty."

"Of course you are, child. Come with me."

He held out his hand and Elizabeth eyed his long, pale fingers in distrust. He wiggled his fingers at her and, reluctantly, she placed her hand in his.

Elizabeth trailed behind him as they walked back through the enclosed, windowless corridors to the huge, cavernous room that seemed to make up Demitri's personal space. They entered the room and Elizabeth shrank back as she took in the sight of Natasha and another vampire—a mountainous creature with a bald head and thick neck. They stood either side of Demitri's huge slab of a desk, their hands crossed in front of their bodies.

"Relax," Demitri instructed them. "She's only a little girl."

"We don't know what she's capable of yet," said Natasha. "She might be able to attack us mentally—play tricks on our minds. I've heard of vampires with such talents."

"She's not a vampire. Not fully."

"I want my drink," said Elizabeth, her eyes shifting from one vampire to the other. She remembered her manners and added, "Please."

Demitri laughed. "Of course. Natasha, the child is hungry."

Natasha scowled at Elizabeth but didn't argue with Demitri. In a blur, she left the room, the door swinging shut behind her. Within seconds she'd returned, the same, long-stemmed, marble cup in her hands.

"Here," she said, handing it to Demitri. Her eyes glowed yellow, her face pale and tensed. Her fangs ran out a little as she forced herself to let go of the vessel.

Elizabeth reached out, a need running urgently through her. Her throat raged, fire closing it over. She wondered if she'd even be able to swallow, but then, as the cup was lifted to her lips and the warm, metallic scent filled her nostrils, saliva flooded her mouth. She grabbed the cup from him and drank. She swallowed the warm liquid with long, deep gulps, relishing in the comfort it brought her poor, burning throat. As she drank, a strange nugget of heat built in the center of her chest. Her heart picked up a notch, thumping loudly, its beat filling her ears.

She'd drained the cup and her stomach dropped in disappointment. Not wanting any to be wasted, she poked out her tongue and lapped around the inside, licking up any last residue.

"Now, now," said Demitri, untangling the cup from her fingers. "Do you feel better?"

"I still want more."

"You can have more, but first you need to do something for me again. Is that fair?"

She nodded and said, "What do I have to do?"

"Only what comes naturally, child. I want you to try to see into the future again, only this time, try to see past your old family."

She scowled. "I can only see things about people I know. My thoughts go to them and what's going to happen just appears in my head."

He straightened and ran both hands through his hair, pushing it behind his ears. He smiled, a smug expression, his fangs glinting.

"Very well. If you only have visions about those you know, wouldn't you say you and I are acquainted now?"

Elizabeth wanted to comment, but she wasn't brave enough. "I guess," she mumbled.

"So how about you think about me? Try to see what my future holds?"

She closed her eyes and exhaled through her nose. The thirst had abated for the moment so she was able concentrate. All she'd been able to think about before was how much she wanted some more of the drink.

The heat at her heart seemed to help her focus. Like a little nugget of strength, she drew from it, pulling its power from her core to her head. She'd never experienced this kind of control before. Previously, the sightings had been random and sporadic, grabbing her wherever and whenever. But now, she was sure she could make it happen—with that strange sensation of power, she could make anything happen.

With her eyes still closed, she felt a strange sucking sensation on her brain, as though her mind was literally being dragged forward.

She was standing in Demitri's room, but more people surrounded her now. Her father stood beside the desk. Her mother was just ahead of her and Demitri stood in front of her mom, their faces only inches apart. Demitri's face was pale, his eyes black and furious. Suddenly an explosion of movement happened near her. Demitri stumbled back, screaming, but that wasn't what caught Elizabeth's attention. Sebastian's yell of pain dragged her eyes to where he stood, a huge wooden stake of some kind protruding from his chest. Terror for her father gripped her heart.

Elizabeth cried out, "Daddy!"

The strange, sucking sensation was back again, dragging her backward now, pulling on her brain and limbs.

Her eyes flicked open in the real world to find Demitri watching her intently. The room spun and she swayed, nausea rushing over her. Unable to control it, she doubled over and vomited hot, thick fluid all over the floor.

Elizabeth's eyes widened.

Blood! So much blood!

She opened her mouth and screamed an ear-splitting shriek. Thick, viscous pools covered the wooden floor— blood that had just come from her. Plumes of steam rose from the emission. In her mind, she remembered the sight of Sebastian with the wooden pole sticking out of his chest. How her mommy had been in Demitri's grasp. Elizabeth wasn't stupid; she knew exactly what her vision meant. Her mommy and daddy were coming to get her. They were going to fight Demitri and his friends, and they were going to lose.

As she lifted her head to search for help, she caught sight of the vampires. Three white, tensed faces with fierce, glowing eyes and protruding fangs stared at the blood.

They lifted their eyes to her.

Elizabeth screamed again and ran.

Instantly, the three vampires were on her. Demitri grabbed her by the shoulders, the male vampire and Natasha landing directly in front of her. She would have collided with them if not for Demitri's hold on her. His grip felt like a band of ice. He gave her a slight shake, but his strength was such that her head whipped back and forth, hurting her neck. Sebastian had never touched her with any kind of force. To experience such strength and cruelty from someone like her own father was terrifying.

With the blood purged, fear washed over her afresh. "Please," she begged. "Please let me go. I want my mommy and daddy."

"Oh, they'll be here. Isn't that what you saw?" Demitri spun her around to face him. "Tell me about your vision, child. It's clear from your reaction that you tapped into something."

She cried, hot tears streaming down her face. Suddenly panicked, she lifted her hand and wiped away the tears. She looked down at the back of her hand and was relieved to find the fluid clear. She'd been almost certain her hand and face would be smeared with red. That she'd been crying blood.

"My mommy and daddy were here," she sobbed. "My daddy got hurt."

Demitri's face brightened.

"Then you need to tell me exactly what happened."

"I told you before," she sniffed. "You and Sebastian were fighting. Everything happened so fast, I didn't see much else."

Slowly, he shook his head. "No, you saw more than that. Tell me or I'll make both you and your parents suffer."

"I don't know anything else!"

Demitri snarled, his maw opening wide and filling her vision with lethally sharp fangs. "Tell me!"

Elizabeth trembled with fear. "My daddy got staked," she said, her voice little more than a whisper. "I think someone killed him."

Chapter Twenty

Hours passed and finally the bright lights of New York City lit up the horizon. Sebastian picked up his pace. Serenity was now only moments away.

He raced through the busy streets, leaping over traffic, brushing past people on the street. They sensed him as he passed, a sudden rush of cold wind on their faces, leaving them shivering and with the impression a ghost had just walked by. Sebastian reached the hotel. He didn't need to stop at the desk to find out if Serenity had checked in or ask her room number. Now she'd taken his blood, they were bound in such a way that he was able to go straight to her. He'd always been focused on her before, had always been able to pick up her scent and the emotions she radiated, even in a crowd, but now the sensation was much stronger. Her heartbeat was like a huge, throbbing base in the center of the building. Sebastian raced up the stairs, pausing for only a fraction of a second on each floor before he burst through the doors of the floor she was on.

He located her room with no problem. Her life force glowed for him, a mental lighthouse he couldn't help but hone in on.

Sebastian paused outside the door and centered himself. He didn't want to charge in, wild and windswept, and upset whatever fragile state she might be in now.

He didn't get to wait any longer. The door opened and Serenity stood before him, her dark eyes wide, her long hair spiraling down over her shoulders. Her face was streaked from crying, her eyes bloodshot.

His heart clenched for her—for her beauty and her fragility. In so many ways, she'd been both his biggest strength and his greatest weakness.

Catching him by surprise, she stepped forward and shoved him in the chest with both hands. The shock of her hitting him made him step back. She would never have been physically strong enough to budge him but, mentally, she'd caught him off guard.

"You told me Demitri wouldn't just turn up and take her," she yelled. "He's got my baby. That monster has her!"

He grabbed her wrists, holding her still. He fixed his gaze on her distraught brown eyes. "It's okay. We'll get her back again!"

"How can you say that? You don't know if that's true. All of the promises you made me about how everything is going to be all right, they're all bullshit! You don't know that anything is *ever* going to be all right!"

He resisted the urge to give her a shake. "Hey, Serenity, she's my daughter as well. Remember, I'm a vampire, I'm not a goddamned superhero."

She hung her head and he let go of her wrists. "I'm sorry. I'm just so frightened for her. She must be so scared."

"Demitri never said he would do anything to hurt her. He wants her to be able to predict the future for him. What would be the sense in harming her?"

"If she's not able to do what he wants, he might."

They still stood in the doorway, Bridget hovering in the room behind.

"Are you going to let me in," he said. "Or do I have to stand in the corridor all night?"

She gave her head a slight shake and stepped back, allowing him through. "I'm sorry," she said again. "This has been one of the worst days of my life. Only Bridget threatening to tie me to a chair has stopped me from going straight to Demitri's club."

He lifted his eyes to where Bridget stood. She gave him a tight smile. "Thank you," he told her.

Sebastian pushed the door shut behind him. The room was almost a mirror image of the one they'd stayed in before. A non-descript landscape print hung above the bed. A small, flat-screen television sat on a dark wood desk, coffee and tea making facilities on a tray beside it.

Serenity went and sat on the edge of the double bed, her head in her hands.

"What are we going to do, Sebastian? Please tell me you have a plan."

He faltered. So far his plan had consisted of going back to see Demitri and demanding his child back. As far as plans went, even he had to admit it wasn't a very good one.

Bridget touched Sebastian's shoulder. "I can help. I know you don't believe in magic, but I can do things."

"She's right," said Serenity, nodding. For the first time since he'd arrived, her eyes brightened. "Bridget, show him."

Sebastian folded his arms across his broad chest, his jaw hardened. This time he didn't complain, only watched with wary eyes. He'd never hidden his skepticism about what Bridget said she could do, but if it made Serenity feel better—

made her think there was hope—then he'd tolerate whatever Bridget thought she could do to help.

Bridget pulled her bag to her lap and delved inside. She took out three stubby candles and a small silk bag with something stuffed inside.

"What's that?" he asked.

Bridget grinned. "Those herbs you love so much. Now hush, I need to concentrate."

She knelt on the floor and positioned the candles in a wide triangle. From the silk pouch, she took a small pinch of the herbs and sprinkled them over the candles. She got to her feet and stepped inside the triangle of candles.

"Now everyone stay quiet," she instructed. "I need to focus."

Bridget bent at the waist and held her hand over the top of one of the wicks of the candles.

She spoke in a low voice. "Lux in tenebris, et tenebrae in luce."

The wick of the candle fizzed for a second, then burst to life. Bridget held her hand over the remaining two candles, repeating the words. Both candles flared.

Sebastian opened his mouth to make a sarcastic comment about being impressed, but a glare from Serenity shot him down.

Bridget stood up straight and crossed her hands over her chest, almost mimicking the same position Sebastian slept in, though she was upright instead of vertical. She spoke in low mumbled tones. "Pone mortale pondus omne et surge Sicut pinna, sicut aer, esto levis."

Sebastian knew enough Latin to get the basic idea of what she was saying.

Cast aside all mortal weight and rise. Light as a feather, light as air.

Her whole body began to tremble. Bridget repeated the words, over and over and before their eyes, she lifted several inches into the air.

Sebastian glanced at Serenity. Her eyes were glued on Bridget, the same bright, transfixed expression on her face. She lifted her eyes to his and smiled. He got the feeling this wasn't the first time she'd seen this trick. Bridget must have shown her what she could do while they were waiting for him to arrive.

Impatience nagged him and he couldn't see how a levitation trick would help them get Elizabeth back. They only had so many hours in the night and sitting here watching Bridget float only wasted them.

"Clever trick, Bridget, but I don't understand how it's going to help us."

Concentration broken, she dropped heavily to the carpeted floor, falling to her hands and knees, and the candles extinguished all at once.

Bridget sat back on her haunches, her long white hair almost brushing the floor behind her. She sighed. "I don't think this will help her, I just wanted to prove to you I was *capable* of helping."

"By doing what? Levitating Demitri out of the way?" He couldn't help the sarcastic bite to his tone.

"No, Sebastian, of course not. I have other things I can do, but they take all of my energy and I figured I'd be better off saving it."

"So what are you thinking?"

"I can create a veil which will protect Serenity from Demitri's eyes."

"What do you mean?"

Serenity interrupted, excited. "He won't be able to see me! I'll be able to walk into the club and take Elizabeth right back again."

"The veil protects good from evil. Makes whatever is good invisible. Serenity will be invisible to Demitri."

"And what about my eyes?" he asked. "Am I considered evil, Bridget? Will she be visible to me?"

Bridget struggled to meet his fierce gaze. "I'm not sure, Sebastian. I know you're not evil, but you are a vampire and you do kill. There's a good chance the veil will protect her from you as well."

"Seriously? And what happens then? Do you really think Demitri will just let Elizabeth walk out of there? He'll turn around and take her right back again."

Serenity blurted, "He won't be able to see her either. I can hold her close to my body so the veil will cover Elizabeth as well."

His eyes narrowed, looking between the two women. "So what am I supposed to do?"

"You need to distract Demitri and the two other vampires somehow so I can steal Elizabeth away."

Sebastian growled, his eyes burning. "I'll need to fight them. There is no other way."

"They can't kill you, can they?" said Serenity. "You've told me enough times that one vampire can't kill another."

"No, they can't kill me, but they can hold me prisoner. Keep me underground in the club and starve me until I have no strength." He shook his head. "Not that it matters, of course. I'll happily switch my own freedom for Elizabeth's." He thought for a moment. "Even if we're able to take Elizabeth, we'll still need to stop Demitri from coming after us."

"What about silver?" said Serenity. "It worked with Madeline."

Sebastian raised a hand. "Serenity, stop. First of all, Demitri is an ancient, older than even Madeline was. You won't be able to trick him easily. Secondly, if you're planning to try to kill him, you can't tell me about it. If I'm involved knowingly in anyway, I won't be able to help you."

"Of course, sorry. But I don't have any amazing plan for how to kill him. I wish I did. Right now, all I'm interested in is getting Elizabeth back." Her voice quivered and she burst into tears.

In an instant, he was by her side, pulling her into his arms. "Hush. We can do this. We'll get her back."

"But what about you?" she cried. "I don't want you to get hurt and I don't want Demitri to exchange Elizabeth for you."

"Don't worry about me." He gave a wry grin. "I'm old enough to look after myself."

She sniffed. "You're not older than Demitri."

"No, I'm not. But you need to concentrate on getting Elizabeth away."

"I could always wait until daylight," she said between sniffs. "If the vampires will all be sleeping, maybe I can find Elizabeth before they wake. Perhaps there is no need for you to get involved."

"I'm not letting you go in there alone, Serenity."

Besides," Bridget interrupted. "If they've got humans working the bar in the day—innocent humans who don't know what they've got themselves involved with—the magic won't work on them. You'll be as visible to them as you are now and all that's likely to happen is they'll call the cops and have you arrested for breaking and entering."

Serenity jumped to her feet. "Why don't we call the cops ourselves? If the vampires will all be asleep in the day, we can send them in to get Elizabeth back."

Bridget raised her eyebrows. "Do you really want that sort of scrutiny? You've been missing for two years and then you come back and someone takes your daughter? How are you going to explain such a thing?"

"Anyway," Sebastian interrupted. "We're not waiting another night before we do anything and I'm not going to let you go into the club alone. Demitri's room is far beneath ground. His age, combined with how far below the surface he is, might mean he can rouse himself from sleep should he need to. I refuse to be asleep, trapped in some closet and hiding from the light while you put yourself in so much danger."

"I don't want to wait any longer either," said Serenity. "Today has been hard enough. Whatever happens, we're getting Elizabeth back tonight." She turned to Bridget. "What if I bump into regular people?"

"They'll just think you're another clubber. If any of them are watchdogs for Demitri and the other vampires, I'm pretty sure they'll fall on the side of 'evil' as far as the cosmic ratings go."

Sebastian held up his hand. "Okay, so I think we've established that Serenity isn't going to go on her own. What now? Night only has so many hours and poor Elizabeth is in the hands of Demitri and his minions."

"I need to concentrate to create the spell, so neither of you can talk while I do it. And I'm going to need some of Serenity's hair."

Serenity raised her eyebrows. "I don't suppose anyone thought to bring any scissors?"

Sebastian lifted one of her curls. "Hold still."

She froze as he wrapped a lock of her hair around one finger. He held the strands with his other hand and gave a sharp pull. Under his strength, the hair fibers split with ease and Serenity gasped.

"Sorry, did I hurt you?"

She laughed, "Just an automatic reaction."

Sebastian handed the lock of hair to Bridget. "How's this?"

"Perfect," she said. "Now listen to me. The veil will only last for an hour, maybe a little more, so you need to get Elizabeth before then. As soon as it wears off, the vampires will be able to see you again."

"How will I know it's working?" Serenity asked.

"You'll feel it like energy around your skin. The hairs on your body will stand on end."

Serenity nodded her understanding.

Bridget rummaged in her bag again and pulled out several clear pockets containing a variety of dried herbs. She dove back in and retrieved a small, black marble bowl.

Bridget lifted her head and caught sight of Serenity and Sebastian watching. "Now you know why I always carry such a big purse."

Serenity flashed a nervous smile. "You're like the modern day Mary Poppins."

The older woman winked. "I prefer 'Witches of Eastwick'. Now, let me focus."

With concentration, she took a pinch out of one packet and a couple of pinches from another. She mixed in Serenity's hair and then lit a candle using the same spell she'd done earlier.

"Let's hope the smoke alarms aren't too sensitive," she said, and then set fire to the hair and herb combination with the candle. The hair hissed and shriveled. An acrid burning stink filled the room.

Sebastian glanced up at the white alarm attached to the ceiling above his head. A small red LED light flashed. Without another thought, he sprang up and tore the plastic device from its holdings.

He settled back on the edge of the bed and tossed the alarm, wires torn from the base, onto the floor. "Problem solved."

Serenity smiled and edged closer to him. He slipped his arm around her waist and together they watched Bridget, still knelt on the floor.

Bridget lowered her head as though in prayer while her concoction burned in the marble bowl.

She murmured her words but Sebastian's keen hearing picked them up. He suspected Serenity would also be able to hear—after all, she had his blood running through her veins. Whether she understood them or not, he didn't know.

"Hanc vela, hanc custodi, hanc ab oculis malorum protege."

Automatically, his mind translated: *Veil her, keep her, protect her from the sight of evil.*

She repeated the words as the hair and herbs burned down to ashes.

His gaze flicked to Serenity who was watching Bridget in rapt awe.

This had better work, he thought. Or they were all out of options.

Chapter Twenty-one

"Are you ready?" Bridget asked Serenity.

Serenity gave the other woman a restrained smile. "As I'll ever be."

Bridget pressed a small, silky pouch containing the ashes of the hair and herbs into Serenity's palm. "You'll need this. When the time comes to activate the veil, split the bag over the top of your head. I'll do the rest."

"How will you know when I've done it?"

Her serious blue eyes rested on Serenity's face. "I'll know. Remember to split the bag at the last possible moment. The magic will only last an hour at the very most. If you use it too soon, you'll run the risk of the effect running out at a critical moment."

With her hand between their bodies, hidden from Sebastian's view, Bridget pushed something else into Serenity's jean pocket.

"What's that?" asked Sebastian, his keen ears having heard the movement.

Bridget looked over Serenity's shoulder toward him. "Just a little insurance policy."

Serenity leaned in and planted a kiss on the other woman's soft cheek. The scent of floral perfume washed over her.

"Thank you."

Bridget shook her head. "Thank me when you're both back here safely with Elizabeth by your side. Until that happens, I won't have done a thing."

Sebastian stepped forward and kissed her other cheek. "I owe you an apology, Bridget. I'm sorry for being such a sanctimonious asshole."

"You weren't," she smiled. "At least no more than any other guy I've ever known."

"Good to know I've not broken the mold."

"Not even close."

They stood smiling at each other. The tension that had been between them dissipated. They were both perfectly aware that without Bridget's abilities and generosity with her time, they'd have no plan to go on.

Serenity took a deep breath, steadying her nerves. "Okay, let's go. Elizabeth is on her own with that bastard and she's probably terrified. She needs us."

Sebastian's strong fingers entwined with hers and she looked up into his chiseled, beautiful face.

"Let's do this," he said.

"Stay safe," Bridget said.

Hand in hand, they walked out of the small room. They took the elevator down to the ground floor and crossed the lobby. A young woman sat behind the reception and she gave them a small smile as they left. Not wanting to appear rude, even though her heart was in her throat and she thought she might throw up from fear, Serenity returned the smile.

Would the receptionist remember her, she wondered. If all this went bad and Sebastian and Elizabeth vanished from society, would the cops track them down here, to this small, indeterminable hotel?

They stepped out onto the street. It was the middle of the night and the streets—while far from empty—were far quieter than the rush hour traffic she and Bridget had arrived in. Taxis swept past them. A young couple, huddled together against the cold, crossed to the other side of the street.

Unlike the other couple, Serenity and Sebastian walked upright and square -shouldered. The cold didn't affect Sebastian and his blood had given Serenity some defense against the night's chill.

Something occurred to Serenity. As they reached the corner of the alley where Demitri's club was located, she pulled Sebastian to a halt. "I want something from you."

He turned to her. "Anything."

"Give me some more of your blood. I'll never be any match for the vampires, but your blood will strengthen me and make me more alert. Surely, it can't hurt."

"What about Bridget's magic? It's a defense against evil. What if, with too much vampire blood in you, the spell doesn't work?"

"It'll just be just a drop or two," she argued. "I won't be a vampire. I won't have killed anyone—at least no one who wasn't asking for it. I don't think it'll affect the magic."

"I wish we'd discussed this with Bridget."

"You know she wouldn't like it, but sometimes we need to make our own decisions."

Sebastian stared at her, his green eyes studying her face.

"She knows her stuff when it comes to witchcraft," continued Serenity. "But this is vampire business."

Sebastian's lips thinned and he gave a brisk nod, making a decision.

Without another word, Sebastian pulled his shirtsleeve up. His face morphed—his fangs running forward and his eyes flashing yellow. He lifted his naked wrist to his mouth, and bit.

With their eyes locked, Sebastian offered his bloodied wrist to Serenity. She took it, her mouth fastening over the puncture wound. Her tongue lapped out and she tasted the cool iron of his blood. Part of her wanted to be repulsed, her brain screaming 'this is blood you're drinking', but nothing about Sebastian could ever repulse her.

The bite healed quickly, closing even while she drank, but she'd still been able to get a few drops. As they slid over her palate and down her throat, she felt their power radiate from her core, spreading over her limbs.

Serenity gasped and dropped his hand, doubling over at the waist. She put her hands on her thighs, trying to steady herself.

"Serenity?" Sebastian's voice came, urgent with worry.

The sound of rushing blood swooshed in her ears, making his voice sound distant and faint. Though she stood still, the world seemed to turn in a slow, lazy swoop. Heat flooded her cheeks and, for a moment, she thought she might throw up, but then everything steadied again. The nausea left as quickly as it had appeared.

Serenity straightened and gave her head a slight shake. "Phew, head rush."

His hand found the top of her arm. "Are you all right?"

She looked up into his concerned face. His dark eyebrows knitted together, his eyes taking on the faintest hint of gold, iridescent in the dim light.

Her muscles burned with strength and her heart beat faster. The warmth that had flared in her cheeks now spread throughout the rest of her body, creating a blanket against the cold. Details leapt out at her—the faintest cracks in the sidewalk beneath her feet, the hint of acrid smoke on the air where something burned in the distance, the scurry of a rat in a trashcan several blocks away.

Gradually, the heightened sensations began to fade. While she still felt stronger and more alert—more aware—than before, she also felt more human.

"I'm fine," she said, offering him a smile, wanting to take the worried expression off his face. He studied her a little longer and seemed to accept her words.

His fingers trailed down her arm and stopped at her hand. "Are you ready for this?"

"I'm ready. I'm more worried about you than myself. You've got to take on Demitri and his two sidekicks. They're not even going to know I'm there."

"We *hope* they won't know you're there. After all, we haven't exactly tested Bridget's spell to be sure it even works."

"It'll work. She wouldn't send us into this if she wasn't one hundred percent confident in what she could do."

"I'm just frightened for you—for you and Elizabeth."

"I guess that's what it means to love someone, to have a family. You always fear for their safety more than your own."

Sebastian smiled and dipped his head, covering her mouth with his cool, firm lips. Serenity allowed herself to close her eyes, to focus only on the sensation of Sebastian kissing her, of the connection, both physical and emotional between them. Reluctant to, but aware of the huge task ahead, they broke apart.

"We're strong together," he told her, looping his fingers through hers. "Our love for Elizabeth makes us stronger than Demitri and his crew. No matter how this ends, we'll get through it. We'll deal with the repercussions and we'll come through it."

Hand in hand, they jogged down the alley toward the entrance of the club. The steady thump of the music could still be heard, but otherwise everything was quiet and still. The double doors they'd waited at previously were closed. The club was clearly popular enough to reach capacity long before closing.

Though no one lurked in the passage or hung around outside the club, the hairs on the back of Serenity's neck stood at attention, every sense afire for the slightest sound or movement. They needed to get inside without being seen.

Sebastian shoved on the closed doors. Right now, the entrance—while probably breaking every fire regulation in the book—was locked. "I guess Demitri is more paranoid than we gave him credit for."

"He has good reason to be."

Using his fierce strength, Sebastian pressed his shoulder against the solid wood. Not wanting to bring any unwanted attention, he gave the door one swift, sharp shove, breaking the lock and cracking the door from its frame.

His arm circled Serenity's waist as he opened the door further and stepped inside the club. Together, they walked through the short corridor and out into the main room. The club was divided into two levels. Gyrating bodies, with arms held in the air and fists pumping in time with the music, filled the main dance floor. The second level was a gallery with a view of the first floor in its center. Here people leaned on the metal bar dividing the upper level from the drop onto the dance floor below. More people danced on this upper level, but most stood watching the dancers below or congregated in groups, talking and drinking.

Music pounded and the stale scent of sweaty bodies filled the air. Beams of colored light cut through the darkness, a flashing strobe causing Serenity to blink.

No one paid the two new arrivals any attention.

There was no sign of any other vampires. Two bouncers stood with their arms folded across their chests, surveying the clubbers, and a couple of humans served behind a bar situated at the back of the club. The place appeared to be devoid of the supernatural.

"Come on," Sebastian yelled over the music. "They must be in Demitri's room."

211

"We should look for Elizabeth first," she shouted back. "If she's being kept somewhere away from the vampires, we should try to get to her and avoid any confrontation with Demitri."

Sebastian nodded and Serenity allowed him to guide her through the club.

Still hand in hand, the two made their way through the crowd of people. Relieved to get out of the deafening surroundings, he headed to the same exit Natasha and Vincent had taken them through. Taking Serenity by surprise, but not having time to explain, he scooped her up in his arms. He moved quickly and whipped open the door and vanished, too fast for any of the partygoers to notice.

They entered a corridor, the air stale with old beer and cigarette smoke—a ghost of the days when smoking was allowed in such places. The music was muffled now, a relief for Sebastian. The beat and volume had been unbearable.

Serenity stood beside him, her heartbeat and breathing now audible. While thankful to be able to hear such things again, he was also aware that if he could hear Serenity, there was a good chance Demitri and the other two might be able to hear them also.

He put a hand out and stopped Serenity. "Wait. I need to see if I can hear anything."

Murmured voices came from a distance, but he couldn't tell if any of the voices were Elizabeth's or if she was close. Even so, he knew the vampires were nowhere near, leaving them free to explore.

Light on their feet, they followed the corridor past the fire escape door, which was also conveniently bolted with a metal chain. Several passageways led off the main one, but Sebastian allowed his senses to guide him forward, Serenity running on her toes beside him.

Elizabeth's scent suddenly flooded his nostrils—her smell distinctive, so unlike any other. She had the strange non-odor of a vampire, but with the iron of life beneath.

Sebastian's nostril flared. Something was different about her smell. The human part seemed fainter, less vibrant, and the bland nothingness one vampire picked up from another was stronger.

The change made him nervous and he picked up his pace, pulling Serenity along.

"She's close, I can smell her."

As he rounded the corner, he realized the sound of her heartbeat was missing. Dread hit him, making his stomach clench. Only two reasons jumped to mind about the reason for the missing heartbeat: Demitri had somehow found a way to make her fully a vampire or she was already dead.

The real reason soon became apparent.

At the end of the corridor, was a storeroom. The door had been left wide open. Boxes and crates of bottled beer and other beverages were stacked high against the walls. Large cylinders of draft beer were pushed toward the back. Just beyond the doorway, several cushions and a blanket lay discarded and rumpled on the hard concrete floor.

The reason Elizabeth's scent had been so strong. Clearly, these few meager items had served as her bedding.

Sebastian left Serenity's side and moved with speed, dropping to his knees beside the blanket. Elizabeth's scent blasted from the material, causing his heart to contract. He hadn't given thought to how much he missed her. He lifted the blanket to his face, taking some comfort in having something she'd touched against his skin.

Serenity touched his shoulder and he turned his face up to her. She bit her lower lip and looked around at the concrete floor and the cold, stark and uncomfortable surroundings.

"This is where they kept her."

It wasn't a question, but Sebastian nodded anyway.

213

"Son of a bitch," she spat. "How could he keep a little girl locked up down here?" Sadness overcame anger and her voice broke. "My poor baby."

"Demitri must have her with him," he said, reached up to cover Serenity's hand with his own. "Assuming they've not taken her out somewhere, she must be in his lair."

Demitri's lair was built directly below the club's dance floor. What must have once been a cellar was now much deeper and, after having money thrown at it from every direction, had been turned into his luxurious room. Though the result was too vast to be called a room—it was more like a hall.

Being beneath the ground and having the noise of the club above, there was no risk of anyone hearing the screams of the victims the vampires fed on. As a further benefit, no safer place from the sun existed than beneath ground. Sebastian had learned that much himself several years earlier when he'd hidden himself away in an underground tunnel system in Turkey.

They took several turns, each time Sebastian following both his nose and the muttered voices he'd picked up on earlier. The corridors were a maze beneath the club, several new branches running from the main one which ran in a square around the outskirts of the club. The ceilings were low, causing Sebastian to duck in some places. The confined space was with lit with harsh, fluorescent strips of lighting.

As they got closer, both Elizabeth's scent and the voices grew more distinct.

At the end of the corridor, the closed double doors of Demitri's cavern blocked the way. Just beneath the subdued voices, Sebastian detected the fast patter of Elizabeth's heartbeat.

Outside of the doors, they drew to a stop.

"I'll go inside and distract them," said Sebastian in a low voice. "You do what Bridget instructed and grab Elizabeth. Don't pause for a second, whatever happens."

Serenity looked up at him, her lips tight with worry, and nodded. They both knew how dangerous this was, how there was a good chance Sebastian might not make it out with them—if any of them made it at all.

He studied her, taking in her long dark lashes, doe-eyes and smooth, soft skin. Her beauty had always been obvious to him, even when she'd been left emaciated and ravaged by Jackson.

She reached up, placed her hands around his neck and stood on tiptoes to place her cheek against his, eyes closed.

"I love you," she whispered, her soft lips brushing against the lobe of his ear.

"I love you too," he said. "And I love Elizabeth. If I don't make it out, make sure you tell her how much I love her."

Taking him by surprise, Serenity pushed his shoulder with the palm of her hand, breaking away from him. "Don't talk like that!"

He caught her by the wrist. Tears trembled in her dark eyes and he imprinted the sight of her on his mind. If things went as he expected and he ended up as Demitri's prisoner, this might be the last time he saw her.

"Elizabeth is on the other side of that door," he said, fixing her with his gaze. "Once upon a time, you told me if you had to choose between her life and your own, you'd choose hers every time. You said you wouldn't want to live in a world with her not in it. I took you at your word and saved her that night in the mine and I did so at your expense. Elizabeth is my daughter as well. At least allow me to make the same sacrifice."

He reached out and traced his knuckles along the fine line of her jaw. Serenity took hold of his hand and pressed his fingers to her lips.

"Okay," she whispered. "Okay."

Inside the room, the voices fell silent.

They'd been heard.

215

"They know I'm here," he hissed.

Sebastian gave her one last, fierce kiss, relishing the taste of her on his mouth, before moving at his vampire's speed, flying through the double doors, leaving them banging in his wake.

He came to rest in front of Demitri's desk,

"Daddy!" Elizabeth yelled, trying to jump up from where Demitri held her on his lap. But the older vampire held her firm, his long pale fingers on her small shoulders. The sight of his old comrade holding his daughter so intimately made him want to leap across the desk and tear the other vampire's head from his shoulders.

In his mind, he saw himself standing over Jackson, plunging his hand deep into the monster's chest to rip out his cold, hard heart. This time it wasn't Jackson he envisioned himself standing over, but Demitri.

But his wishes were empty. He could no more rip Demitri's heart out than he could his own. Sure, he could fight Demitri, attack him, but if he tried to take the vampire's life, his strength would melt away and he'd be left weak and helpless.

The blonde, Natasha, stood just behind the huge black leather chair Demitri sat in, her hand resting on the back. Her fingers, tipped by blood red nails, drummed the leather.

Upon seeing Sebastian, no surprise registered in Demitri's handsome features. Instead, a slow smile spread across his face.

"Sebastian! We've been waiting for you. How good of you to grace us with your presence. Of course, your clever child here had already told us you were on the way."

Elizabeth's lower lip poked out, her small face crumpling. Tears trembled in her dark eyes, matting together her thick lashes. The look was so reminiscent of Serenity that it stung his heart.

"I'm sorry, Sebastian," she said.

His lifted his hand slightly, wanting to comfort her but not daring to take a step closer to Demitri until he'd assessed the other vampire's intentions.

"It's okay, Elizabeth. None of this is your fault."

Natasha moved forward, bringing herself in line with the chair. Sebastian wondered where the other vampire, Vincent, was.

"What shall we do with him, Demitri?" asked Natasha. "Bury him beneath the floor? He could be there for centuries and no one would ever hear him screaming."

Sebastian snarled. "You couldn't do a thing to me, and you know it. I'm stronger than you'll ever be."

She snorted. "Not with Demitri's help you're not."

Demitri lifted a hand to silence her, releasing one of Elizabeth's shoulders. Sebastian watched his every move, his mind whirring over ways in which to get Elizabeth away from him.

"Hush, Natasha. We already know how this is going to play out, thanks to our little Dhampyre here. We must wait for her mother to get here before we make any decisions."

Sebastian stiffened. If this thing had gone to plan, they shouldn't even have been aware of Serenity's presence.

Chapter Twenty-two

Serenity stood on the other side of the door, listening to the voices of the vampires. It became clear Demitri was aware of her involvement in trying to get Elizabeth back, she just wasn't sure how much he knew.

Feeling faintly ridiculous despite her fear, she took the small fabric pouch from her pocket. Sweat slicked her palms, leaving damp patches on the silky material. Her heart felt as though it had crawled into her throat, its pounding filling her whole body. The amount of adrenaline pumping through her veins made her sick, but her only focus was Elizabeth and Sebastian. No matter how frightened she was, she'd do anything to get them back.

Bridget had stitched the pouch shut—apparently necessary to keep in the magic—so she tore at the stitches with her blunt nails. At first the cotton held, but then the threads began to fray until they finally popped.

Please let this work, please let this work...

She repeated the chant over and over.

I'm doing it now, Bridget, she called out in her mind, hoping somehow her thoughts would be transported through the ether and Bridget was doing her part of the process.

Serenity pulled open a split in the pouch. The thought that she was doing something people on the outside might view as crazy washed through her again, but she ignored it and tipped the contents over her head and shoulders. Bridget had burned the hair and herbs down to a fine powder and Serenity barely felt the dust fall over her.

She held her breath, expecting a different sensation to wash over her, but there was nothing; no tingling over her skin, no prickling of the hairs on the back of her neck. Nothing.

Oh God, it's not working.

She knew it as certainly as she knew her own name. She didn't understand much about magic, but when she'd been in its presence the air had been charged. Right now, she felt no different than if she'd just sprinkled the contents of a teabag over her head.

Her stomach sank and her throat closed with despair. She heard a thin, whining sound and realized it had come from her own mouth. What did they have now? What should she do? She could hardly leave Sebastian and Elizabeth here and go back to the hotel to see Bridget and find out what had happened.

She reached back into her pocket and fingered the second pouch Bridget had given her—the 'insurance' Bridget had thought to give her.

Had Bridget somehow known she'd need it, that the spell wouldn't work? Surely Bridget wouldn't have sent them in knowing the magic wouldn't work.

No, Serenity shook the thought from her head. The vampire blood must be to blame. *Damn it.*

She couldn't just turn her back and walk away from her family. The idea was unthinkable. She had no other choice; she needed to go in, face Demitri, and get her daughter back.

Serenity closed her eyes for a moment, centering herself. To show fear to the vampires was like waving a chunk of steak in front of a tiger's face. She needed to go in with her shoulders back and her head held high.

Taking a deep, shuddery breath, she forced her legs to move. She placed her hands against the double doors and pushed.

The moment she entered the room, Demitri's gaze turned to her.

"Mommy!" Elizabeth cried out in delight, her dark eyes brightening.

Sebastian spun to face her and she crossed the room toward him, wanting to take her place beside him in front of the evil bastard who sat behind his pretentious desk with her daughter on his lap.

Though she trembled all over, she put her hands on her hips and stared back at Demitri.

"Give us our daughter back, you son of a bitch."

"What are you doing, Serenity?" Sebastian exclaimed. His eyes had taken on a glint of panic she was unused to seeing in his face.

"I won't simply exchange your life for Elizabeth's. I love you both and I intend on taking my whole family home with me."

Demitri threw back his head and laughed. "This is all too good to be true. The whole family here together. How touching." He released his grip on Elizabeth and she sprang from his lap and raced over to Serenity.

Serenity scooped her up in her arms, burying her face in her daughter's soft hair. Elizabeth clutched her, her arms around her neck, her legs locked around Serenity's waist.

"I'm sorry, Mommy," she mumbled against Serenity's neck.

"Shhh, you've got nothing to be sorry for."

"I told them what was going to happen. He gave me blood to drink, and I really liked it, and that's why I told them."

Sebastian's head flicked back to Demitri, glaring at him, eyes blazing. "You fed her blood?"

Demitri shrugged. "I needed to make her vampire side stronger."

"You sick piece of shit."

"Now, now, Sebastian. I know you, remember? I know all the things you used to get up to before you went all…" He made a circular motion with his hand as if searching for the word. "Humanized on me."

Wanting to keep her hands free, Serenity untangled Elizabeth's limbs from hers and set her down between herself and Sebastian. Sebastian reached down and placed his large palm on Elizabeth's head. The little girl looked up at him with wide, adoring eyes and Serenity wanted to cry. She couldn't let anything tear them apart, she simply couldn't.

Elizabeth tugged on Sebastian's shirt. "You're going to get hurt, Daddy. I saw it!"

Serenity felt as though someone had just punched her in the stomach, an automatic 'oh' of shock bursting from her lips. Sebastian, however, didn't react to the news, at least not on the outside.

"Shhh," he stroked Elizabeth's hair. "I'm going to be just fine. You wait and see."

"But I saw it happen! I saw you getting hurt."

Demitri watched, making no effort to stop Elizabeth from telling them. Perhaps he felt sure the future couldn't be changed, that her telling Sebastian of his fate wouldn't affect the outcome.

Serenity prayed he was wrong.

Demitri walked around his desk and stopped in front of Serenity. Like Sebastian, the vampire seemed to take up more space than a real person—as though his aura were a tangible part of him. His long dark hair shone like silk and, as she watched, he reached up and tucked it behind his ears. His slightly too broad nose did nothing to diminish his features, instead making him appear even more masculine. His dark eyes, with their gold rims, bore right through her.

He stopped—his body only inches from hers—and stared into her eyes, focusing on her with his intense gaze. She forced herself to stare back, hoping he didn't pick up on the tremors which seemed to wrack through her body.

Demitri lifted a hand and touched her cheek with cool fingers. Beside her, she heard Sebastian's sharp intake of breath. The air between them seemed to stiffen as Sebastian held himself back from what Serenity felt sure was his desire to attack.

"Maybe I should keep you too," said Demitri. "You are very beautiful and it's been awhile since I had a human companion."

From behind Demitri's desk, one hand still resting on his chair, Natasha glared at Serenity.

Serenity forced herself not to flinch from Demitri's touch. "I'll stay with you if you let me take care of my daughter."

"Serenity!" Sebastian's voice came, shocked. The pain she heard in that solitary word burned through her heart.

Demitri laughed again, clearly enjoying the show.

"If he won't give her back to us," Serenity continued, talking to Sebastian, but her eyes remaining on Demitri's face. "I'd rather be here with her willingly, than risk leaving her alone. We both agreed Elizabeth was the most important person in all of this. You should know I'd never leave her if I had any other choice."

Though she didn't want to meet Sebastian's gaze, didn't want to see the pain in his eyes, she turned her head.

Their eyes met.

"What are you doing, Serenity?" he almost begged.

"What needs to be done."

222

"Well," Demitri said, clapping his hands together. "If that is all agreed, I guess Sebastian is free to leave."

Sebastian's fists clenched at his sides. "I'm not going anywhere."

Demitri opened his arms wide. "So, welcome to the fold, Sebastian. You hand Elizabeth and Serenity over to me and you can become one of my underlings."

Sebastian snarled, his fangs protruding. His face was stark white in his anger, his eyes burning. "Never!"

"No? And may I ask why not? After all, the rest of your friends and family have decided my way is the best way."

At the word 'friends' Sebastian's eyes narrowed and his forehead creased, a line appearing between his dark eyebrows.

Behind them, the door flung open and the big, bald vampire, Vincent, strode in holding Bridget by her upper arm. In Bridget's other hand was the small rucksack Serenity had packed, the one that was full of Elizabeth's precious belongings.

"Oh God, Bridget," Serenity cried. "How did they find you? I'm so sorry you got caught up in this."

No wonder the magic hadn't worked, she thought. Vincent must have found Bridget before she'd got the chance to use it.

Demitri smirked. "Oh, don't worry. Bridget has been caught up in this from the start. How else do you think I knew all about Elizabeth?"

Sebastian shook his head, the line remaining between his eyes. "Bridget, what's he talking about."

Tears shimmered in her eyes. "I'm sorry, Sebastian. I never meant for it to come to this."

Vincent had let go of her arm, but she made no attempt to get away, she just stood at his side.

"I'm so sorry. Vincent is my son and I had to do it. Demitri threatened to make him suffer if I didn't help him. Demitri had already heard rumors about Elizabeth and wanted to find out more about her. He made Vincent put me in your home to watch how things developed."

"What do you mean, 'put me in your home?' I employed you, no one put you there!"

"Where did you find her, Sebastian?" Demitri interjected.

The bewildered expression remained on his face. "Another vampire recommended her."

Instantly everything fell into place for Serenity. "Someone you knew," she said, directing the comment at Demitri.

The vampire gave her a charming smile that never reached his eyes. "Well, of course."

"I can't believe you'd do this to us, Bridget." Sebastian said, staring at his employee. "Elizabeth treated you like a mother and all the time you were spying on us."

"I'm sorry, Sebastian. I couldn't believe it when you said you planned to bring Serenity here to try to make her better. At first, I hoped you were talking about a different vampire, but it was obvious you weren't. I tried to tell you not to come, but you wouldn't listen. What was I supposed to do?"

"Tell us outright what was going on!"

"I couldn't! Demitri told me that if I said anything, he'd destroy my son."

"You lied to us! I should kill you right here!"

"No!" cried Elizabeth, clutching at her father's leg. "Leave her alone!"

Demitri watched the exchange with an amused smile on his face.

"Anyway," continued Bridget. "I thought you'd find out about the 'arrangement' when you brought Serenity here. I thought Demitri would make his intentions clear. But then you came back and said everything was fine so I thought perhaps Demitri had changed his mind. After you didn't say anything, I hoped you'd sorted something out between you."

"I didn't say anything," said Sebastian, glowering. "Because I knew you'd disapprove." He barked laughter. "I was actually worried about what you'd think."

"You were worried about what I'd think because I'd already warned you not to come. Yes, I played my part in this, but I tried to make things right. You were the one too pigheaded to listen."

"Now, now, children," said Demitri raising both hands. "Let's not fight among ourselves—although Bridget, please understand your attempt to warn Sebastian has not gone unnoticed. I'm almost tempted to make a meal of you myself for that little piece of betrayal."

As if to prove his point, Demitri darted toward Bridget and hissed. Serenity drew in a sharp breath of shock, certain he'd attack Bridget, though she was pleased the proximity of the vampire to her family had been increased.

Vincent stepped in front of his mother, his face hard, his fangs drawn.

Bridget put out a hand and touched his arm. The vampire, probably knowing he was out of his depth, slunk back down like a whipped dog.

"Better," said Demitri, his expression matching the one on Vincent's face seconds before. "So, Bridget, would you like to explain to me your reason for trying to stop Sebastian's coming here?"

"Isn't it obvious? I didn't want them to find out the truth."

"Why? What did you think would happen?

"The worst. Sebastian might kill me for betraying him and then you would do whatever you wanted with my son."

Serenity still struggled to think of Vincent as being Bridget's son. The big, hulking vampire was nothing like the sweet, young man she'd pictured when Bridget had been talking about him. This guy didn't look like he needed protecting from anything.

"Anyway," Bridget said. "I never trusted you. Having Sebastian and Serenity on my side was like a little bit of insurance." She turned to Serenity, her bright blue eyes locked on Serenity's face. "I hope you'll forgive me, Serenity. Sometimes we all need a little insurance when it comes to protecting our children."

Insurance.

The tiny pouch Bridget had given her felt like a rock in her pocket, as though the shape protruded, huge and obvious. A brief flare of heat warmed the material of her jeans, as though the contents had reacted to Bridget's words.

Earlier, before Sebastian reached the hotel room, Bridget had explained what the pouch contained: powdered silver combined with vervain and wolfsbane. The tiny molecules would stick to a vampire's skin, burning them. The only way to get it off would be to immediately take a long shower or plunge into water. Unless Serenity had the unfortunate luck of using the pouch either in the bathroom or near the coast, the vampire would become incapacitated before he reached help.

They'd needed to keep the contents of the pouch and the reason for it being in Serenity's possession a secret from Sebastian. Not only would he not want Serenity to place herself in any kind of danger, but if he knew he was taking part in any plan to kill the other vampire, he would be left weak and helpless.

But could she trust Bridget? After everything that had happened, perhaps the older woman was setting her up for more failure.

Serenity glanced down at her daughter, still between her and Sebastian. Elizabeth had one arm coiled around Sebastian's leg and she hid her face behind him. Sebastian had been the one taking care of Elizabeth this whole time; he was the person she sought comfort in.

Sebastian had saved Elizabeth in the mine, now it was Serenity's turn. She wouldn't allow them to be torn apart—

she needed to take any chances she had. And right now she only had one.

Demitri was fast and strong—more than Sebastian even. If the older vampire even got a clue that she was up to something, he'd be able to stop her. She needed him to be distracted, but by what? She couldn't communicate with anyone else to tell them she needed a diversion.

She only had herself as a distraction.

"None of this matters," she said. "We're all together now, why can't we just learn to live together? Elizabeth will be here to show you the future, Demitri. I will be here for both you and Elizabeth."

Demitri's eyes flicked to Sebastian. "What about him?"

"What about him? It's his choice if he doesn't want to stay with us."

"Perhaps I should do as I originally planned and bury him in the cellar beneath the club. I could put him there with Bridget and Vincent. We could take bets on which vampire gives in and feeds from her first," he laughed. "I'm guessing it would be Vincent. After all, he's still so young and Sebastian has had centuries of self restraint. How ironic it would be if the son she betrayed everyone to protect eventually killed her."

"No!" Bridget yelled. "He would never do that!"

The uncomfortable expression on Vincent's face told Serenity that was exactly what he would do.

Beside her, Elizabeth began to cry. "I don't want Bridget to get hurt."

Not wanting to use her child, but seeing no other option, Serenity ducked down beside Elizabeth and pulled her into a one-armed embrace. As she crouched, she pulled the pouch from her pocket.

"Shhh, Elizabeth," she said, "Don't be frightened, everything will be all right."

Elizabeth started to pull away from her mother but Serenity gave her a tight squeeze—one that was a little too brusque—and Elizabeth seemed to get the message. She put her arms around her mom's neck and stayed that way.

With Elizabeth's body blocking Demitri and Natasha's view, she got to work on picking at the stitches.

With the pouch being so tiny, the process was frustratingly fiddly. Pinching the body of the pouch between her thumb, pinky and ring finger, she used her index and forefinger to scratch away at the fine thread.

The argument continued around her and for that she was thankful. Without the angry voices, she was sure the vampires would hear the slight but insistent sound.

"Don't expect me to go down without a fight, Demitri," said Sebastian. "If you think I'm going to just allow you to lock me up or bury me somewhere and walk off with the woman I love and my daughter, you can think again."

Demitri snorted. "Woman you love? Who do you think you are, some modern day Lothario? You're a killer, Sebastian. You're not human. You don't have a human heart to even love with, so how can you tell me you love her?"

"My heart may not be human, but I still have the capacity to love."

"Oh, please. It's not real. What you experience are simply memories. They're emotional echoes from your human life. You're acting and feeling the way you do because you think it's how you're *supposed* to think and feel. In truth, you're no deeper than the rest of us."

"Bullshit!"

The first stitch popped on the pouch. Even to Serenity's ears—their acuity improved by the vampire blood—the *snick* of the thread breaking sounded horribly loud. She paused for a moment, waiting to see if Demitri or Natasha had noticed, but they were all too caught up in the argument.

She went back to work while she kissed Elizabeth's hair, muttering reassurances to her. She tried to make her actions seem no less natural than any other mother comforting her distressed child.

"Do you think by keeping Serenity and Elizabeth, you'll have my reason for wanting to live?" said Sebastian. "Is that really what you're looking for, Demitri? Your existence is empty and you've seen something in the way I care for these people that makes you want to claim them for yourself?"

"Hilarious, Sebastian. Truly."

"They'll never give you want you want, Demitri. They'll never love you."

The final stitches gave way and the neck of the pouch opened.

Serenity gave her daughter a final, fierce kiss and rose to her feet, though she kept the hand holding the pouch hidden behind her back. "That's not true, Sebastian. If Demitri wants us, we will stay. Elizabeth is young enough to come to think of him as her father over time and I will surely learn to love him."

"Serenity!" His green eyes glowed yellow.

"I'm sorry, Sebastian, but if this is what needs to happen for Elizabeth and I to stay together and for you to walk away from this, then that's what we need to do"

She stared into his eyes. She hoped he understood that she didn't mean what she was saying, but from the pain she saw shimmering in his eyes, she thought he believed her. What she was about to do next would push him to the edge of his restraint. She prayed he would trust her enough not to try to interfere.

Serenity pulled her long hair to one side, exposing the pale line of her throat. "Why don't you taste me, Demitri?" she offered. "If I'm to be yours, don't you think you should sample me first?"

She lowered her lashes, looking out at him from behind the dark fringe. "You know I have a thing for vampires. Sebastian just happened to be the first one I came across. But now you're here. You're older than Sebastian and so much stronger. I can't help myself, I find that sort of power irresistible."

"Serenity," Sebastian growled. "Stop this."

She took a couple of small, slow steps toward Demitri, and he held his ground. From behind the desk, Serenity sensed Natasha's fierce-eyed glare, obviously unhappy about Serenity trying to step in on her territory.

"I told you before, those desires lost interest for me a long time ago." The vampire's black eyes smoldered. He lowered his head, almost bull-like, to look down at her, his dark eyebrows knitted together.

Her tone was teasing. "How long has it been, Demitri?"

He narrowed his eyes at her, suspicious, but not before his gaze traveled down over her body, lingering over her high, firm breasts, her rounded hips, her long thighs. With both hands, he pushed his long, black hair behind his ears.

"You can have me, Demitri," she continued. "If that's what you want. You can taste me and take me in whatever ways you want. All I ask is that you allow me to be here for my daughter."

From behind, she heard Sebastian's low growl, emitted from somewhere deep in his chest.

Please trust me, Sebastian, she willed him. *Trust that I love you.*

Hidden loosely in the palm of her hand was the pouch; the opening cupped between her thumb and forefinger. She knew her chance would be brief, barely even a second. She needed to be close enough to Demitri for him to not be able to stop her once she'd sent the powder airborne.

Demitri stepped closer so that only a couple of feet separated them. He tilted his head to one side, his full lips curling in a lopsided smile of victory. He reached out a hand and touched Serenity's cheek. She lowered her face into his embrace.

Sebastian's rage was palpable. He wouldn't hold out much longer.

"Demitri," she said. "You have no idea what your touch does to me."

Then she threw the pouch's contents.

Chapter Twenty-three

Demitri caught her arm before she'd managed to lift her hand more than six inches. His ice-cold fingers wrapped around her wrist, his grip so strong it sent agonizing sparks of pain up her arm. She cried out in agony, sure he'd cracked the bones. For a moment, she thought he'd rip her arm off, but the small movement she'd managed sent the contents of the pouch into the air like a puff of smoke.

Only a fraction of a second passed and the dust of silver, vervain and wolfsbane settled on his skin. Demitri released his grip and stumbled away, a scream of fury ripping from his throat. His hands clutched at his face and a horrific hissing filled the room, together with the stench of burning flesh. Smoke poured in streams from between the vampire's fingers.

Still standing behind the desk, Natasha screamed.

Vincent and Bridget stood frozen in place, watching events unfold with wide eyes.

"Let's get out of here," Serenity yelled and bent to scoop up Elizabeth.

A loud crack and snap of fractured wood cut through the air.

"Look out," shouted Bridget.

Serenity spun just in time to see Natasha—who was no more than a blur—flying across the room, one leg of Demitri's giant desk held out like a spear.

Or a stake.

"Sebastian!" Serenity cried out, but he'd been too concerned with getting his family to safety to notice the oncoming threat to himself. He turned in an almost perfect symphony of movement for the splintered end of the desk leg to drive through his right shoulder.

"Daddy!" screamed Elizabeth.

Pain ricocheted through Sebastian's shoulder, a white-hot bloom of agony. Elizabeth's cry filtered to his ears, but she sounded distant. He'd not experienced such pain in a long time and the injury drained the strength from his limbs.

He glanced down to find the table leg protruding from his shoulder. It was large and had shattered his shoulder and collarbone into splinters. Sebastian gritted his teeth and took hold of the wood with both hands. With a tightened jaw and a yell of agony, he tore the leg from his body. The wood came free with a wet, sucking sound and he threw it to the ground.

His head swam, but he forced himself to stay conscious. He would heal quickly, but not quickly enough. Blood flowed from the gaping wound, though already the flesh had started to knit together.

Sebastian focused on Natasha. She stood, her eyes flicking between Demitri, still in agony, his face now unrecognizable, Sebastian and Serenity. Her mind apparently made up, she focused on Serenity and hissed, "You bitch!"

The vampire leapt at Serenity.

Elizabeth stood watching, pale faced and terrified. He was too badly injured to try to save her and Natasha clearly had her sights set on Serenity. All Sebastian could think was that Elizabeth needed to get as far away from all this danger as possible.

"Run, Elizabeth!" Sebastian yelled. "Run!"

The little girl spun on her toes, one way and then the next. Natasha collided with Serenity, knocking her to the ground, and Elizabeth ran.

The blonde hit Serenity like a brick wall and Serenity flew backward. She smacked against the floor, the air bursting from her lungs, and the vampire landed on top of her. The blonde's face was chalk-white, her eyes burning yellow with hatred. Her jaw had lengthened and thickened, her fangs protruding from her mouth. She snarled in hatred and lunged for Serenity's throat.

Serenity squeezed her eyes shut, preparing herself for the pain of razor-sharp teeth piercing her skin. But the teeth snapped shut, missing her throat, and then Natasha was dragged off her.

Sebastian, she thought with relief. She rolled to her side to find Sebastian still bent over, his hand clutched over the rapidly healing wound in his chest. Bright blood covered his pale fingers—a terrifying amount of blood.

Confused, she looked to find Natasha grappling with Vincent. Though the two vampires couldn't inflict a mortal injury to each other, they could still fight and the sounds of their clash echoed around the large room. They were a similar age so, despite Vincent's obvious advantage in size, their strengths were evenly matched. Vincent took hold of Natasha's throat and pushed her backward, her feet dragging along the floor as he used his momentum to crash her against a wall. Natasha tore his hands from her throat and flipped him over so he landed on his back while she held him down.

Bridget stood with a hand over her mouth and wide, worried eyes. Clearly she was still terrified for her son's safety, despite Natasha not being able to kill her vampire sibling.

Serenity risked a few seconds to look around.

Where was Elizabeth?

For once, she didn't have time to think about her daughter. This might be the only chance she'd get to put an end to this once and for all. All she wanted was for them to be able to live in peace. If Demitri survived, that could never happen.

Demitri's face bubbled, his eyes milky and blind. He thrashed around the room, his hands clawed above his face, as though he wanted to tear his own skin from his skull. All of his vampire's grace had left him as he staggered around, his head whipping from side to side.

The table leg, still coated in Sebastian's blood, lay on the floor a couple of feet away from Serenity. She got to her hands and knees and crawled toward it. Her hand wrapped around the thick post, but it was too heavy to lift one handed. She got to her feet, crouched, and used two hands to hoist it up.

Serenity lifted her head to find Sebastian watching. He could play no part in this, but he gave her the briefest of nods before turning his face.

Serenity channeled all her energy, all her anger, and lifted the splintered end of the table leg. Natasha and Vincent continued to snap at each other, so she took advantage of their being distracted.

With a yell of fury, she ran across the room. Demitri seemed to sense her coming and spun as though to attack. The sharp end of the leg drove directly into Demitri's chest. Serenity felt the initial resistance, then the 'pop' of his skin, followed by the crunch of rib-bones and, finally, the soft, sickening suck into his heart.

For a moment, everything stood still.

As though in slow motion, Demitri fell backward. He hit the ground with a crack. It sounded as though a slab of marble had hit the floor instead of something that used to be human.

As he lay there with the huge table leg protruding from his chest, what looked like a gray moss crept over his face and hands, crawling up his arms. His long, black hair turned to spider webs, as fine as spun candy.

Their fight forgotten, Natasha left Vincent and rushed to Demitri's side. She dropped to the floor beside him.

"Oh no, Demitri, my love."

She reached out and touched his now gray cheek. The moment her fingers made contact with what had once been his skin, Demitri crumbled to dust. The table leg fell to the floor with a clatter.

With blazing eyes, Natasha straightened, her gaze focused on Serenity.

"You fucking bitch," the vampire spat.

Sebastian appeared between Natasha and Serenity. The hole in his shoulder had now almost completely closed over, though through the tear in his shirt, the skin still looked pink and twisted with scarring.

"Back off, Natasha. Demitri is gone. Either you get out of here, or you'll be the one locked in the basement with the door chained in silver."

Her eyes flicked between Demitri's remains and Sebastian.

"I won't let you get away with this," she hissed. "You haven't seen the last of me."

Sebastian tilted his head to one side and raised an eyebrow. "Yeah, sure. You could at least leave with an original line."

Not waiting any longer, Natasha vanished through the door, slamming it in her wake.

Serenity looked around the room. "Elizabeth! Where the hell is Elizabeth?"

Chapter Twenty-four

Blind with panic, Elizabeth ran.

The corridors felt like a never-ending maze. She ran down their length and came to a t-junction. She took one turn and the next, with no idea whether she was heading in the right direction. She ran past the storeroom where she'd been kept, seeing the small pile of blankets and cushions on the hard, concrete floor. Briefly, she wondered if she should stop, curl up on the cushions, and wait for Sebastian and her mommy to come and find her. But then she remembered Sebastian's instructions to run. She'd risked their lives before by not listening to what Sebastian had told her to do and she didn't want to put any of them in that situation again.

Elizabeth kept going, air whistling in and out of her lungs. The air smelled damp and seemed devoid of the oxygen she needed.

Past the storeroom, she found another door. She pulled on the metal handle. At first she thought the door was too heavy for her to open, but finally it gave way and opened onto a stairwell. The music, which had always been faint in the background, blasted louder.

Elizabeth followed the sound and raced up the stairs. She kept one thing in mind: music meant people and people meant help.

Her small legs pumped up the stairs, her thigh muscles burning. She rounded one flight, and then a second before another big, heavy door blocked her way.

She took hold of the handle, the metal cool and smooth beneath her palm. She gave it a yank and again the door resisted. Relief filled her as it opened on the second pull.

Music, voices and hot air blasted at her. She darted through the door and into darkness, flashing lights and loud music. Half-naked bodies were crammed into every space, but they seemed to move as one, in time with the loud, pounding music. Elizabeth pushed past their legs, grabbing at arms, trying to get someone's attention.

"Help me, help me," she cried. "Someone's trying to hurt my family."

But the music was too loud and she received only confused glances from jaded, glazed faces. She still wore her pajamas—the same ones Demitri had snatched her in—and the sight of a barefoot child in her nightclothes didn't fit in with the party-goers normal reality. A few people stopped and nudged their friends, nodding at the small child suddenly among them, but no one offered her any help.

Elizabeth pushed through the bodies, her slight frame slipping between legs—women in short skirts and high-heeled shoes, men in jeans and sneakers. The air was hot and thick, tinged with a mixture of body odor, perfume, and the same stale scent that had been so overpowering in the storeroom where she'd slept.

She reached the shiny, silver railings that separated the balcony from the dance floor below. Three horizontal bars, each with a couple of feet between them, divided the upstairs clubbers from those below. The railings were easily high enough to prevent any adults from falling over the top, but allowed plenty of space for a six-year-old to crawl between them.

Elizabeth leaned against the second bar and looked out over the sea of writhing, dancing bodies. The dancers held their hands aloft, punching the air in time with the thump of the song.

In the crowd, she spotted Sebastian, turning a slow circle, his hand knotted in his hair.

"Sebastian!" she yelled, leaning out over the crowd. "Sebastian! I'm up here!"

But the music was too loud. Even though Sebastian had hypersensitive hearing, the power of the sound system drowned out any ability to pick out individual voices.

Wanting him to notice her, Elizabeth climbed up onto the lowest bar. The metal felt cold against the bare soles of her feet. The second bar pressed against her ribcage and she leaned out as far as she dared, waving her hands to catch his attention. Her daddy didn't only have great hearing, his eyesight was sharp as well. If she could only get him to notice her, he would come up and take her away from all of this.

But then she saw the familiar blonde head of Natasha in the crowd, standing only feet from where her father searched for her. Caught up in his mission to locate his daughter, he'd missed the presence of the other vampire.

"Sebastian!" she yelled again, stretching out just a little further. "Watch out!"

Her foot slipped on the silver rail and she teetered forward, barely balanced on the edge. Her heart lurched into her throat as she thought she was about to fall head first, but then she regained her equilibrium. She lifted her hand once again to wave and someone knocked into her from behind.

Elizabeth tilted over the edge, her hands grappling for the bars.

And fell.

Movement caught Sebastian's attention and he looked up in time to see Elizabeth's body plummeting through the air. He ran with a burst of speed, but something collided with him. He barely registered who had stolen those precious moments from him—Natasha!—before he threw her away. The younger vampire had done no more than interrupted his run, but it had made all the difference. Natasha glared at him with fierce yellow eyes and disappeared back into the crowd.

Only a foot ahead, Elizabeth made contact with the dance floor, her body hitting with a sharp crack that sickened him to his core.

All around, people screamed and backed away from the small child lying on the ground. Though Elizabeth's eyes were open, her neck was kinked at a horrific angle, the bones of her vertebrate creating sharp lumps just beneath the skin. One of her legs was disjointed at the knee, the lower leg sticking out at what should have been an impossible angle. Her left arm was trapped beneath her body, but her right arm lay beside her head, her hand curled up and her fingers twitching.

Someone switched off the sound system and the crowd's cries of shock echoed around the room.

Sebastian fell to his knees beside her.

"Oh God, Elizabeth. My sweet girl."

She blinked at him. "Daddy?"

"Everything is okay, sweetheart. I'm here. You're safe."

A small spasm of shock wracked through her small frame. "I fell," she said, her voice weak.

He forced a smile. "I know you did, silly."

From behind, a scream louder than everyone else's cut through the room.

"Elizabeth!"

Serenity pushed her way through the crowd. The clubbers parted for her, allowing her through. The party atmosphere had vanished, replaced by one of tense anxiety.

Her eyes widened when she caught sight of her daughter lying on the floor, so badly hurt. All the color drained from her face and her hands covered her mouth. She ran to Elizabeth's side and dropped to the floor, opposite Sebastian.

"Oh God, what happened?"

"She fell, Serenity. From up there."

They both looked upward to the massive drop between the balustrade and the dance floor, and then back down at their daughter. They both knew what the huge drop meant.

No one could survive it.

Serenity felt as though someone had reached inside her chest with clawed hands and ripped her heart in two.

A thin, keening noise emitted from her throat and she hovered over Elizabeth, wanting to pull her into her arms, but terrified of making her injuries worse.

It doesn't matter, a little voice spoke inside her head. *Her neck is probably broken.*

She rocked over her daughter, her hands fluttering to cup Elizabeth's cheeks. Her skin felt cold to the touch—too cold.

"No, no, no. Oh, my baby, my poor little baby."

Please, God, this can't be happening, it wasn't real. Take it back, take it back. Please don't let this be real.

Anguish and a desperate sense of denial tore her in one direction and then the next. She wanted to not believe her own eyes, to hope and pray this was a horrific nightmare she'd wake from at any minute. But she knew it wasn't. Unrealistically, she willed for them to take a step back in time, to unravel the last few minutes and start again. Just a couple of minutes, that's all they'd need. Long enough for her to have made a different choice and run up to the next level or for Sebastian to have caught Elizabeth.

A bubble of blood bloomed between Elizabeth's lips and burst, splattering her pale skin with flecks of bright red.

"Mommy…"

"Everything's okay, baby. I'm here. You're going to be fine."

"It hurts, Mommy." She gave a couple of thick coughs and winced at the pain.

Serenity felt Elizabeth's pain so viscerally it was like her own. She'd give anything to switch places with her daughter; to take away the suffering and make her well again.

Elizabeth's short life flashed through Serenity's head: Elizabeth as a tiny baby, so helpless but still an individual, changing every day. Elizabeth as a chubby toddler, taking her first steps, arms extended, confident her mother would be there for her if she fell. Elizabeth as a preschooler, creating her own pictures for the first time, always so proud to show Serenity what she'd achieved.

Serenity thought of the years she had missed. Years she'd never get back. Years she'd now never be able to make up for.

She couldn't take this. She *refused* to take this. One thing had healed her when she'd been at the brink of losing who she was forever. Surely the same thing would help their daughter now.

Serenity forced herself to lift her gaze from her daughter's horrific injuries and pain-stricken face, and focused on Sebastian.

"Feed her your blood! It helped me, so it might heal her as well."

He looked up at her, aghast. "You want me to feed her vampire blood? She's so close to death; what if she turns?"

"I don't care!" Suddenly she was filled with fury toward him, rage that he'd even hesitate. "I don't care what she is. I just want her to be with us. Why are you even arguing this with me? Would you rather watch her die?

"A child vampire, Serenity. That's what you're asking of me."

"I don't care!" Her voice was a screech of hysteria. "I want my baby girl. If she dies, I'll die with her, I swear I will."

"It's okay," a voice came from behind.

They both turned to find Bridget stood behind them, her face pale and strained, visibly shaking. "She's a Dhampyre—she's already part vampire—she can never be turned by vampire blood. She'll always be just what she is."

Vincent appeared behind her and placed a hand on Bridget's shoulder. Whatever Bridget had done to them, however she betrayed them, she still obviously cared for Elizabeth and seeing the little girl so badly hurt had shaken her to the core.

"Do it, Sebastian," she encouraged. "She's dying. What do you have to lose?"

Sebastian's head tilted back, lifting his chin. When he lowered his head again, his jaw shape had changed, his fangs—long and sharp—protruded from beneath his curled upper lip. The vampire's eyes burned in the flashing strobe lights.

Around them, nervous mutters rose from the crowds of onlookers. People began to back away, widening the circle. The already tense atmosphere became even more charged, prickling with nervous energy.

Sebastian lifted his wrist to his mouth and bit, deep and hard.

Screams and shouts of 'what the fuck, man' broke from the crowd. People turned away and pushed at each other in their efforts to get away. Panic spread from one person to the next, picked up like a communicable disease. Before some people even knew what they were running from, the clubbers began to pour through the exits, pushing and shoving each other.

Serenity barely noticed the chaos around them. All her attention was focused on her daughter and the vampire who needed to save her.

Elizabeth's eyelids fluttered. They open briefly, but only to reveal her eyes rolling back in her head, flashing bloodshot whites.

"Oh God, Elizabeth," Serenity cried, her voice breaking with a sob. "Do it, Sebastian!"

He held his wrist to Elizabeth's pale lips. Blood dripped from the gash—he'd needed to bite deep. Elizabeth didn't have the strength or ability to suck and he couldn't risk the wound healing before she had taken what she needed.

Drops spattered. Elizabeth's eyelids fluttered again and her tongue snuck out, catching the droplets. The moment the first drop slid down Elizabeth's throat, color bloomed in her cheeks. She gasped and her eyes shot open. With renewed strength, she managed to lift her head, her mouth seeking sustenance.

Sebastian lowered his wrist and Elizabeth's mouth locked around the wound.

As she fed, her bones knitted back into place, the horrific lumps in her neck popping back into place with short, jerking movements. Her leg twisted back around, locking back into place. The blood melted away from her skin and her hair curled into ringlets.

The wound in Sebastian's wrist healed and he pulled his arm away.

Elizabeth stared up at them, her dark eyes clear and fresh with wonder.

"Mommy?" she said, propping herself up on her elbows. "What happened?"

Serenity burst into tears and grabbed her daughter, pulling her into her arms.

"Oh, my baby girl. I thought I'd lost you. My sweet, sweet baby."

"Mommy!" she said in an exasperated tone. "I'm not a baby."

Serenity kissed her hair, dampening the soft strands with her tears, laughing and crying at the same time. "No, I know you're not. You're my big girl. My big, brave girl."

Elizabeth looked to Sebastian to be rescued from her mother's onslaught of affection. He held his arms out to her and she untangled herself from Serenity and scrambled into them. Sebastian wrapped the little girl in his strong embrace. His eyes found Serenity's and she gave him a smile.

Thank you.

"Has anyone seen Natasha?" Sebastian asked. "She got in my way when I was trying to catch Elizabeth. She tried to attack me but must have realized she was no match for me. I just threw her back into the crowd, but then she disappeared."

"She's gone," said Vincent. "She was like a sibling to me and I can tell when she's still around. I don't know where she's gone, but she's nowhere in the club."

Beside her son, Bridget sniffed and wiped away tears from her cheeks. "I'm so sorry you had to go through this," she said. "I never meant for any of this to happen. I'm so glad she's okay."

Sebastian handed Elizabeth back to Serenity and rose to his feet.

"How could you do this to us, Bridget? We trusted you?"

"I'm so sorry." More tears pooled in her eyes and spilled from the corners, trickling down her cheeks. "I didn't know what else I was supposed to do. I love you and Elizabeth, but Vincent is my son."

"He's a grown man—no, worse, he's a vampire."

"He's still my child. No matter how big he is, or what he's become, he'll always be my child. Just like Elizabeth will always be your child, even when she's a grown woman. Would you ever choose someone else above her?"

Sebastian shook his head.

"Well," she continued. "How can you expect me not to do the same thing?"

"You still betrayed us. I should kill you now!"

Instantly, Vincent was in front of his mother, eyes flashing yellow. Sebastian squared before him, the vampires eyeing each other, snarling.

Elizabeth gave a shriek of fear and Serenity wrapped her arms across her daughter's narrow chest, pressing Elizabeth against her legs.

"Hey!" she shouted. "Quit it, you two. You're scaring Elizabeth."

The vampires glared at each other but backed down.

"I've got a question," said Serenity. "How come Elizabeth never saw any of this about you, Bridget? Why didn't she have any visions about you?"

Bridget gave an apologetic shrug. "Another spell, shielding me from her. Each day that passed, I wondered if someone would notice, realize that Elizabeth saw things for everyone else but me. But Sebastian was so caught up in his search for you; I guess the thought never crossed his mind."

"Or maybe I just trusted you, Bridget," he said. "Maybe I never thought to question anything about you."

"Please don't think I left Elizabeth unprotected. Every night, before I left, I covered her in the same protective spell I'd hoped Serenity was going to be able to use. I didn't know for sure that Demitri planned to come and take her, but I didn't want to take the risk so I hid her from him. That night you came back from taking Serenity to him, you said everything was fine, that it was all sorted, and I believed you! I thought Demitri hadn't said anything to you so it was all over. That's why I didn't do the blanket that night, though I wish to God I had."

"Whatever steps you took to try to help doesn't change that you were reporting back to Demitri about an innocent little girl you were supposed to be taking care of."

"Demitri said he'd never hurt Elizabeth, he was just interested in her, in what she could do. Though I knew him

245

taking her was a possibility, I never actually thought he'd do it!"

Sebastian couldn't say much. He'd also underestimated Demitri.

"We need to get out of here," Serenity interjected. "If someone hasn't already called the cops, they will soon."

Chapter Twenty-five

True to Serenity's word, as they left the club, the sound of approaching sirens cut through the night air.

They had more pressing issues to deal with and both Sebastian and Vincent knew it. The night sky had lost its inky black, morphing to a deep indigo blue.

Dawn was coming.

"Here," said Bridget, handing Serenity the bag containing Elizabeth's things. Even though the little girl had been fed vampire's blood and was protected against the cold, she still needed some proper clothes.

"Thank you," said Serenity. She fished out Elizabeth's comfort blanket. "Here you go, sweetie."

Elizabeth grinned in delight and took the cloth, pressing the soft material against her face.

Quiet until now, Vincent spoke. "What are you going to do, Mother?"

"I'll be okay, especially now that I don't have to worry about you. I'll fly back to Los Angeles. No one is going to stop an old woman in connection to strange goings-on in a club."

She put her arms around her son's neck and gave him a brief, fierce hug.

"I'll see you soon," he told her.

She nodded and kissed his cheek. "Stay safe."

The big vampire gave her a brief, tight-lipped nod and then vanished in a blur before them.

"We have to go too," said Sebastian, feeling the approaching dawn with an anxiety akin to insects scuttling inside his veins. "It's almost light."

She nodded. "I know. Will I see you again?"

Elizabeth tugged on the sleeve of his jacket. "Please, Daddy. Don't make Bridget go away."

"It's okay, Elizabeth," said Bridget. "Your father is only doing what's best for you."

He looked down into Elizabeth's dark eyes. She wasn't crying but her eyes had taken on the wet, shimmering look of someone who wasn't far off. He turned to Serenity, trying to gauge her opinion.

"Bridget did what she could to help us," Serenity said. "Yes, she should have come clean with us, but Demitri had her son. As she said, it's only natural to do whatever you can to help your child."

Sebastian pressed his lips together. "Okay," he relented. "I assume you realize you can't have your job back, but if you want to stay in touch for Elizabeth's sake, then you can."

Both Bridget and Elizabeth's faces broke into a smile.

"Thank you."

"You only get one chance," he warned. "Don't ever cross me again."

"I won't, Sebastian. I cross my heart."

He glanced at the sky and something deep inside him jarred. "We have to go."

"We can't go back to the hotel," said Serenity. "It's too close to the club. Someone might match our description."

"No, we need to get away from here."

The sirens grew louder.

Bridget threw them a final glance and blew a kiss at Elizabeth, before turning and hurrying away.

Sebastian caught them up in his arms and fled. They crossed the big city, an increasing fear mounting in Sebastian's heart. To be caught out in the open like this, with no bolt hole and daylight approaching was tantamount to one of his worst nightmares. He couldn't just find another hotel. The cops might be on the lookout for them and he couldn't risk getting caught in a hotel room in the middle of the day.

Ahead, they approached the huge, concrete square of the entrance to the Brooklyn-Battery Tunnel. Something inside him relaxed. Underground. They'd be safe underground.

He skirted the outside of the four lanes of traffic, sticking close the wall. Within seconds, he found a door to a service tunnel and ripped it open. A small nook was set back in the wall and he pulled Elizabeth and Serenity into it with him.

Exhausted, Serenity had no more questions for him. Together they slept: Sebastian sitting upright, but deep in his undead slumber; Elizabeth and Serenity curled into each other, their heads resting on Sebastian's lap. They'd been through a harrowing time—both mentally and physically— and with only the steady drone of traffic in the background, broken by the occasional siren, they slept soundly.

Serenity jerked awake to find Sebastian looking down at her. Her hand reached out to touch Elizabeth, to reassure herself that Elizabeth was both alive and still human—or at least as human as she ever had been. Elizabeth stirred beneath her mother's touch and Serenity let out a sigh of relief.

"She's all right," said Sebastian. "She's safe."

Serenity nodded and pushed herself to a sitting position, careful not to disturb Elizabeth too much. Her muscles groaned in protest, stiffened from the hard surface she'd slept upon and from the cold.

"Come on," he told her. "Let's wake Elizabeth up and go home."

Serenity smiled. "Home. I like the sound of that."

He lowered his face to hers and kissed her. "Me too."

Together, they woke their daughter.

Wrapped around Sebastian's strong body, they left the tunnel, and then the city, far behind.

They stopped for food within the hour—both Serenity and Elizabeth hadn't eaten in over twenty-four hours and were starving. Serenity watched Elizabeth closely, wondering if any new need or thirst for blood would surface, but Elizabeth tucked into a cheeseburger with all the enthusiasm of any other half-starved child.

Soon they were off again, traversing the country from the east coast back to the west. By the time the lights of Los Angeles came into sight, Elizabeth had fallen asleep once more on Sebastian's shoulder.

Finally, they reached their house. Sebastian set Serenity down on the gravel while Elizabeth still slept on his shoulder. To Serenity, the big house looked like the best place in the world.

Serenity stepped through the front door and into the kitchen, surveying the carnage Sebastian had caused. She lifted her eyebrows and he gave an apologetic shrug.

The damage didn't matter; they were home and safe.

Without waking her, Sebastian took Elizabeth straight up to bed. She would be happy to wake up the next morning in her own room with Serenity there to take care of her.

Serenity began to pick up pieces of marble from the kitchen floor. Sebastian's cool hand on her arm stopped her and she turned into the circle of his embrace.

"Leave it," he said. "I'll sort it out later."

"I don't want Elizabeth to come down and cut her feet on any sharp pieces."

"I said I'd clean it up."

"But what about—"

"Serenity," he said, cutting her off. "She's not going to get hurt. She's safe."

She shook her head. "I can hardly believe we almost lost her. Seeing her lying on the floor, all broken like that..." Serenity's voice broke and tears filled her eyes.

"Everything is okay now."

"I know, but I don't think I'll ever get that image out of my mind. I don't think I've ever been so scared in my life."

"I felt the same way. I might not be able to show my emotions in the same way as you, but that doesn't mean I don't experience the same thing."

Serenity sniffed and nodded. "I understand."

He held her closer and she pressed her cheek against his chest, relishing in the solidity of his body; it was her wall against the rest of the world.

"The thing is," she continued, "I let her down in the club when I thought she was going to die. I wasn't thinking of her in those moments, I only thought of myself, of how I was going to cope if I didn't have her in my life. I've always believed I put Elizabeth's needs first, but right at that moment I knew becoming a child vampire wouldn't be what would be best for her. To be caught as a six-year-old child forever would be horrific. But I didn't care; I only wanted her. I couldn't stand the thought of losing her."

"Hush," he soothed her, his large palm stroking her hair. "You wanted to keep your daughter with you. Any mother would react the same way."

"No, I don't think they would."

"We all have our weaknesses, Serenity. Perhaps your love for Elizabeth is your weakness. Perhaps my love for you is mine. But in our weaknesses we must also find strength."

"I'll always find strength in you," she said. "I always have."

"We find strength in each other," he said. "That's what family is all about."

She nodded against his chest. "But we're safe now, aren't we? No more Jackson, no more Demitri. Just us together."

"Yes, just us. We deserve a happy ending and I intend to make sure we get it."

Serenity's thoughts turned briefly to Natasha and her parting promise:

I won't let you get away with this… You haven't seen the last of me.

She shook the concern from her head. The other vampire was younger and weaker than Sebastian. She wasn't a threat to them.

Serenity lifted her arms and wrapped them around Sebastian's broad neck. Her fingers laced into the soft, dark hair at the base of his neck. He smiled, his green eyes lighting. He bent his head to hers and kissed her, soft and slow and deep. All of Serenity's worries melted away. For once, she felt at peace.

They were together and they were safe.

For the moment, nothing else mattered.

Please keep reading for the first chapter of Marissa Farrar's novel, The Dark Road, which is now available to buy.

What starts as an adventure for Sasha Mills turns into a terrifying fight for survival ...

Emotionally blackmailed by the cold-footed fiancé she hasn't seen in a year, Sasha abandons her life in London to track him in Siem Reap, Cambodia, where he's teaching.

While in Bangkok, locals react strangely to her request to travel the following day, insisting it is a not a good day to travel despite numerous posters advertising buses running every day. Ignoring the warnings, Sasha assumes some kind of bank holiday and offers a large amount of money. She secures a seat on the solitary bus heading for Siem Reap.

Thrown together with a random group of international backpackers, including the handsome Josh, Sasha is no longer certain of what lies ahead as they cross the Cambodian border and the roads turn into dirt tracks.

Soon after, a storm like none she's ever witnessed before descends upon them. When one of their group disappears off the side of the road, Sasha realizes she has more than just the warnings of land mines to worry about.

One by one, the travelers lose their minds as they are plunged into the terrifying secrets of the Dark Road.

Reviews for The Dark Road:

There's enough mystery, mayhem, twists and turns to keep you thriller fans happy, while those of you who don't typically feel the need for speed will love the detailed descriptions of exotic locales. There is definitely sense of verisimilitude as you read Farrar's words that evoke sight, sound and smell with seeming ease. The dark story of the dark road has the power to keep you up at night with your heart in your throat. - **Thrillers Rock**

Want to get on a thrill ride with a bit of paranormal, fantasy and horror? Then look no further than Marissa Farrar's The Dark Road! This book is an on edge horror and suspense ride and it's one you won't want to miss. I really enjoyed this book, the characters, the plot, it's one of those stories that you grow to love because you are on the journey with the characters. As the reader, you become their eyes and ears of the characters, exploring with them and plot, dialogue flowed naturally. Farrar has traveled far and wide and after reading the book, I know now why the visions for this book were so clear and crisp. Farrar is an author to watch out for as with her travels, I expect to see more books come into fruition. Go and catch The Dark Road! - **The Pen and Muse**

If you like fascinating locales, ancient temples, curses, and long-dead kings, The Dark Road is another MUST read! Join a group of travelers and immerse yourself in a frightening, night time world. A group of backpackers take a harrowing bus ride along a "road" that leads from Bangkok, Thailand to Siem Reap, Cambodia. After crossing into Cambodia, one of the group goes missing from the road, and it isn't long before the remaining travelers realize they will be in the fight of their lives, and it's anyone's guess as to whether or not they will make it through the night. You need to read The Dark Road or you will be missing out on an adventure and a half! - **The Scribe's Desk.**

Chapter One
The Phone Call

When the phone rang, Sasha Mills was tucked on the sofa, a half-empty glass of wine sitting on the side table, and Merlin, her Siamese cat, curled up beside her. She'd been expecting the call, but all her muscles still tightened in anticipation as she reached across and picked up the receiver.

"Hi, baby." Nick's voice was starting to become more familiar than his face.

"Hi, you," she said, squashing the phone between her ear and shoulder, settling back into the comforting arms of the sofa. "When are you coming home?"

Sasha asked every time he called. The question was usually just her teasing him, but this time she was serious.

For the past twelve months, Nick had been teaching English to children in Cambodia. In a week, he was due to fly home to the flat they shared in London—the flat they *used* to share. For the last year, Sasha had been living alone.

They'd been happy together for almost two years before he left, but Nick had become disillusioned with the rat race and decided he wanted to do something to make a difference in people's lives. Having gone straight from university into work, Sasha thought him spending a few months discovering the world outside of London was a great idea. She supported his decision and suggested Cambodia. She'd spent a number of months traveling the country in her early twenties and the experience left her with a lasting impression of the innocence and strength of the children.

It hadn't taken long for Nick to arrange some volunteer work teaching English to Cambodian children in a remote village. Within weeks of making the decision, his bags were packed.

Now, only silence met her question and a sickening sensation churned with the wine she'd drunk. Her right hand flicked unconsciously to her left and she twisted the diamond solitaire binding her third finger.

"Nick?"

He sighed down the phone."Look Sash, I've been thinking. Why don't you come out and join me for a bit? You could work out here. They're always looking for more teachers…"

Acid rose from her stomach and burned the back of her throat. They'd had this conversation before. The first time had been six months ago when he'd been first due to come home. He was only supposed to have been gone a few months. Sasha could have gone with him. Nick wanted her to, but she'd already finished that chapter of her life and didn't want to retrace old steps. Naturally, she was upset when he left, but she'd believed the experience would be good for him, good for *them*. He would return more fulfilled. Sasha never contemplated the idea that he wouldn't want to come back.

"Please don't do this to me, Nick. You know I can't."

"Of course you can, Sash. We can short-let the flat and your mum would look after Merlin. She dotes on that cat."

Sasha sighed. "It's not about practicalities. My life is here and I don't want to go away again. It would be like putting my life on hold."

"You don't have much of a life, Sash. You go to work, watch television and go out drinking in bars. No one is going to notice if you're gone."

Sasha bristled and spoke through gritted teeth. "I may not be out changing the world, but I happen to love my life."

"More than me you mean." Bitterness tainted his voice.

"Don't forget, you're the one who left me, Nick!"

"I wanted to make a difference."

"How noble..."

They fell silent, hurt and anger buzzing through the phone line.

Eventually, Sasha asked, "So what are you really saying, Nick? That you don't want to come home?"

"I want you here with me."

"Just be fucking straight with me will you," Sasha yelled. "Are you coming home or not?"

"I can't leave here, Sash. These people mean too much to me."

"And I don't mean shit!" She swallowed hard, trying to dislodge the burning lump choking her.

"Don't be ridiculous."

"I am *not* ridiculous!" She trembled with anger. "It is not ridiculous to want my fiancé home, or to not want to traipse off to some foreign country at the drop of a hat."

Nick spoke again, his voice distant and even. "I'm sorry but I'm not coming back, not yet at least. I've changed my flight back to London. I'm going to Bali for a couple of week's holiday instead. I want you to come, but if you're not here by the time I leave, I'll assume you don't love me enough to make the effort."

He hung up.

Heat rushed to Sasha's cheeks and her mouth dropped open.

The sheer nerve! He could at least have come home for a couple of weeks, spent some time with her. Now, not only was he not coming home, but he also expected her to give up *her* life to fly out to him and go to freaking Bali!

Sasha yelled in frustration and flung the phone across the room. The handset landed with a crash and Merlin, who had been sleeping soundly, oblivious to the drama unfolding around him, shot out of his seat.

"Oh, I'm sorry, Merlin! I'm sorry, baby. I didn't mean to scare you."

Sasha got up and tried to coax the shivering Siamese cat from under the television stand. He let out a pitiful yowl. She reached under and pulled him out by the scruff of his neck. Clutching him in her arms, she buried her face in his soft fur and let the tears come.

Despite not seeing each other for a year, Sasha believed Nick to be her future. She'd thought it from the moment they met, but now that future seemed to be disintegrating. What he'd said about her life hurt and she was bitterly disappointed about not having him back in London.

Was she being selfish for not going? Was Nick right in thinking her simple, normal life was not enough? Or was he the one being selfish by asking her to give up everything to be with him?

Sasha didn't know what to think.

She had less than eight days to decide what to do. In eight days, she'd either be sitting at home crying while he boarded a plane to fly away from her, or she'd be on a plane herself, going to meet him.

Her boss would go mad.

Was she seriously contemplating this?

Yes, she thought. *Why not?*

She could fly to Cambodia, on to Bali, spend a couple of weeks with Nick, remind him what he was missing and then come home again. After all, it didn't have to be forever. Just long enough to save their relationship. Perhaps the trip wouldn't be such hardship; she imagined loads of women would love to be in her place.

Sasha's tears subsided and she wiped her face in her cat's already-damp fur.

The next morning, Sasha jumped on the tube for the short ride to her office near Angel Station. She'd been working as a recruitment consultant for almost three years now. There shouldn't be any reason why she wouldn't be able to take some time off, but she couldn't ignore the nerves tugging at her insides. Sasha caught herself chewing at her nails, a habit she'd dropped years ago. Disgusted, she pulled her hand away.

Her boss, Alison Killery, though only a few years older than Sasha, was one of those focused, career-minded women who always made Sasha feel slightly inferior and intimidated.

Sasha got into work, went to her own desk and sat down. She waited for Alison to drink her first cup of coffee and trawl through her emails before she got up the courage to approach.

Alison glanced up before Sasha reached her desk.

"Hey, Sasha," Alison said, smiling. "Everything all right?"

Sasha smiled back. Her heart thumped audibly and sweat slicked the palms of her hands.

"Actually," she said, "I have a huge favor to ask."

"Sounds ominous," Alison said, raising her eyebrows.

Sasha took a deep breath. "I need the next three weeks off." She hurried on before Alison cut her off. "I've not had a holiday since last year. I've got days I need to use up and Nick is still in Cambodia…"

"Nick is still in Cambodia?" Alison frowned. "Isn't he supposed to be coming back next week?"

"Yeah, but he's sick." The lie slipped out and Sasha's cheeks flushed with shame.

"Oh, no." Alison's genuine dismay made Sasha feel even worse. "The poor thing. It's nothing serious, I hope."

Sasha shook her head. "They don't know yet." Her mind ran through numerous potential illnesses. "I think they're testing for malaria."

"When do you need to go?"

"As soon as possible," Sasha said.

Alison leaned forward and tapped some keys on her computer. She frowned at the screen.

"Tony is supposed to be taking a long weekend next week. No one else is off, so I guess we can survive without you."

Sasha stopped herself hopping up and down, and clapping with excitement. Instead, she tried to put on a concerned, yet relieved face of a worried fiancée.

"Thanks Alison, I really appreciate it."

She turned away from the desk and walked back to her own, keeping her smile tightly locked behind her lips. The small lie meant she couldn't start raving about her trip to her colleagues. And she would need to tell everyone Nick hadn't contracted malaria when she got back.

At least she was able to go.

Sasha spent the rest of the day trawling the Internet, trying to find a flight. She secured a flight from London to Bangkok, but had a three day wait before flying to Siem Reap

During her travels years ago, she'd flown from Bangkok to Siem Reap, in Cambodia, but traveling by road hadn't been as safe back then. Plenty of people caught buses between the two countries now. Perhaps that would be a better way to go? She'd leave the day after she flew into Bangkok and gain a whole extra day.

Sasha typed an email to Nick letting him know of her plans. The village Nick taught and lived in was miles away from any technology and he went into one of the larger communities once a week to use the phone or computer. He normally picked up his emails and made phone calls on a Sunday, and as today was Monday, he would only get the email the day before, or even on the day she arrived in Cambodia. The timings weren't ideal, but she had no other way of contacting him. Maybe he would have enough sense to check his emails sooner considering the circumstances. If he really did want her to come, and missed her like he said he did, surely he would make the effort to check every day hoping to hear from her?

That evening, Sasha picked up the phone to call her mother. After three rings, her mum answered.

"Hello?"

"Hi Mum, it's me."

"Hello, Sasha-love. How are you?"

"I've got a favor to ask," she said for the second time that day.

"Oh yes?"

"Nick has asked me to go away with him for three weeks and I wondered if you would like to flat-sit?"

"What do you mean, 'Nick has asked you to go away'? Isn't he supposed to be coming home?"

Sasha inwardly cringed. She didn't want to explain things to her mother. Her mum wouldn't hesitate to point out Nick's flaws and right now Sasha didn't want to hear them.

"Yes, but there's been a change of plan. He wants us to take a holiday together before he comes home."

She tried to tell herself she wasn't telling another lie; technically the trip would be a holiday and Nick was still going to come home at some point.

Her mother's pause told her more than words could, disapproval radiating through the phone.

"Please Mum. Merlin would hate to be here by himself for three weeks and getting someone to pop in and feed him isn't the same. You know how he hates to be left by himself."

Her mother huffed air out of her nose, snorting into the phone. "Well I suppose I could do with some time away from your father." She lowered her voice. "He's caught a cold and he's had the damn football on all day. All he seems to do these days is sit in front of the television and complain."

Sasha smiled. She knew her parents loved each other, but they'd been married over thirty years and sometimes even they needed time apart.

"So, is that a yes?"

"When are you leaving?"

"In two days."

"Wow, Sasha!" Her mother didn't even try to hide her surprise. "That's short notice."

"It's been a bit of last-minute thing. You won't need to get here until the day after I leave. You've still got your keys haven't you?"

"Yes, of course."

"So will you do it?"

"I suppose so."

"Thanks, Mum," Sasha said in relief. "I love you, and tell Dad I hope he gets better soon."

She didn't wait for her mum to say anything else. She didn't want to push her luck. Instead, she simply said her goodbyes and then sat back, wondering what the hell she was getting herself into.

About the Author

Marissa Farrar is a multi-published horror and paranormal author. She was born in Devon, England, loves to travel and has lived in both Australia and Spain. She now resides in Devon with her husband, three children, a crazy Spanish dog and two rescue cats. She has a degree in Zoology, but her true love has always been writing.

Her dark take on a vampire romance, Alone, was first published in 2009 and has now been re-launched together with the rest of the books which are now the 'Serenity' series.

Her short stories have been accepted for a number of anthologies including, Their Dark Masters, Red Skies Press, Masters of Horror: Damned If You Don't, Triskaideka Books; and 2013: The Aftermath, Pill Hill Press.

If you want to know more about Marissa, then please visit her website at www.marissa-farrar.blogspot.com. You can also find her at her facebook page, www.facebook.com/marissa.farrar.author or follow her on twitter @marissafarrar. She loves to hear from readers and can be emailed at marissafarrar@hotmail.co.uk.

CAPTURED

CAPTURED

www.ingramcontent.com/pod-product-compliance
Lightning Source LLC
Chambersburg PA
CBHW021956170626
46808CB00001B/178